"I'll stand guard," said Abe.

Duff rolled his eyes. "As you wish." He sat on the ground and lowered his legs into the cave mouth. "If I have to fight a bear in this one, I'm going to be very upset with you."

"I don't think there are bears this far south."

"Bigfoots, then. If I have to fight a sasquatch, that's on your ass."

"I'll take that chance."

Duff started to wiggle into the hole. "If I die in hand-to-hand combat with a Bigfoot, tell everyone I died doing what I loved."

Sean Patrick Little

BOUGHT THE FARM

An Abe & Duff Mystery

SPILLED INC. PRESS

Published by Spilled Inc. Press, Sun Prairie, Wis.
Printed and bound in the United States

ISBN: 978-1-312-27549-2

Other books in the Abe & Duff Mystery Series:
The Single Twin
Fourth and Wrong
Where Art Thou?

For Kaija

BOUGHT THE FARM

An Abe & Duff Mystery

1

THE HOSTESS BLINKED twice and rolled her eyes when Abe Allard told her he was eating alone. It might have been an involuntary reaction. Maybe it was purposeful. It didn't matter. Abe was used to that reaction. On Saturday nights restaurants usually expected groups or couples out on dates, maybe some families out for a weekly gathering or celebration. They rarely expected sad-eyed, middle-aged men carrying a book. Abe was used to it, though; he was no stranger to eating alone. Over the past year he'd grown to appreciate it. It was a good time to sit and reflect on life, maybe read a chapter or three in a book, maybe do a little people-watching. He wasn't forced to make conversation. He wasn't forced to listen to anyone's troubles or open up about his own. When he inevitably slopped sour cream on his shirt, there was no embarrassment, only mild annoyance at his long-suffering gracelessness.

The hostess checked her seating chart. She glanced over her shoulder at the restaurant behind her. It was only at fifty-percent capacity. She sighed and made an X on a table with a dry-erase marker. She grabbed a menu and spun on her heel. "This way."

She seated Abe at a small table on a long row of small, square two-person bistro tables which could be shoved together to accommodate larger groups, if necessary. On one side of the table was a long bench seat running the length of the tables. On the other side were spindly wrought-iron chairs with padded seats. Abe chose the bench side of the table because it faced the door. The hostess told him his waitress would be right with him.

Two tables to his right was a woman a few years younger than himself. She was dressed simply in a dark blue skirt and white peasant blouse. Fancy, but not overly so. Her hair was trimmed in a stylish modern cut. She was drumming her fingers nervously on the table and skimming the menu. She also bounced one of her legs. She was keeping her anxiety from appearing on her face, but it was coming through loud and clear in her body language. A second menu was on the other side of the table from her. A half-empty glass of red wine showed she was trying to relax before the other party for her evening arrived.

Abe thought about telling her to relax in a friendly sort of way but realized there was no easy way to tell someone you don't know to relax, especially in a restaurant where you've just been seated almost within nose-punching range. He chose instead to open his book and start reading. His chosen tome for the evening's entertainment was *The Best New True Crime Stories: Serial Killers*, an anthology of stories about some of the worst individuals society had ever birthed.

The waitress arrived. She was a petite blond, college-aged, with an expensive manicure, probably a student at UIC which wasn't too far from the restaurant. She asked Abe if he'd like something to drink. Abe went with ice water, as much as he would have liked a diet soda. He was almost forty-six. If he wanted to be asleep at a decent time, caffeine after five o'clock was no longer an option for him. Hell, caffeine after two o'clock, for that matter. That waitress bustled away from the table. Abe cracked the cover of his chosen tome and adjusted his bifocals.

"Looks like a heavy-duty book."

Abe turned to his right. The nervous woman at the table was smiling at him. She nodded toward the book. "You do a lot of reading on serial killers?"

Abe closed the book again, holding his index finger inside it to mark the page. "Some. I try not to make it a habit."

"I am addicted to true crime podcasts. I listen to like ten of them every week." She pulled out her phone. "Do you mind if I take a picture of the cover? I'd probably like to read it."

Abe held the book out for her, and she leaned over and snapped a picture. He told her, "I checked out this one at the library just down the street. I'll probably finish it within the week and return it promptly."

"Noted."

Abe figured she was chatty enough that he might be forgiven for prying. "Pardon me for being forward, but you look a little nervous. First date?"

She shook her head and reached out for the cocktail in front of her, something brown and fizzy with a plastic spear holding two cherries. "Third date, actually." She winked at him when she said it.

"Oh." Abe had no idea what she was implying. He felt himself blush, anyhow. Women could do that to him. He should have outgrown that sort of discomfort by now, but it was so deeply ingrained in him he did not believe he ever would. "Third date is a big one, right? I don't think I ever actually dated. I just sort of ended up with someone, and there were no real dates because we were in college together."

"Well, third dates are usually the date where you make that leap of faith. Is this relationship real? Is this going to be a thing? Are you actually dating now, or are you just friends? Is it time to consummate the relationship?" She clamped a hand to her mouth. "I'm sorry. I get chatty when I'm nervous. It's a bad habit. You didn't come here to listen to me babble."

"No, it's fine." Abe tried to sound reassuring. "I don't mind, honestly. I spend a lot of time in silence, so this is a welcome change."

The woman flashed Abe a genuine smile. "I appreciate that. Maybe I can discharge all my nervous energy before my date gets here. You seeing anyone? I noticed you're not wearing a ring."

"No."

"Bachelor?"

"Divorced."

"Me, too. It's so hard, isn't it? You spend years building a life just to tear it down and start all over."

"Exactly."

"I hope I'm not being too nosy. I'm Patty, by the way. If you call me Peppermint Patty, I'll punch you." She held out a hand.

Abe shook her hand. "I'm—"

"Abe!"

Abe had not just yelled out his own name; someone had beaten him to it, someone with a painfully familiar voice. Abe turned his head to see his ex-wife Katherine standing ten feet away with the hostess.

Abe looked to Katherine, then to Patty, and back to Katherine. It did not take a detective of Abe's caliber to put together this puzzle. Patty was there to meet Katherine. It was their third date. It had been Katherine's recent reckoning with her long-buried homosexuality that led to Abe agreeing to seek an amicable divorce between them. Amicable or not, Abe felt a deep stabbing pain in his gut, and a cold sweat broke out on his back. He wanted to be anywhere but that restaurant at that moment.

"You two know each other?" Patty looked to Katherine, then back to Abe. The pieces fell together for her. "You're her ex?"

Abe could feel his face getting warm. He was sure his cheeks were tinged with a deep pink. "I am." He pushed himself to his feet. He pulled a five dollar bill out of his pocket and threw it on the table. "I'm sorry, Katherine. I honestly had no idea you were going to eat here tonight. I'll go."

Katherine held out her hands and gestured for Abe to sit. "Oh, no. No. That's fine, Abe. Please, join us."

Abe looked down to Patty. "No, thank you. I really don't want to be a third wheel. I'll go." He started to walk to the door. If Katherine was out on a date, Abe reasoned he might be able to go hang out with his daughter at his old house for a bit. "Where's Tilda?"

"She's out with her friends tonight. Where's Duff?"

"Who knows?" Abe was not his partner's keeper. He took two more steps.

Katherine moved toward him and grabbed his sleeve. "Abe, please stay. We can pull a table over. It won't be a problem."

Abe and Katherine remained friendly after their divorce. They had too much history and a child between them to make a clean break, but it did not mean that Abe wanted anything to do with her new romantic life, especially since he knew that Katherine was dating frequently, and he had not even had so much as a single match on a dating app. She seemed happy and fulfilled, she was active and energetic for the first time in years. He was miserable and lonely. He did not need to witness her social prosperity firsthand, and he did not want her to witness his sadness.

Abe pulled Katherine's hand from his wrist. He chose to invoke the pet name he'd called her for years as a way of reassuring her. "Kittykat, I'll be fine. Enjoy your night."

"Are you sure?"

"I'm always sure."

"You're never sure."

"I'm sure about this." Abe let half of his mouth curl into a smile. "I'll be fine. Honest."

"I'll call you tomorrow." Katherine looked concerned, but she knew when Abe's mind was made up. They were no longer married. She knew she had relinquished any right to have a say in how he spent his nights. It did not mean old habits didn't die hard, though.

"I'll answer."

"Okay, then." Katherine curled her fingers at him in a small wave.

Abe nodded, turned on his heel, and left. He did not look back.

Instead, as he often did whenever he felt a perverse need to balance the karmic scales between Katherine and him, he went to Chick-fil-A to get a sandwich and waffle fries. It was a petty thing, buying food from a company that went out of their way to make life more difficult for LGBT people, but Abe only allowed himself that treat when he felt he was slighted by the universe a little more than normal. He tried to be an ally, and he felt he was. He usually went with Popeye's or maybe even McDonald's when he wanted chicken sandwiches fast, but every so often he let himself have one of Truett Cathy's originals, a simple pleasure. He cleansed his guilty conscience by reminding himself of all the good things the Chick-fil-A organization did that never got as much press.

Abe took his bag from the smiling teenager in the drive-thru window. She dropped the requisite "My pleasure!" before he could even thank her. He pulled forward in the lane just far enough for the next car to pull up. He stabbed a straw through the plastic lid and took a deep swig of Coke. Despite keeping a continual eye on his waistline, which was thinner than most men his age but still needed work, Abe had allowed himself the joy of an original Coke, and the sugar blast punched him square in the mouth. It was such a small, pointless joy, but it seemed to mainline endorphins into his veins. He would have difficulty sleeping later, but the hit of dopamine the icy Coca-cola sent to his brain might have been worth it.

Abe pulled into a parking space in the restaurant's lot and let the car run while he listened to the news on NPR Illinois. It was nice enough of a night that he cracked the driver's window an inch and let in some fresh air. Spring had arrived in Illinois. Even the mountains of snow in the parking lots had melted away, and the daytime temps were in the upper sixties every day, although the overnights were still drifting down into the forties. There was still another month or two before summer would hit and the true Chicago would emerge, the hot, sweaty Chicago where the heat baked the brains and made the world smell like burnt asphalt. Abe liked summer, but he also liked not having sweat run down his back and inner thighs, so he was split on the matter.

A text popped up on his phone. It was Katherine. *Patty's in the restroom. Are you sure you're okay? I'm so sorry, Abe.*

Abe thought about it and texted back. *No worries. I hope you're okay. I'm fine.*

He set his phone down for a moment. Then he picked it back up. *By the way, Patty is hoping your night leads to sex. Just thought you should know.*

He set his phone back into the passenger-side drink holder on his battered minivan. He was pleased with himself; let it never be said he wasn't a good wingman for his ex-wife.

ABE OPTED NOT to go back to his apartment after his meal. He did not feel like being alone, so he chose to go back to the little one-bedroom apartment that served as the office for Allard and Duffy Investigations. Given the fact there were a dozen or so baseball games being played at that moment, it was likely his partner, CS Duffy, was watching at least one of them in the apartment or at the bar down the street. Either way, Abe could usually find him because Duff was a creature of habit.

Abe found Duff sitting in the office at his desk. He was watching the small TV they kept mounted on the far wall for news programming or the weather channel. A baseball game was indeed on the TV. To Abe, it looked like the white team versus the red-and-gray team, whoever they may be. The sound on the TV was off, however. A local news update was scrolling across the bottom of the screen, something about a hijacked delivery truck. Duff was wearing his favorite pair of faded blue jeans, too. Usually, he favored a pair of stained basketball shorts and bare feet in his off-hours, no matter the time of the year. His sneakered feet were perched on the corner of his desk, and he was leaning back deeply in his chair. Duff did not look at Abe when he walked in the door, but instead held up a finger for silence.

Abe caught the sign and closed the door carefully. He lowered his voice to a sibilant hiss. "What's up?"

Duff tilted his head in several directions listening for stray sounds. Not hearing any, he returned Abe's whisper. "No idea. Someone's coming, though."

"How do you know?"

"Cesar told me."

Cesar Salazar was the owner of the taco stand on the first floor of their building. He was often Abe and Duff's eyes when they weren't in the office. He would warn them about *gringos* who may have been looking for them.

Abe moved to his own desk. "What did he say?"

Duff dropped the whisper. "I was over at Wheels's place earlier. When I got bored, I came home. Cesar was still in the stand. He said some old white guy went up the stairs, knocked on our door, tried the knob, and then left. He was driving a white pickup truck, regular cab, with Wisconsin plates."

"And he came this late on a Saturday night?" Abe knew that meant it had to be someone who knew Duff stayed in the office all the time. Someone who knew there was a better-than-average chance Duff would answer the door. "Ideas?"

"One, specifically: Buddy Olson. But why would he drive down here?" Duff lifted his ever-present cap and scratched his head. His lip curled slightly as he pondered this. Buddy Olson was Duff's mentor and a father-figure to him in many ways. He was a retired county sheriff and helped them with a case over the border in Waukesha County the previous year.

"If it was Buddy, maybe he was in town for something else and tried to stop by to say hello."

"No one says hello to me."

"Buddy might."

"He would have called first, don't you think?"

There was a knock at the door. Abe and Duff both swung their heads toward it. "I guess we'll find out." Abe opened the door and revealed Buddy Olson in all his glory.

The old sheriff was decked out in Wrangler jeans and a snap-button khaki work shirt that barely contained the ample belly formed from years of desk work, too many doughnuts, and too much beer. He also wore a shabby tan houndstooth blazer that hadn't been cool since the early Eighties. "Evening, boys."

Duff nodded at the sheriff. "I assume this is a business call?"

Buddy stepped into the room and shut the door behind him. "What makes you say that?"

"Your left arm is hanging just slightly differently than your right. I'm betting you've got a gun in a shoulder holster."

Buddy pulled back the left lapel of his jacket to reveal the wooden stock of a heavy-duty six-gun hanging low beneath his arm. "Old habits die hard. I rarely go anywhere without one. Too great a chance of running into guys I arrested, even if we're all getting up there in years."

Buddy Olson waded into the room and sat in the chair opposite Duff's desk. He nodded toward the empty chair behind Abe's desk as he did. "Have a seat, son. This is going to take some explaining."

Abe did as commanded. He lowered himself into his chair and leaned toward Buddy. "Something bad went down, didn't it?"

"Well, it did, and then again maybe it didn't. I'm not sure."

"You drove two hours down here to talk to us about something that you're not sure about. You feeling alright? Is this a senior episode? Should I look into a memory care unit for you?"

Buddy calmly extended his middle finger at Duff. "That's for you, you ungrateful little prick. I got more brain cells firing than you got burrito wrappers in that wastebasket. Now shut the hell up and listen."

Buddy adjusted himself in his chair, his belly fighting for air against the buttons of his shirt. "You hear about that murder-suicide that went down last week just outside of Madison?"

Abe and Duff exchanged a glance. They hadn't. It wasn't unusual, though. Chicago news overrode most stories from Wisconsin. What was surely a front-page story for the *Wisconsin State Journal* would be buried deep in the *Chicago Sun-Times*, if it were even printed at all. Unless it was a border battle in sports, most Wisconsin news got put on the back-burner in Illinois. "Not at all," said Abe. "Was it a big deal?"

"Pretty big for Dane County."

Duff was already on his phone searching Google. His expression changed to mild shock. "Was this the same Arthur Laskey from your staff back in the day?"

"The same." Buddy's face darkened. "Art was a good boy. I've known him for years. He started his law enforcement career with me. I know he wasn't the type to do something like this."

Duff read from the first paragraph of the story. "Dane County deputies were called to the home of Arthur and Michelle Laskey outside of Blue Mounds for a welfare check and discovered the bodies of the Laskeys dead from an apparent murder-suicide."

"Ouch." Abe could not help but wince. He hated hearing about domestic violence.

"When did this happen?" asked Duff.

"Last week Wednesday night." Buddy ran a hand through a surprisingly thick shock of white hair standing it up on end. "The Dane County investigators finally concluded their investigation yesterday and declared it murder-suicide."

"You don't think it was, and you want us to look into it," said Duff.

"You remember Art and Michelle, don't you? They'd just gotten married around the time when…when all that stuff went down in Waukesha."

Duff nodded. "Unlike your dementia-riddled self, I don't forget things. I remember them."

"They were together for thirty-something years. I'd never seen a couple more in love. They were the gold standard for marriages."

Duff kicked back in his chair and put his feet on his desk, as was his usual thinking position when at his desk. "Well, that's just it, isn't it? Thirty years is a long time to be in love. Maybe they stopped being in love. Maybe things were darker behind the scenes."

"Brave public face." Abe knew a lot about putting on a brave face to family and friends.

"I doubt it," said Buddy. "You didn't see these two like I did. They were never angry at each other. They didn't fight. They were never anything but each other's biggest fan."

"Abe's my biggest fan."

"No, I'm not."

"My true fans would deny they were my biggest fan."

Buddy ignored them. "When those two first got together, it looked like they thought the sun rose and set in each other's pants. They went at it like coked-up rabbits. Last time I saw them, they still had that look in their eyes. Maybe they weren't as grabby as they once were, but it was pretty clear that they were a couple who still enjoyed each other in the Biblical way."

"You mean they liked to drive moneylenders from the temple together?" said Duff.

"More or less."

"Why did the cops call it a murder-suicide, then?" asked Abe.

"Two shots. Each to the side of the head. Close range. Michelle was still holding the gun when they found them."

"Any prints on the gun besides hers?" asked Duff.

Buddy shook his head. "That doesn't mean much, though. You know that. First thing I'd do if I was trying to stage a murder-suicide was make sure the gun was clean, then I'd press one of the victim's hands on it."

"There would have been powder burns on her hand. Did the medical examiner check for it?" asked Abe.

"Allegedly. Said there was. I'm not buying it, though." Buddy's eyes narrowed to slits. "If there wasn't, though, that means the Dane County ME was in on the killing in some way."

"Do you think he might be?" asked Abe.

"Maybe. He's a slippery sort of cuss, I hear. From what I know of him, he's a little greasy, but I've never met him."

"Was Arthur still putting on a uniform?"

"No. Took early retirement after a pretty bad back injury sustained in a car wreck during a chase about eighteen or twenty years ago. He was getting a fat monthly disability check and working part-time at a hardware store in Mount Horeb."

"That's west of Madison, right?" asked Duff.

"Yes. Not too far from Madison." Abe had been there a couple of times while he was in grad school, once with his mother not long before her passing. They had gone to a Christmas store and several antique shops. It had bored Abe greatly, but it made his mother happy. At that point in her cancer treatments, any joy for her was worth any amount of Abe's own boredom.

"They had the life they always wanted to live. Big old country house. Lots of land for hunting in the fall. The kids were finally out of the house. They were traveling and seeing the world. There was just no reason for them to end up like this. It smells fishy to me." Buddy thumped his fist lightly on the armrest of the chair.

"Are you sure you're not buying it because this is one of the stages of your grieving process?" Abe knew that Buddy could be firmly in the denial stage of grief. He was refusing to acknowledge the possibility things were not picture-perfect behind the scenes.

"You don't think I haven't thought of that?" Buddy was a former sheriff with more than forty years of carrying a badge. He had been around the block and then some. He knew grief intimately.

"I guess the better question is what do you want us to do?" asked Duff. "Dane County Sheriff's Department isn't going to like some retired sheriff with no jurisdiction poking around in their investigation."

"That's why I want to hire you two jokers. Go up there and poke around in my stead. Be my eyes and ears."

"What if we find out the ME's report is accurate, that it was a murder-suicide?" Duff dropped his feet down from the desk. "Maybe your gut feeling is wrong."

Buddy held up his hands in a half-assed shrug. "Then so be it. At least I'll sleep better at night."

"You know what helps me sleep at night? Cookies."

"Oh, I'm no stranger to Oreos, friend." Buddy jostled his belly. "But I'm afraid a few sleeves of those aren't getting the job done. I just need to know the truth, whatever it is."

Buddy reached into his ugly jacket and pulled a stack of bills from the interior coat pocket. He tossed them onto Abe's desk. "That's six grand, cash. That should be more than enough to get you started. Figure this out in less than six days, and you can keep the change."

"What if it takes us more than six days?" asked Duff.

"Then you're not who I thought you were."

"Start the clock, I guess." Duff checked the time on his computer. "It's almost seven. We could be in the Madison area before eleven if we hurry."

"You want to go now?" Abe checked his own phone screen to double-check the time. "Why don't we get a good night's sleep and go first thing in the morning?"

"If we slept in a hotel in Madison, we'd be able to start all the earlier tomorrow."

"It's Sunday tomorrow. There won't be much traffic if we're out around dawn. We'll be in Madison in time for a late breakfast."

Duff's eyes narrowed. "I'm not having breakfast with the church crowds on a Sunday. Are you insane?"

"Fine. We'll get McDonald's."

"I'm good with that." Duff looked to Buddy. "You coming with, Big Shooter?"

Buddy pushed himself out of his chair. "I'm gonna drive home and sleep in my own bed. I'll be available by phone if you need me, but I'd better not start poking around in some other sheriff's business without invitation. Not unless you find a reason for me to poke around in someone else's business, first."

"Got it." Duff gave him a Cub Scout salute.

Buddy paused at the door to their office. "Oh, boys—one other thing: Bring your hardware."

Abe glanced toward Duff's room where there was a safe in the closet that held both of their guns and a few boxes of ammo. Neither Abe nor Duff liked their guns, nor did they carry them regularly. Typically, the weapons came out of the safe once a year for about two days. One day for them to practice on the range, and the next day to shoot for real at a qualification session for their PI licenses. Then, the guns were cleaned, oiled, and put back in the cabinet. They were not very good marksmen, usually only qualifying by the skin of their teeth, more luck than skill. "You think it's going to be that serious?"

Buddy's big shoulders bobbed once. He held out a hand and rocked it from side-to-side in a noncommittal motion. "Maybe. If it was what the Dane County investigators are saying it was, then those irons aren't going to need to get hot. But if it wasn't a murder-suicide, then it was two murders, and anyone who doesn't have any qualms with putting a slug in a former cop's brain wouldn't hesitate to execute you two."

"Execute me?" Duff clutched at invisible pearls. "But I'm lovable."

Buddy held up his hand and rocked it side-to-side again. "Ehh." He stepped out of the office and began to close the door. "Stay in touch, gentlemen." The door closed and clicked as it shut.

Abe walked to the door and double-checked it to make sure it was locked. "You think there's anything to be concerned about?"

Duff was already gazing into the distance, his thinking face making his visage blank and impassive. "Yes. I know Buddy; he doesn't jump to conclusions lightly."

"But a double murder disguised to look like a murder-suicide that fools investigators? You can't possibly be buying that." Abe knew from long years of experience that staging a murder-suicide was difficult, if not impossible. People who did not want to be murdered usually would not cooperate with the murderer. Telltale evidence like powder burns and gunshot angles would be off and small details like tear-streaks on the cheeks of the victims would often give clues to a prolonged fit of fear.

Duff's eyes snapped back into focus, and he looked at Abe. "It's a long shot, I admit. But he just threw a big wad of cash at us to make sure the investigation was accurate. Given the odds are with us that the investigation was likely accurate, I'm going to go up to Madison, check some boxes, lay an old man's fears to rest, and come home with a few extra bucks in our pocket. What say you, old sport?"

"It's not like I have a life," said Abe. "I go where you go."

"How was dinner, by the way?"

"Don't ask." Abe flopped down in his chair. He swiveled it to face Duff. "Katherine was meeting a date there."

Duff was suddenly interested. "Oooh! Hot girl-on-girl action. Nice. How was that?"

"Embarrassing. For the briefest of seconds before Katherine showed up, I'd been talking with the woman she was seeing, and because my gaydar is nonexistent, I was dumb enough to think she was actually starting to flirt with me a little."

"Well, that was your first mistake, Quasimodo. Esmerelda will never love you; she loves Captain Phoebus."

"If either of us is Quasimodo, it's you. You're a lot closer to having a hunched back. And you're shorter than I am. If anything, I'm Claude Frollo, all thin and gaunt with hard, small eyes, and repulsing women with my age and station."

"You do realize that means I get to toss your ass off the top of Notre Dame, right?"

Abe shrugged. "There are worse ways to go."

"So, that's a maybe, then?"

2

ABE SLEPT RESTLESSLY. He often had trouble sleeping the night before he had to travel. He was constantly possessed by fears of oversleeping or of missing a flight despite the fact he almost never flew anywhere. He worried about packing for extended trips. He worried about forgetting something he would need like his wallet or his house keys. He would obsessively make lists and pore over the lists several times while stacking everything he thought he would need in piles. Then, he would pack them in a bag, only to wake up in the middle of the night, take everything out of the bag, and repack them one more time while going over the list yet again. It was certainly some form of OCD, but Abe never bothered to seek help for it. He had enough psychology training to know what it was, he knew methods to help others work on minimizing its impact, but he could not turn those methods on himself no matter how hard he tried. Physician, heal thyself, indeed.

In the morning, after he showered and dressed, Abe would inevitably go through his travel bag one more time, re-rolling his socks into perfect tubes so they took up less space in his suitcase. He prided himself on his packing abilities. He could Tetris-together a multitude of things in a small satchel by rolling, flattening, and compartmentalizing things. He checked and double-checked his list. He added a warmer coat in case it got cold, as it often did during the Midwestern spring. He added a raincoat, just in case. Lastly, he went to the bathroom and added his toiletries he would need for three days, including a razor and shaving cream. He did not like shaving at hotels, but if they were there long enough that he needed to do it, he would be prepared.

These efforts were in stark contrast to his more chaotic partner, of course.

When Abe arrived at the office promptly at the stroke of six, Duff was still asleep. Abe opened the door to his room and flipped the lights on. "You wanted to go last night! I told you to be ready at six!"

Duff sat bolt upright in the recliner that served as his bed and central video-game chair. The TV mounted on the wall was playing an infomercial about granite cookware that was supposedly better than Teflon. "I'm good to go. Just let me get my pants on."

Duff popped out of the chair flinging blankets off him and to the floor. He was still wearing his Carhartt hoodie from the day before and a pair of socks that looked like they were in need of laundering. He grabbed a pair of jeans and stepped into them. He slipped on his shoes. "Let's go."

"What about a toothbrush? A change of clothes?"

"Good point." Duff scooped a few things off the floor of his room and put them in a plastic bag from CVS. He wandered into the bathroom and grabbed a toothbrush. "I'm sharing your toothpaste," he informed Abe. Duff picked up an old disposable razor and inspected it. He grimaced and tossed it into an overflowing garbage can. "And maybe your razor."

"Over my dead body. You can buy a new one when we get to Madison."

"Fair enough." Duff closed the door to the bathroom. Abe could hear urination and then the sound of the toilet flushing. Duff threw open the door. "All set."

"Really?"

Duff looked at the dangling plastic bag in his hand. "Yeah."

"What if it gets cold? What if it rains?"

"Then I'll get cold and wet. This is the Midwest. I'm used to it." Duff shouldered past Abe and opened the door to the office.

"Hold up." Abe held up a hand. Duff closed the door. They both turned and looked at the wall of the office where just beyond was a small bedroom closet in Duff's room, and at the bottom of that closet, buried under Carhartts of various colors and stain-levels, was a small, square, dark gray gun safe.

"I suppose we better." Abe walked into Duff's room, swept the clothes and other, more terrible items off the safe, and then knelt to key in the five-digit passcode to pop the lock. The door opened and the two steely harbingers of doom lay inside, both harmlessly unloaded.

Abe pulled out Duff's Walther PPK, a gun Duff insisted on due to a lifelong affinity for all things James Bond. Abe's weapon of choice was a standard, black steel Smith & Wesson snub-barreled .38 with a six-bullet cylinder. The guys down at the gun range kept telling him he should upgrade to something fancier, maybe a Glock or a SIG Sauer nine-millimeter, but Abe liked the classical model. It was simple. It looked like the gun Jim Rockford carried. Growing up without a father figure, Abe often looked to television heroes for guidance, and *The Rockford Files* was on in reruns every day after school. Every day at four o'clock, it was Abe, a glass of milk, an unheated Pop-tart, a nineteen-inch Zenith TV with a fuzzy picture despite the tinfoil on the rabbit ears, and Jim Rockford.

Abe handed Duff the Walther. It was a small gun and looked like a toy in the big man's hand. Duff held it by the end of the grip between his index finger and thumb like it was a dead rat. "Now I am become Death, destroyer of worlds."

"It's not quite the atom bomb, Oppenheimer."

"If I shot you in the head right this second, it would fuck up a lot of people's worlds. Yours. Mine. Kathrine's. Tilda's. Hell, it'd fuck up Cesar's world because then who would buy his tacos every day?"

"I suppose that's true. Cesar's greatest fear is you keeling over from a heart attack because he just bought a new Mercedes and needs to make payments." Abe handed Duff two filled magazines for the Walther and took a box of loose bullets for himself. "Is that enough bullets for you?"

"If I can't hit it in twelve shots, it's going to kill me anyhow, so I doubt that thirteenth bullet is going to make or break it."

"You ever feel like maybe we should go to the range more often, maybe practice a bit?"

Duff snorted. "What on Earth would make you feel like we should start getting good at anything?" Duff found a shoulder holster on the floor of his room, shoved the gun into it, and stuffed it into the shopping bag with his clothes and ammo magazines.

Abe slipped his belt-clip holster onto his side and gingerly stuck the unloaded revolver into it. He pulled on a coat to hide the gun and shoved the box of bullets into the coat pocket which he promptly zipped shut.

Duff approved. "Very Barney Fife of you."

They walked down the stairs to street level. Already it was turning into a glorious spring day. The sun was tinting the horizon with vibrant pinks and oranges. The Sunday morning traffic was light, so the city was relatively quiet. The songbirds were seeking mates in full force, so the traffic din was punctuated with warbles, tweets, and chirps. It was still cold enough to see breath as they exhaled, a gentle reminder that winter wasn't over until it decided it was over. Winter in Chicago was a tenacious beast.

El Muro, the little taquería housed on the first floor of their building, was already serving customers. The walk-up window was always busy on weekdays from neighborhood patrons on their way to work, but on Sunday it was a little slower. Rodrigo "Sally" Salazar, a portly house painter who was one of Duff's drinking buddies and a cousin to El Muro's owner, Cesar Salazar, was at the window in paint-spattered whites held up by bright red suspenders. He held up a cup of coffee in salute to Abe and Duff. "Buenos dias, gringos! What brings you out of hiding so early on a Sunday?"

"Your mom," said Duff. "She said she needed someone to take naked pictures of her, so we volunteered."

"Shit, you could have just asked me. I got some." Cesar stuck his head out of the walk-up window. "Too many, really. Tell your mom to stop sendin' them to me. It's weird."

"Fuck all of you." Sally said. "No really, you guys working on a case or what?"

"Don't know for sure; maybe it's a case, maybe it's not. Either way, we're going up to Wisconsin for a few days to check some stuff out."

"Someone steal some cheese?" Cesar popped back out of the window with a pair of foil-wrapped breakfast burritos, a bottle of water, and a can of diet Coke.

"You figured it out. We're investigating grand theft cheddar. We're going to look for a guy who hasn't taken a shit in a week. He'll be the prime suspect." Duff took the burritos from Cesar and passed him a pair of fives.

"You're packing your gun?" Cesar jutted his chin toward the bag in Duff's hand. The Walther in the holster was clearly visible against the thin plastic. "Must be some serious cheddar."

"No, we're taking the guns in case we need to make Swiss cheese. We'll just shoot up the cheddar a bunch."

"How's a bullet gonna make orange cheese white?" Sally said.

"Scares the hell out of it, that's for sure."

Cesar and Sally looked at each other and burst out laughing. "You fuggin' guys," Sally snorted. "Be safe, eh?"

"Will do, Sally." Duff gave the good-natured painter a nod and strode past him.

Abe and Duff got into their minivan, *The Bad-Luck Charm*. It was a decade-old Toyota Sienna that, through no fault of their own, had several smart dents, a missing front license plate, and a cracked side window Duff had fixed with Flex-Seal tape, because late-night infomercials were an extremely effective form of marketing on him. It was the kind of car that attracted damage. Two weeks ago, Abe had been driving it down the Dan Ryan Express and a large seagull decided it had more than enough of life because it dive-bombed the front windshield. Abe didn't hit the bird; the bird tried to play chicken with a two-ton minivan and lost. It left a considerable chip in the top of the driver's side windshield with its beak. Or its skull. Or maybe it was carrying an ice climber's piton. Something dinged the living hell out of the glass. That was the sort of luck the van had. If a semi was driving in front of Abe, it was a question of when, not if, a rock was going to shoot out from beneath one of its tires.

At least the interior was clean. For all his faults in personal grooming and laundry-folding, Duff was meticulous when it came to the interior of the car. He hated to see scraps of paper or stains. Some days, when Abe was hard at work on the boring research stuff that kept their investigations office afloat, Duff would go down and hand-scrub the industrial carpeting in the van because he felt it was getting dingy. He couldn't be bothered to clean his room, but the van must be clean.

Abe started the van. It gave a squeal of protest due to the cold but turned over and began chugging along. All the cosmetic damage had not affected the engine, and Toyota did build long-running vehicles. Abe was grateful for that.

It was a little less than three hours to Madison. Abe guided the minivan out of its parking space and headed west. It would not take much time to get to Highway 90, and then it was a clear shot to Rockford and all points north.

WHILE THEY DROVE northward, Buddy Olson texted Abe and Duff the home address of the Laskeys. He sent them the names, addresses, and cell phone numbers of their two adult children, as well: Marcus Laskey and Marybeth Collier.

The home address was listed as being northwest of a little town called Mount Horeb, once a very rural farming community that had over the years transformed into more of a gentrified bedroom community for professionals who worked in Madison, although it remained surrounded by picturesque rolling hills of farmland. The farmhouse the Laskeys were living in was just outside of a town called Blue Mounds, which was a ramshackle conglomeration of a few old houses next to a few newer subdivisions at the base of the tallest point in Dane County, Wisconsin, and one of the highest points in the entire state: Blue Mounds State Park. It was a local landmark, an unmistakable giant hill of trees that swelled out of the landscape and towered above the lower-lying farmland.

Eons ago, a sizable chunk of Wisconsin went untouched by the Ice Age glaciers that encroached over most of the north-central states. This region was called the Driftless Area, and Mount Horeb and Blue Mounds were on the eastern edge of that region. Thus, the landscape around them was quite different

17

from even that of Madison, only a few miles to the east. East of Madison, the land was largely level and flat, bulldozed by countless centuries of ice migration. Around the southwestern edge of Dane County, there were hills and valleys with twisting creeks and rivers winding through the flats. The farmland was ridiculous, with slopes sometimes jutting up at thirty-degree angles or better, forcing farmers to adopt precarious tilts on their tractors to get the strip-farmed fields plowed.

Abe and Duff elected to book a hotel in the town nearest to Mount Horeb, a little bustling suburb of Madison called Verona. Given it was a Sunday, reservations were not a problem. Duff used his phone to select a single room with two queen-sized beds but noted that check-in was not until after three in the afternoon. This gave them time to scout the area and look at the farmhouse.

The Sunday morning roads were beginning to get busy when they arrived at the hamlet of Mount Horeb. The early services of the local churches were letting out and minivans and cars were starting to clog the streets, either leaving the early Mass or heading to the later one. A large number of people were out on bicycles, trying to take advantage of the sun and early spring temperatures to start getting back into distance-biking shape.

Duff went on a rant when he saw them. "Why do all these bicycle idiots buy expensive bikes and get the little cute Tour de France outfits like they're expecting the peloton to chase them? When I was a kid, all you needed was a shitty bike from the hardware store and a pair of cut-off jeans. Shirts were optional, depending on how fat you were and how much you liked road rash. I always wore a shirt."

"I'm sure the neighborhood was grateful."

"They pretty much insisted. I think there was a petition."

Mount Horeb was a contradiction. On one hand, it was still heavily rural, with nearly fifteen solid miles of farmland separating it from Madison, and family-owned dairy farms dotting the countryside. Placid and unbothered, scores of black-and-white Holsteins grazed in fields and watched cars wind down county roads. On the other hand, Mount Horeb was becoming heavily modernized as people who worked in Madison sought a quieter style of life, escaping the more crowded suburbs for the slightly larger yards and pastoral vibe of the country. Mount Horeb was evolving into a more hip, vibrant community and quickly becoming less bucolic. After a town gets its second yoga studio, any claim to still be rural gets tossed out the window.

Newer subdivisions surrounded Mount Horeb's older homes, and the town was expanding eastward, toward its neighbor, Verona. Madison began to creep toward being a modest megalopolis, quietly swallowing up the small suburbs like Middleton, Verona, Fitchburg, and Sun Prairie as it expanded so that travelers hardly knew when they left Madison's limits and passed into a new town.

Chicago was like that, though, a true monument of urban sprawl. Abe and Duff were used to the expansive divisions of neighborhoods and small towns in the suburbs being ignored in favor of simply being labeled as Chicago by outsiders. Madison was a long way from that level of stretch.

Abe entered the little town on its most eastern edge, drifting off the highway onto an exit ramp next to a Chevy dealership. Beyond that was a hotel, a few homes, and what comprised the start of the retail shopping district of Mount Horeb, a grocery store, a newly built strip mall, and a sign pointing to a golf course.

Abe drove the main drag slowly. It had been almost twenty-five years since he'd last seen the town. It had changed drastically. From his memory, the town had once ended at the golf course with only cornstalks and hayfields beyond it. Now, it was a swollen tick of a little burgh, with various shops and buildings mixing in at the edges of the subdivisions. The subdivisions themselves were nothing special. A halfway cognizant eye could pick out the eras in which the houses were built. Most of the ones near the highway were less than ten years old. Further in, the eras were more clearly delineated, moving from the late 1990s to the 1970s, and further in toward the center of town were the old brick structures that were easily more than a century old, although they still held their shape and looked grander than most of the postwar homes.

The oldest section of the main street through town looked like a lot of small towns in the Midwest. It was anchored by brick structures, including a former performance hall and theater, a towering, three-story, Queen Anne-style building with a bulging circular corner tower. Like many American towns established in the late 1880s, the smaller shops and restaurants down the central street were square-fronted. Cars lined parking spaces on either side of the street, and pedestrians strolled down the sidewalks, although not too many pedestrians. It was a Sunday morning, not even ten o' clock, so apart from the occasional jogger or dog-walker, human forms were limited.

Beyond the main street's shops were houses, many dating back to the 1920s or 1930s, and beyond that, a large hardware store and a liquor store, and then the farmland started up again. Abe cruised the whole drag slowly, but it took less than five minutes to get from one end of town to the other.

Abe liked the place a lot. "I can see the appeal of a town like that." Abe and Katherine had once dreamed of small-town life early in their marriage, especially when it came to raising a child, but with Abe's general failure to be a lawyer and the founding of his private investigations practice headquartered in Chinatown, it was never meant to be. The idyllic life escaped him.

"Needs more sports bars. And people. And traffic." Duff once was banished to the legitimate North American wilderness where he had been forced to endure his teen years, and thus had had a great distaste for the outdoors, the cold, and any lack of Internet connectivity. At that moment, the pungent smell of freshly spread manure flooded the van. Duff tucked his nose inside his sweatshirt. "And fewer cows."

Abe drove county highway ID out of Mount Horeb and found Blue Mounds shortly thereafter. The mound for which the town was named was visible for miles around, a long, low hump jutting out of the ground a quarter-mile high on the horizon. As they drew closer, the mound seemed to disappear, becoming more of a hill than an obstacle in the landscape. It was still a good-sized, steep hill, but it looked more impressive from afar, as so many things often do.

Following the directions on Duff's map app, Abe turned off ID and onto county road F, moving toward Brigham County Park. Duff read the Wikipedia entry about the park off his phone as they drove. "Says it was named after Ebenezer Brigham, the first permanent European resident of Dane County." Duff exited the app and stuck it back in his pocket. "There's a name you don't run into too often: Ebenezer. You think Charles Dickens ruined it for everyone, sort of like how Hitler ruined the name Adolf?"

"Probably."

"Could you imagine having the Hitler surname now? People do, you know."

"I do know."

"You'd have to be constantly saying, C'mon, fellas—I'm a good Hitler. I bet that'd get tiresome quickly."

"You think a lot about names, don't you?"

"I do." Duff refused to use his given name, the one his CS Lewis-devotee father had saddled him with so many years ago. "I'm still thinking we should have cool, macho nicknames. It might help our cause."

"I don't think anyone would buy us having cool nicknames."

"Whatever you say, Hawkeye."

"Hawkeye as in the Marvel archer, Natty Bumppo from the James Fennimore Cooper book, or the guy from M*A*S*H?"

"Take your pick."

Abe shook his head. "No one will call me Hawkeye."

"I just did. Now you start calling me Grendel."

"No."

Abe turned down a small, one-lane road and found the Laskey residence. It was a quaint white farmhouse set near the top of a ridge, but far enough off of the county road that it looked distant and small to any traveler who might see it. There were three out-buildings visible from the road: a dilapidated old barn, a low machine shed, and a pole barn that served as a two-car garage. The pole barn doors were open, and two vehicles were inside, a late model, black, Ford F-150 pickup and a sporty blue Subaru WRX with a tailfin.

"Those aren't cheap rides," said Abe. "But they're not going to break the bank, either."

"That's a Ford with the Raptor package," Duff corrected him. "That Raptor package adds like twenty-grand to the sticker. That's easily a seventy-thousand-dollar truck, maybe seventy-five. In my abject poverty, I have not been out pricing pickup trucks as much as I'd like to be."

"The WRX is only a thirty-five-thousand-dollar car." Abe had been out pricing cars, but not to buy. Never to buy. He liked cars, but he was never one to be flashy. Having a car with a tailfin made a statement, and Abe knew he was not that kind of guy. He was solidly a minivan or PT Cruiser-type of guy. Maybe, in his flashiest moments, an '87 Jeep Wagoneer-type of guy. He was comfortable with that, though. Those kinds of guys paid the bills on time. Those kinds of guys didn't come home with black eyes after pissing off the wrong guy at the bar.

"Figure the truck was Art's, and the WRX was Michelle's?"

Abe turned the minivan down the Laskeys' long driveway, creeping forward on the engine's impulse power. "That's probably the most likely scenario."

Abe pulled the van to a stop in front of the garage. Duff was out of the van before Abe could put it in park. The big man stood on his toes and sniffed the air like a prairie dog. "Smells weird."

Abe shut off the van. He stepped out and sniffed the air, as well. It was crisp and cold with hints of cow manure and wet earth. "Smells like the countryside."

"Ah, that's it. I miss the smell of urine, dead fish, and diesel fumes. And where is all the screaming? I miss the screaming." As if to punctuate the change in environment, in the distance, a cow began a long, mournful lowing. Duff began to whistle the theme to *Green Acres*.

The front door to the house was still wrapped with yellow crime scene tape. A legal notice from the Dane County Sheriff's Department was still taped over the edge of the door, sealing the home from nosy neighbors.

Abe and Duff walked to the house and peeked through the window of the door. The house was on a raised stone foundation so the windows on the first floor were all six-and-a-half feet off the ground. There was no peeking in the windows. Abe glanced through the round portal window of the door. There was a small entryway that looked like it served as a mudroom, and past that was a larger living room. Although the crime scene was more than a week old, it had not been cleaned. A large, dried pool of blood had turned a dark brown on the light oak floor.

"Well, there's your crime scene."

Duff used his hands around his eyes as a shield against the light and pressed his nose to the window. "Yep."

"See anything?"

"Nope."

They backed away from the house. "I don't suppose there's a ladder around here," said Duff. "Maybe we could try to get in on the second floor."

"Or maybe we respect the legal sealing of a crime scene by the prevailing local law enforcement for once."

"Why would we do that?"

"Because we don't like prison."

Duff waggled a finger at Abe. "There you go again. Always with the good ideas." He walked toward the garage. "We can at least poke around the other buildings. No crime scene tape on them."

Abe stood at the base of the concrete steps leading to the small porch at the front of the house. He looked around the property for a moment. A chill crept up his back. He had been in and around many murder scenes over the years, but a murder in Chicago is a little different than a murder at an older farmhouse down a long driveway near a little-traveled road. There was no sound in Abe's ears outside the wind in the trees in the valley behind the house and the distant birdsong of the early-arriving sparrows, robins, and warblers. He reasoned the near silence of the empty countryside was throwing him off. There was no dull, moaning drone of traffic punctuated by the occasional horn honked in anger. There were no voices. There was only blue sky, birds, and breeze. It felt wrong, almost. Eerie.

Duff seemed unfazed by the change in environment. He had spent years in a boys' home in the Canadian wilderness, and he had once told Abe that when the snow fell thickly up there, it was like being in an acoustic chamber, and all sound just died a quiet, still death. It would get so silent that he could hear his heartbeat in his ears.

Abe followed Duff into the garage. Around the corner, parked next to the WRX, was another surprise: a very large Harley-Davidson touring motorcycle, complete with leather storage bags mounted behind the seat and a big front fairing. The cycle was mostly black with white accents, and it looked new. "Another twenty grand, would you say?"

"At least." Duff looked around the garage. "This has to be at least a hundred-grand in recently purchased motor vehicles, you realize that?"

"Retirement must be good."

Duff's left eyebrow arched high on his forehead. "Yeah. Sure. Retirement. Hang on." Duff stormed out of the garage, taking a sharp turn around the corner. A moment later, there was a pair of loud thumps on the side of the corrugated tin garage. Duff's voice called to Abe through the metal. "Hey, come look at this."

Abe stepped out of the garage into the chilly wind and walked around to the rear of the garage. Under a blue plastic tarp was a large Manitou pontoon boat.

"I guess this is what he needed the F-150 for," said Duff. "What do you expect? Another fifty grand?"

Abe shrugged. He had no idea; he never priced out boats. A sports car was already an unattainable dream. Buying a boat was just more salt for the wound. "Sure. Let's go with that."

"So, we're already up to a hundred-and-fifty-grand in vehicles at this place. You want to bet on whether we're going to find more expensive stuff when or if we get into the house?"

"It is a lot of money, but there might be an explanation. Inheritance? Smart investing? A lucky pump-and-dump of cryptocurrency? Small lottery win? Someone wins two-hundred-grand in the Powerball, and it doesn't make the news."

"Sure, I suppose. Maybe this is all legit. Or maybe Buddy is right, and something is a little hinky about these people."

"Remember what you told me about jumping to conclusions when we first started working together?" Abe knew Duff remembered. Duff had a memory even better than Abe's.

"Don't do it."

"That's right. Work from a hunch if you have to, but let the facts lead you where they may."

They walked back to the garage. The F-150 was locked, but the WRX wasn't. Abe opened the driver-side door and peered into the car. Duff opened the passenger door and slipped into the seat, immediately popping the glove compartment to see what he could find. It was a nearly new car, only fifteen thousand miles on it. The only thing in the glove box was a copy of the Laskeys' insurance card and the owner's manual. Abe popped the small trunk, but inside there was only a winter-weather kit, a necessity for southern Wisconsin cars.

"Disappointing," said Duff. "Might be some more stuff hidden in here, but we'd have to start taking the car apart."

"I suggest you don't do that." A woman's voice froze Abe and Duff.

They started to turn, but the voice shouted another command. "Slow. Do it slowly and show me your hands."

A cop. Had to be.

Abe and Duff both slowly moved their hands out away from their sides to show they were empty. Then, both moving very slowly, they turned to see a young woman in khaki slacks and a dark brown Dane County sheriff's deputy uniform shirt holding a gun. She had her finger in the safe position, so she wasn't looking to shoot them, Abe figured. The gun was pointed toward the ground near their feet, but it would take a fraction of a second for her to raise it and end their lives if they did something stupid, and that was more than enough of a deterrent.

"Who are you? And why are you here?" The deputy's dark eyes were narrowed. They reminded Abe of an angry cat. She looked to be in her mid-twenties, with short, dark brown hair with reddish highlights and high cheekbones. A gold deputy's badge sat high on the left side of her shirt, almost to her shoulder. She was small, a full head shorter than either Abe or Duff, but she looked like she was tougher than both of them put together. Something in her stance, something in her posture said she could hurt them if she needed to, and she wouldn't need the gun to do it.

"I'm Abe, this is Duff. We're private investigators." Abe looked back to the end of the driveway and saw a Dane County Sheriff's SUV parked at the top of it. That was how the deputy had been able to creep up on them.

Duff inclined his head toward Abe. "Slappy's got a PI license in his pocket. He'll show it to you if you promise not to shoot him."

"Got any weapons on you?"

Duff inclined his head toward the van. "They're in our van. Unless you're talking about my razor-sharp wit."

"Take the badge out, then. Slow."

Abe reached into the front pocket of his slacks with two fingers and withdrew the thin badge folio he carried there. He did it slowly and cautiously. With one hand, he opened the folio to show the small Illinois PI license and badge.

"That badge is shaped like a stink bug."

"It's not really a badge," said Abe. "It's more like a little sigil pin or something. It's not supposed to be a badge, and we're not supposed to call it a badge, but we all do."

The deputy lowered her gun, pointing the barrel at the ground next to her. She strode forward and took the folio from Abe's hand. "What kind of name is Aberforth?"

"Medieval."

"Illinois. What are you FIBs doing up here, then? Illinois license is good in Illinois, not Wisconsin."

"For the purpose of establishing an investigations business, yes. For the purpose of conducting an investigation the license is good in all states, provided we follow all state and federal laws and municipal edicts." Abe held out a hand, and the deputy handed him the folio.

"What about you, Chuckles? What's your name? Where's your license?"

"I'm Duff. License is in the van, I think. Maybe Aberforth has it. I don't know. Don't really care, honestly. I try never to carry the damn thing if I can help it."

"You don't carry your license?"

"You'd be surprised at how little people care when you burst into a room, tell people you're a PI, and then flash that rejected Cracker Jack prize. Besides, I'm more interested in hearing about the breakup you just went through. What happened?"

That was a left jab the deputy didn't see coming. It caught her off guard. It rattled her. She hesitated. "What breakup?"

Duff, hands still raised in the air, pointed at her left hand with his index finger. "There's an indentation on your ring finger where the ring used to go."

"I don't wear a ring while I work."

"Yeah, you stick it in your right front pocket. I can tell because there's a pretty good ring-shaped wear mark on your left thigh right about where the bottom of that pocket would be, but there's no ring in there today. So, I assume you either broke up with someone recently or you left it at home. I'm betting, just from the looks of the ends of your fingernails, that you've been suffering some major anxiety lately, so I'm going to have to guess that you broke up with someone. Did he cheat on you?"

The deputy relaxed and holstered her service weapon. "That's some good observation. Maybe you guys really are private investigators."

"I'm going to guess the breakup was less than a week ago, right?"

"Eight days, actually. Last Saturday night."

"Bummer. I was close." Duff lowered his hands. Abe followed his lead.

"I'm Shelby Ree. You can call me Shelby. Don't have to call me deputy. Why are you two at a crime scene?"

Abe said, "We were hired by a friend of the Laskeys to do our own investigation into their death."

"Really? Someone thinks it's suspicious?"

Abe heard a change in the deputy's tone. There was no hint she might be curious about his statement. There was an edge to what she said, a very dry, wry sarcasm. "I guess you don't like it, either."

Shelby Ree stared hard at Abe for a long moment. "Let's just say I'm not a fan of the official story."

"Oh, do tell," said Duff. "We'll come back to that breakup later."

Ree chewed on her lower lip for a moment, looking from Duff, to Abe, and back to Duff as she did. She gave a shrug of her shoulders. "What the hell. Why not?"

Shelby snapped the leather strap of her holster back over the top of her gun. "I knew the Laskeys. They were nice people. In no way, shape, or form do I believe for even one second that Michelle Laskey killed Art and then herself. She didn't have it in her. She didn't even like guns. She was a pacifist. She was a trained mediator. If she and Art fought, it was done with love and jokes, not guns. They were sarcastic and droll. They liked to tease each other, but you could tell, even though they were in their early sixties, they were still knocking boots on the regular."

"Well." Duff's mouth curled into an ill grimace. "There's an image I won't be able to scrub from my brain."

"I'm just telling you; they were still in love. They acted like teenagers. I was out here on patrol a few weeks back, and I saw Art's pickup come up over a hill at me. Michelle was actually sitting in the middle of the seat, snuggled right up next to Art, no one else in the truck with them. It was just the two of them cruising down the road like they were still dating."

Duff's face contorted into a clenched-teeth grimace. "Are they one of those couples who sit together on the same side of a booth at a restaurant? I hate those people. Face each other! Look each other in the eye!"

"Ignore him; he was never loved, and his heart is a stone," said Abe. "What makes you think the investigation is wrong?"

Ree kicked at a rock on the ground in front of her. "Didn't say it's wrong. I just didn't come to the same conclusion, is all. Maybe they're right. I just don't think so, but I have nothing but a gut feeling to base it on."

"Trust those instincts. I do." Duff took a couple steps toward the farmhouse. "Can I get in there?"

Ree shook her head. "Not until someone says so, unfortunately. The investigation just concluded on Friday. The Laskey's kids own the house now, technically. They are getting a crime scene cleaner to come out to clean up their parents' blood so they don't have to see it. Earliest you might be able to get in there would be tomorrow night, I think."

"What about the barn and the shed? Can we get in there?"

"Sure," said Ree. "Don't think you'll find anything, though. Deputies went through there the night of the incident and said they were both empty."

"No offense, but most sheriff's deputies I've met have heads emptier than that there barn." Duff froze, his face warping in a look of horror. "Did I really just say *that there*? Am I turning country?" He snapped his fingers at Abe. "Boy, go rassle me up a Garth Brooks CD, a jug of your finest moonshine, and a pair of leather shitkickers, would you?"

"What-kickers?"

"Boots." Ree held out her right foot. "Usually cowboy boots, although we call our tac boots shitkickers often enough around here."

"Colorful." Abe felt a sudden longing for Chicago.

THE BARN WAS indeed empty. It was an old, weather-beaten hag of a building. Once it had been the heartbeat of a small family farm, home to dairy cows, chickens, cats, dogs, and maybe a few sheep or goats over the century or so since it was first built. But, as it so often does, time changed the landscape of the area. When the family that farmed that plot of land grew too old, no one showed up looking to replace them as tillers of soil and milkers of cattle. Instead, someone showed up looking for a sanctuary from the hustle of Madison and a quiet place to enjoy their nights and weekends in the relative security and serenity of a small town. The barn, no longer needed and kept full of hay and the body heat of the cows to help insulate it in the winter, quickly fell to disrepair. The limestone and mud-daubed foundation of the building began to crack and splinter. The boards in the haymow swelled and shrank repeatedly from decades of rain, heat, and cold until the nails could no longer hold the boards to the beams and they simply fell away. Now, the building was a gap-toothed monster, missing every third or fourth board, and the once bright red paint that made it stand out like a beacon amidst green fields was weathered down to the wood, so the predominant color of the barn was a dull, earthy gray tinged with a hint of red.

There was still a thick layer of hay in the mow, but it was ancient and moldered, dusty and foul. The second Abe set foot in the building, his sinuses jumped to life with a visceral reaction against the mold and dust. He sought the handkerchief he kept folded in his back left pocket and pressed it to his nose and mouth. It was a weak filter against the elements, but it was all he had.

The barn looked like all the old barns around Wisconsin. The base level was the milking parlor, a series of rusted metal stanchions where cows once were milked twice daily. There was a gutter running the length of the barn on either side of the central aisle for whatever they dropped behind them to get swept out of the place. There were still old, rusted pipes hanging from the ceiling. The pipes had once been shining stainless steel, kept to food-grade levels of cleanliness for running milk to tanks. Now, they were no longer serviceable for anything, save recycling.

When the trio walked into the barn, Abe and Shelby Ree hung back by the sliding door that served as the entrance. Only Duff crept inside. A few old windows, the glass long ago broken out of the panes, served the light from outside in glowing shafts thick with dust that seemed to do a slow, swirling waltz in what little breeze made it into the building.

"See, empty." Ree pulled her flashlight from her utility belt and clicked it on, sweeping the shadows in the far corners where the light was hesitant to go.

"Is it though?" Duff was standing in the middle of the large, concrete, central aisle. He was turning in a slow circle, eyes cast to the ground.

Abe, who had spent practically every day with Duff for more than twenty years, knew that tone immediately. It was the sound of him noticing something that the police had overlooked, either through haste or incompetence. "What did you find?"

"Not certain, but there's more here than just nothing." Duff pointed at the floor on one side of the barn, past the stanchions. "Look at the dust."

Abe and Ree walked into the barn and stood next to Duff. They looked where he was looking and saw a messy floor, an old slab thickly covered with a layer of dust and dirt.

"It's messy. So what?" Ree held the beam of her Maglite on the spot.

Abe could see what Duff was seeing. It was faint, but it was there. "It's messy, but it's all messy in one direction. There were slide marks in the dust, as though something large and heavy with a flat bottom had been slid into place there, then slid out again. "Boxes. There were stacks of boxes there at one point."

"Yup. And not overly long ago, too."

Ree squinted at it. "How did you see that?"

"Well, first I opened my eyes, and then I looked at it," Duff said. It was a matter-of-fact statement. "You see, unlike most cops I know, I didn't burst in here with a gun drawn looking to shoot someone. That helps clear the mind somewhat so things that are perfectly obvious stand out a little more."

Ree appraised Duff with a glance. "You're something of an asshole, aren't you?"

"Yes, he is," said Abe. "And you're far from the first person to reach that conclusion."

"The first person to figure it out was my mom. I like to say I learned from the best."

"Storing boxes isn't a crime," said Ree. "Might have just been a pile of stuff they were saving to take to Goodwill."

"True. Maybe the boxes are important, maybe they're not. I don't know. However, I do know there were boxes in this barn at some point in the last few weeks, and they're no longer here."

"So…boxes equal murder, then?" said Ree. "I'm not buying it."

"I'm not buying it, either. I'm just saying there were boxes here. That's all. Let's go check the other building." Duff turned on his heel and walked out of the barn.

The old machine shed was in similar shape to the barn, although in its heyday it had been painted white, not red. Much like the barn, it had seen better days. Once, the long, low building had housed things like tractors, plows, and hay-rakes, as well as the tools and parts to fix them when they broke. Now, the building was empty, and time had worked its hateful magic on it. The ridge of the sloped roof had broken in the middle, and while the building remained standing, it had a sickly swayback look to it.

At the far end of the shed was an old, wooden worktable. A few odds and ends Art Laskey must have used were on it: a toolbox with an assortment of tools, a chainsaw that had seen better days and was taken apart for repair, and a reciprocating saw that needed a blade. A generator stood to the side of the table, and a portable work light sat atop the generator. Next to the generator was a large rock auger outfitted with a wicked-looked conical tip with hooks and barbs meant to grind through stone. The rest of the shed was empty.

Ree hit the shed with her flashlight and swept it around the room. This time, knowing what to look for, she spotted it immediately. She pointed with the beam of the Maglite. "Boxes."

The same patterns of dust disturbances from the barn could be seen in the dirt on the floor of the shop, although it was harder to see because the floor of the machine shed was just earth packed hard as concrete from decades of use. The building was well barricaded from the elements, though. It had not lost boards like the barn. It was still a fitting shelter from the wind and rain. The marks on the ground were faint, but they were there. Just as faint in hard-packed clay were a couple of sets of boot prints. Judging from the pattern on the sole, they were tactical boots favored by police.

"They walked right over it. Didn't even see it." Ree shook her head sadly.

"You think it means something, then?" asked Abe.

Ree shrugged. "I don't know. Ask friggin' Sherlock over there."

Duff also shrugged. "Don't know. I'd like to get into that house. Maybe I'd learn something valuable. Maybe I wouldn't. Marks in dust don't mean much in and of themselves, but until it's nothing, it's not nothing."

"Can't get in legally until you're given permission. Maybe tomorrow." Ree holstered her Maglite and spun on her heel, walking back out into the brisk breeze of the early spring morning.

"We have the contact info for the Laskeys' kids." Abe searched his phone for the text from Buddy. "We could call them. Can we get access if we get verbal permission from the next of kin?"

Ree shrugged. "If I hear it from the owners of the house, which would be their kids, I technically have no right to stop you from cracking the seal on the door."

Duff waggled his eyebrows at Abe. "Now we're cooking with gas. Get on the horn, Silverhand. Talk to the people."

"No. No nicknames. We're not nickname people."

"Aren't Abe and Duff already sort of a nickname?" Ree looked slightly confused.

Duff was undeterred. "They're not cool nicknames. How 'bout you call me Iceman, and you can call the killjoy over there Slider?"

"I've told you a thousand times, no *Top Gun* call signs."

ABE HATED MAKING calls like this. Duff had zero qualms about talking to strangers, getting into people's faces, or otherwise making them upset, but he also had no tact and no desire to be tactful. Talking to the child, even an adult child, of a newly deceased person required tact, especially from a stranger, and even more so when that stranger calls from out of the blue with no preparation. This was the sort of thing Abe would have preferred to do face-to-face, but if a crime scene cleaner got into the house before he and Duff did, who knows what possible evidence might be lost. It was imperative they get into the house.

Abe walked a few paces away from Duff and Ree while he dialed the first number Buddy had texted them, the number for the Laskeys' son, Marcus. It went straight to voicemail. Abe left a stilted message. "Hi, this is Abe Allard with Allard and Duffy Investigations. My partner and I would like to talk with you or your sister about the possibility of getting into your parents' house to conduct an investigation sometime today or tomorrow morning before the cleaners get to it." Abe left his number and a request for Michael to return his call. Abe hated leaving that sort of message. It felt cold. With most people not answering their phones when strange numbers popped up on the calling screen that was becoming more and more commonplace, though. Abe rarely got people on the first call anymore. Leave a message; if they want to talk to you, they will call back. Even more concerning was the number of times Abe called a line and got a *voice mailbox full* recording. That meant that people weren't deleting messages, possibly not even listening to them anymore. It was text or nothing for many people.

Abe hit the link for Marybeth Collier's number. She was the Laskeys' daughter, their second child. According to Buddy, she had married while she was young and given the Laskeys a pair of grandchildren. Marybeth's phone rang three times, then jumped to voicemail. That meant she saw the call come in, but manually deferred it to the recording. At least she saw the call hit her phone.

Abe left the same message as he did for Michael. He kept his phone in his hand hoping one of the two would call him back quickly. "I tried."

The three of them stood there staring blankly at each other for several seconds. Ree finally broke the silence. "I guess I should get back to work, then." She pulled a business card from her pocket and scrawled a number on the back. "That's my personal cell. I'd appreciate it if you guys kept me in the loop on this."

"We'll do our best." Abe took the card from her and handed her one of his own cards. "Both our cells are on there."

She pocketed the card and turned and strolled back to the big SUV the county gave her to aid with serving and protecting.

Abe and Duff walked back to *The Bad Luck Charm*. "Well, I guess we could go back to Mount Horeb and look for lunch or something. It's getting on towards eleven. Culver's is open." Abe started the van.

"Or, better yet, we could pretend to leave, do a loop back, and do more poking around." Duff pointed at the deputy's SUV turning left on the road. "Follow her back to that main road we were on. Turn the opposite direction she does."

Abe did as instructed. The deputy turned right, heading back toward Blue Mounds. Abe went left. They drove until the deputy's SUV was out of sight, and then Abe pulled a three-point turn in the nearest driveway. He drove back to the Laskeys' house.

"Pull the van around behind the house."

Abe knew better than to ask questions. When Duff had a plan, it was usually best not to argue with him. Abe steered the van through the gap between the house and barn and crept over the grass. The van rocked a little from the uneven turf of the yard, but it was nothing concerning. When the van was fully hidden behind the house, Duff told him to stop and throw it in park.

"What are you doing?"

"I'm using the van as a stepladder so I can look into the windows."

Abe was no expert on the weight rating of minivan roofs, but he had a good idea that Duff's frame was probably a little much for it. "You think that's really a good idea?"

"I'm not going to step into the middle of the roof. I'm going to use the roll cage frame. If the roll cage can't support my weight, it's not going to support the van's weight if the damn thing flips over."

"Why test it, then?"

Duff gestured at the cracked window and the damage to the front quarter panel. "What? Am I harming the resale value?"

What was a little more damage to an already battered van? "Fine. Go ahead."

Duff left the van and walked around the driver's side. He opened the rear door and used the seat in the back as a steppingstone to vault himself to the van's roof. For a man his size, he accomplished the move with surprisingly little effort or struggle.

The van's roof protested. The sound of the metal panel flexing and compensating for the sudden and unwanted weight was thunderous. Duff quickly oriented so he was standing on the edge of the van's body where it was strongest, and he was leaning precariously to the house, supporting his weight against the framing around one of the windows.

Abe shut the rear door of the van to help give the cage extra support. "What do you see?"

"Pretty much what we saw from the other window. Big dark stain on the floor. Crime scene evidence markers. Not much else."

Abe thought of the vehicles in the garage. "How's it look money-wise?"

"Big-ass TV on the wall. Looks like a top-of-the-line OLED. It's probably a five-or-six-thousand-dollar TV."

"Well, that's a start."

"Can we get one of those bad boys for the office?"

"No. Keep looking."

Duff turned back to the window. "Leather couch. Leather loveseat. Those ain't cheap, but they're not going to break the bank, either. Looks like refinished hardwood floors throughout the first floor. Most of these old houses had hardwood floors, so that's not too unusual. The refinish job is, though. That's some big money."

"So, they were definitely well-off, and it wasn't just about the cars they drove. I'd like to get a look at their bank statements," said Abe.

"I'm betting they did a lot of cash transactions. Easy way to launder a lot of dirty money is big-ticket cash purchases like TVs or furniture. Big enough to get rid of small piles of cash, but not big enough to alert the feds." Duff lowered himself to a crouch, flopped onto his stomach on the edge of the roof, and then slid his legs off and dropped to the ground. "We need to get into the house. I don't know if it will help or not. I don't know if we'll find anything new, but we need to get in there and poke around."

Before Abe could tell him it was a bad idea Duff was making tracks for the still-sealed back door of the farmhouse. "You're breaking and entering, and that's still considered a crime scene as long as that tape is up. That's a felony."

"Wouldn't be the first time," said Duff. "And I'm not going to break the tape."

"Then how are you getting in there?"

Duff waggled an eyebrow. "I could see the door from the window. The window next to it isn't latched. We just have to slide it up. Pull the van below the window, I'll get into the house, and then you can pull the van away from the house. Go hide it behind the pontoon boat and wait for me."

Abe could already feel heartburn at the back of his throat. He carried antacids in the van precisely for moments like this. He knew Duff was right, though. They needed to get into the house sooner than later. "Let me try calling the Laskeys' kids one more time. Maybe they'll answer."

As if the universe had heard Abe's nervousness and wanted to put him at ease, Abe's phone started to ring. He looked down at the screen and saw Marybeth Collier's name on the screen. He answered it as fast as he could. "This is Abe."

There was a small voice on the other end. "My name is Marybeth Collier. My parents were Art and Michelle Laskey. Is this the private detective who called me?"

"Yes, it is. Mrs. Collier, I'm sorry about having to call you so impersonally and ask about getting permission to enter your parents' home, but my partner and I were hired to investigate their deaths, and inspecting the house is very important to that investigation."

There was a pause. "Who hired you?"

Abe put the phone on speaker so Duff could listen. Duff started recording the conversation with his own phone, using his big body to block the wind from getting to the microphone. "Do you know a man named Buddy Olson? He was the sheriff of Waukesha County for many years."

"Of course. Buddy and my dad were old friends."

Abe hesitated. "Buddy doesn't believe your parents died the way the Dane County investigators say they did."

There was a long pause, a dreadful silence. Abe started to think Marybeth had ended the call, but finally he heard a sharp, pointed sob. She had been crying. In a shaky voice, she said, "Neither do I."

Abe let out the breath he didn't know he had been holding. "That makes three of you, then. Mrs. Collier, can we have permission to search your parents' home? We promise, we will not disturb anything, and if we find anything pertinent, we will let you know."

"Can...can you wait for me? I'll come right over. I have a spare key."

Abe and Duff exchanged a glance. Abe knew what seeing a crime scene in a bloody state could do to a loved one. "It's not going to be pretty, you know."

"I know. I just...I want to know." There was a long pause. "I have to know."

"We'll wait for you, then."

"I only live a few miles away. I'll be there in ten minutes."

The phone went dead in Abe's hand. He dialed the number for Shelby Ree. She snapped up the line in one ring. "What?"

"We got ahold of the Laskeys' daughter. She's letting us into the house."

"I'll be right there."

The phone went dead again. Abe pocketed it. "I suppose I'd better get the van off the lawn."

"We could just tell them that a sudden micro-tornado put it there."

"We're not in Kansas, Dorothy. I don't know if anyone will buy that."

"Not even if I click my heels together? What happened to the magic of Hollywood?"

3

MARYBETH COLLIER DROVE a minivan. Unlike Abe and Duff's uniquely abused ride, hers was in pristine condition. It was a black Chrysler Town and Country with dust on the side panels, a side effect from living on and around so many gravel driveways. Marybeth pulled the van to a stop in front of the garage, parking next to the Dane County SUV. When Marybeth exited the van, she did not look anything like what Abe had anticipated. She was a diminutive sprite of a human, barely more than five feet tall with a thin, waifish frame. For a petite woman who had birthed two children, she still looked like a teenager. She was in her early thirties, but she was clearly motivated by health and kept herself in excellent physical shape. She had a short haircut, which only served to emphasize her size and features. She was a pixie come to life.

Shelby Ree introduced herself to Marybeth, and Abe and Duff followed the deputy's lead. Abe expressed his condolences for her loss. He could see her eyes were still red from crying. At the moment, she seemed more angry than sad. Her jaw was set, and her fists were clenched. Through gritted teeth she managed to say, "They should still be here."

"You think it was murder then?" Duff was interested.

"I do. Someone killed them and made it look like my mom went nuts, but she wasn't nuts. She never was. She was flawless. She was superwoman. Everyone loved her."

"And you told this to whoever was investigating this case?" asked Abe.

"I did. The detective didn't seem to care. He kept saying the facts were the facts."

"Sounds like Andruzzi," said Ree. "Paul Andruzzi. That's his catchphrase. He's an arrogant prick."

"Good detective, though?" asked Duff. "I don't care if he's the biggest douche canoe on the planet as long as he puts the right guys behind bars."

Ree thought for a moment. "He does alright. He doesn't get a lot of tough cases. Most of the time, pinning a bullet on someone is pretty cut-and-dried around Madison. He does okay with most of the murders he gets, but he's useless when it comes to things like theft or assault. He takes a statement, and then ignores it unless someone calls him to say they found the car, or the bike, or the whatever-it-was that got picked."

"Sounds about right." Duff had a general distaste for most police detectives. He butted heads with many over the years. "Can you get me a copy of Andruzzi's reports and maybe a copy of his murder notes?"

"I can try. No promises, though. You know how some of those guys are." Ree turned back to Marybeth. "Are you sure you want to do this, Mrs. Collier? If you give us permission to unseal the house, we can go through it, and you won't have to see anything."

"No. I have to see it. I need to see it."

Ree took charge. "If you have the key, let me have it, and I'll go in first."

Marybeth handed over a small bronze key without protest. Shelby Ree ran the edge of the key over the tape seal to break it and pulled open the screen door. She unlocked the inner door and opened it into the mudroom.

A dank smell hit Abe, the smell of blood. He was very familiar with it. The smell of large amounts of blood was coppery and very rich. It had a wet heft to it. When that blood dried, much of the weight and metallic tang evaporated, turning rank and fetid as it spoiled and dried. Eventually, that rankness would go, but not for a time. After the cleaners did their thing, all foulness would be replaced by the false clean scent of chemicals. The house would eventually return to a normal smell, but only for those who didn't know what happened inside of it. Those who knew, they would always smell the blood faintly, a permanent afterimage in their memory.

Ree stepped inside with her right hand gripping the handle of her holstered service weapon. "This is the Dane County Sheriff's Department. Anyone here? Hello?"

There was only a still, eerie silence in the home.

Duff followed Ree as the second person to enter, followed by Marybeth, and then Abe. Tears were already streaming down Marybeth's face as she crossed the threshold. When she saw the dark stain in the living room, she broke out into sobs and collapsed. Abe was ready for it. He caught her under her arms and helped lower her gently to the floor. She turned and clutched at the front his shirt, burying her face into his chest. "I shouldn't have looked."

"Let's get you back outside, then." Abe helped the poor woman to her feet and shielded the rest of the house from her with his body. He gingerly walked her back to her van. She wept fiercely the whole time.

Duff and Ree surveyed the house. There were six yellow evidence tents the size of a deck of cards in various places around the room. One was tagged on the wall near a bullet hole. The rest were on the floor in and around the blood stain.

"Pretty simple scene, I guess." Ree nudged one of the tents with her foot. "If it was a double-murder and not just a murder-suicide, then it looks like it was professional, or committed by someone with some experience, at the very least."

"That's just what I was thinking." Duff used a chair as an assist to help him get down on one knee. He groaned as he did.

"You alright?"

"As alright as I get, I guess. My knees are shot."

"Yeah, no shit. Maybe try less sugar. I hear good things about Keto."

"You can take my gun. You can take my dignity. You can even take my will to live because it was never that strong to begin with, but you will never get my Zebra Cakes." Duff flopped to his stomach and turned his head to the side, eyeballing the floor at an angle from floor-level.

Ree crouched next to him. "What are you doing?"

"Resting. It's been a long day." Duff pushed himself to his knees, and then used the chair to get back to his feet. He walked to the center of the nearby kitchen and did a slow three-sixty.

"Crime scene is out here." Ree watched him with her hands on her hips.

"Crime scene is the house. The house is all around us." Duff opened the dishwasher. He opened one of the cabinets. His face lit up. "Score!"

"You find a clue?"

"No, better!" Duff pulled a box of Little Debbie Swiss Cake Rolls from the cabinet. "You want one?"

Ree's nose wrinkled with disgust. "Dude, you're stealing from the dead."

"Correction: I'm stealing from the next of kin. The dead own nothing; they're dead." Duff peeled the wrapper from a box and pulled one of the cakes out, biting it in half. "I love these things."

"You can eat at a crime scene?"

The big man shrugged. "If there's Little Debbie snacks available, I can eat at a crime scene." He strode out of the kitchen and toward the stairs to the second story. "To the bedroom!" He still carried the box of snacks. Ree followed Duff upstairs.

The master bedroom was in disarray. Detectives had tossed it during their investigation, and while it was not quite as messy as it would have been during a full search for something like drugs or guns, it was still a level-two disaster area. Clothes were strewn across the bed from when they emptied the dresser drawers. The closet in the room was messy, but it was tough to tell if it was from a search or if that's just how it was to begin. Boxes had been opened, shuffled through, and hastily stacked again, most of them with lids akimbo.

Duff went to the drawer of a nightstand on what was clearly Michelle Laskey's side of the room. He opened it and shut it quickly. "Whoa. Found the sex toys. I guess they were still actively banging. Good for them, I guess. You were right. Good call."

"Told you." Ree opened the drawer on Art's nightstand. "What am I looking for?"

"Hell if I know; you'll know it when you see it." Duff lowered himself to the floor again and used the light on his phone like a flashlight to look under the bed.

"Well, at least tell what you think we're looking for. Where's your head in this?"

Duff sat up on his haunches. His face contorted as he sought the right words. "Murder-suicide is the most statistically likely cause of death."

"But I said—"

"I know what you said, but I'm telling you that statistically speaking, this sort of death is most likely murder-suicide. I'm not saying it is. I'm just quoting stats. It's very easy to think a couple who have been together for a long time can get on each other's nerves. Hell, most mornings I'm shocked Abe hasn't already spread my brains across the wall of our office."

"I can understand why."

"But if someone killed both of them, then we have a lot of questions. The first would be why. What's the motive? Why did this couple have to die? What did they know that they weren't supposed to know? Who did they screw over? What did they do that was so heinous that someone felt the need to end their involvement with this planet?"

"That's a big question."

Duff pushed himself back to a standing position. "Exactly. If we can't find something that makes us think this poor couple got involved in something shady that might have resulted in a professional level hit on them, then the only thing we're left with is the painful truth that Michelle Laskey shot and killed her husband and then herself."

"And what are you thinking right now, then? Did she do it?"

Duff looked around the bedroom one last time before heading for the door. "I don't think so."

Ree followed Duff down the upstairs hallway and into the little upstairs office next door. "Explain."

Duff sat at the large, leather chair and opened the computer on the desk. It sprang to life, but it was password-locked with a PIN code. Not seeing a handwritten set of numbers on a nearby Post-It, Duff closed the machine. "The marks in the barn and the shed. They're suspect. It's not one mark. It's a lot of them. The Laskeys were storing a lot of something, but what was it, and why? That's the question. Might be nothing, but if it's not nothing, then I'd bet it factors into why someone killed this couple."

Duff started rooting through the drawers attached to the large, wooden desk. He found a bunch of hanging files in the biggest drawer and riffled through them. In another drawer, he found a stack of paid bills for the utility company and the Internet provider. The police had already combed through the office, so there was nothing interesting to be found. "The money, too. Look around. They had been doing a lot of spending lately. That truck and car in the garage are both less than two years old. That Harley is less than three. I don't know boats, so the pontoon boat in the back might be new, I don't know. I'm betting it is, though. This TV on the wall—big money. That couch and loveseat—big money. The floors—money. They've been spending a lot lately. Where the money came from might have a logical, innocent answer. And then again, it might not."

"And if it doesn't have a simple answer, then it factors into this case, doesn't it?"

"You got it." Duff pointed finger guns at Ree and winked. They left the office and headed downstairs. "Also, if Michelle Laskey did do it, why did she do it in the middle of the living room? I knew the Laskeys when I was a kid. Michelle was petite, like her daughter. Art was a big guy, tall and muscular, and he was a trained cop. According to Buddy, he was shot at close range. If Michelle did that, she would have had to surprise him. If she was going to surprise him, it would have been a lot easier to kill him while he was sleeping or watching TV or something. The middle of the room, that sets off all kinds of alarm bells in my head."

"You see the world weird, don't you?" Ree gave Duff a hard stare.

"I see it as it is. Most people don't. They see it as they want to see it, or as it makes the most sense to them." Duff appraised Ree in return. "Do you see it weird?"

Ree gave a noncommittal bob of her head. "I'm half Native and a cop. I see everything as a possible threat."

"That's probably not a bad way to go through life. Can't get surprised that way."

"You already know something else, don't you? Something you didn't tell me."

"How can you tell?"

Ree crossed her arms over her chest. "Call it a cop's intuition."

Duff beckoned her over with a crooked finger. She followed him into the kitchen. He opened the dishwasher. "What do you see?"

Ree squinted into the dishwasher. "A few cups. Plates. Silverware. A pretty light load."

"Look again, gaijin."

"Gaijin is Japanese."

"I was going to call you Tonto, like going for a whole thing where I'm the Lone Ranger and you're my sidekick, but I figured that might be construed as insensitive."

"You're right. You would have caught a TASER to the face for that." Ree bent over and scanned the dishwasher again. "I see cups, plates, and silverware. Stop with the Where's Waldo game and just tell me what I'm looking at."

"There are three cups, three plates, and three forks in addition to a pie pan and an ice cream scoop. And not just any cups: that's good china; that's not goofy gift mugs with funny sayings or grandchildren's pictures on them."

"Holy shit. You're right. Michelle baked a pie. They had someone over here probably the day of the incident, didn't they? Someone they wanted to impress." Ree opened the fridge. A Tupperware container with the uneaten part of the pie was on the central shelf.

To add support to his claim, Duff started opening cabinet drawers in the kitchen. He quickly located the cabinet with the everyday mugs, the ones the Laskeys would have used when it was just them, and further down the row, in a far more impractical place for daily use, was another cabinet where expensive china was stored, the same type that was in the dishwasher. "Michelle did a small load spacing out the cups because she didn't want them banging into each other and chipping."

"Genius."

"I know. It's a curse," said Duff.

"Not you, dummy. Her."

Duff was not bothered by Ree's slight. "I'm still a genius. Just not one who does the dishes too often."

"How do you manage that?"

"I eat like ninety-eight-percent of my meals off of wax paper or tinfoil wrappers."

"What about the other two percent?"

"Restaurants with actual plates instead of burger wrappers."

"Classy."

"I should write a book about it."

MARYBETH COLLIER CRIED for a solid five minutes. She was wracked with full-body sobs that rippled through her as though they were going to break her in half. She sat in the driver's seat of her van with her arms crossed on the steering wheel, her face buried in her forearms.

Abe knew better than to say anything. He stood next to her and patted her back gently. He wanted her to know he was there, but only barely. He stood still and let her have her sadness. He knew from his psychology classes that grief was a powerful and terrifying emotion. It manifested in many shapes and forms. No two people suffered grief alike, and no grief was more or less valid than any other grief. It was not a game of oneupmanship; it was an unbearable burden for everyone.

Abe never knew his father. His mother only ever told him his father was tall, and she did not know him long. Abe's mother had died of cancer shortly before he and Katherine had married. Abe's grief had been profound, but also tempered by the fact that he and his mother had been distant most of his life. It was not by choice or design. His mother often worked two or three low-wage jobs just to afford a lousy apartment on Chicago's north side to keep food on the table and clothes on Abe's back. She would wake him up for school in the mornings but be gone for work before he was dressed. She would return in the evenings when it was time for him to sleep. Occasionally on the weekends they might do something fun together, but she used the weekends to catch up on sleep or go grocery shopping so they would have something to eat. Abe never minimized his mother's sacrifices for him. She had no life of her own until he went off to college, a gift only made possible by scholarships and grants because he was a straight-A student. Abe had planned to become a lawyer and earn enough money so his mother could stop working, but the cancer diagnosis ended that dream. Abe missed his mother, but it was only the sadness that came from missing out on the life she never got to live because so much of herself went into working for Abe's future. She would have loved being a grandmother to Matilda. She never got to enjoy that time in her life, and that's what generated most of Abe's sadness over her passing.

Marybeth was obviously close to both her parents. Abe could feel her sorrow radiating off her in palpable waves. Each sob was intense. It was the sound of utter loss.

After she expelled enough grief, her sobs reduced to sniffles. She pulled herself far enough out of the mire of sadness to seek a tissue from a box in the area between the two front seats of her van. She dabbed at her eyes and wiped her face. "Sorry about that."

"You have nothing to be sorry about. I'm sure this has been the worst week of your life." Abe stepped aside so Marybeth could exit her van.

"It has been. By far. The worst part has been telling my children that they can't go ride the four-wheeler with Grampy anymore."

"I could imagine." Little alarms went off in Abe's head. Four-wheeler? There was no four-wheeler in the garage, barn, or shed. Where was it? "Did you already take that over to your house?"

"Take what?"

"The four-wheeler?"

Marybeth blinked at Abe, not fully understanding. "What? No. It's over in the little shed." She pointed at the machine shed with the badly sloping roof.

Abe slowly shook his head. "I don't think so. Did your brother take it, maybe?"

As if she did not trust Abe's words, Marybeth started storming toward the shed. "I doubt it."

Marybeth stopped at the entrance of the machine shed and shook her head incredulously. "It was right here! It was right god-damned here. What happened to it?"

"Did someone else take it, maybe? Did a neighbor borrow it?"

Marybeth's sorrow was replaced by rage. "No, some stupid son of bitch knew my parents were dead, and they knew my dad kept the keys in the stupid thing. Probably just came over here one night after the cops left and just drove it home. One of the neighbors probably has it in their shed waiting for the heat to die down." Marybeth spat on the ground. "Bunch of fucking animals around here."

"It doesn't sound very *Green Acres* of them."

"What's that mean?"

"It's an old TV show. I'm old."

Marybeth walked back to the van seething over the pilfered ATV.

"This was a standard four-wheeler, right?" asked Abe.

"Yeah. Just a little Honda Rancher. Pretty basic, but my dad liked to take around the fields or use it for plowing snow off the driveway. The kids loved it, though. Grampy would set them on the seat in front of him and he'd drive up and down the gravel road like a maniac. Gave my mother a heart attack to watch him do it, but the kids would laugh and scream. It was better than Disneyland to them."

That sounded like fun to Abe even now. He would have liked to try it out, at the very least. He'd never even sat on one, let alone tried to drive it. City life was a very limiting in terms of motorsports one might enjoy. Since they were talking about it, Abe decided to gently broach the subject of the vehicles. "Your parents had some nice toys in that garage."

"Oh? The car and the motorcycle? Yeah, they liked their fun, alright. Dad was always cruising around on that motorcycle rain or shine. He'd disappear for hours, just him and the road. Mom liked to go fast in that little car. She would take it down this one road out by Daleyville—it had the wildest camel hump hills—and she would drop the hammer on the gas pedal. Felt like a roller coaster."

"These are all new vehicles. I mean, bought in what, the last year or two?"

Marybeth shrugged. "I don't remember. Maybe. Mom and Dad were always doing stupid stuff like that. They'd buy a new truck, keep it for two or three years, and then trade it before the warranty ran out. Dad hated paying for repairs."

"Makes sense," said Abe, but he did not mean it. That was the kind of thing only people with a lot of money could afford to do. Abe's own finances meant that he drove a vehicle until he couldn't possibly drive it anymore. As long as there was a minimal chance the engine would turn over again, it remained in service. "They must have been pretty well off."

Marybeth's head snapped around, and she stared at him with narrowed eyes. "Are you insinuating that I'm getting an inheritance from them? That I'm benefiting from their death?"

Abe held up his hands like Marybeth was holding a gun on him. "No, not at all. I was just saying that they had a lot of new vehicles. I was just wondering where they got the money for all of them, and maybe that might be the reason someone killed them."

"My dad was good at investing. He knew about stocks." There was an edge to Marybeth's voice. She was defending her parents' honor.

Abe needed to defuse the situation. Marybeth was getting angry. A vein was starting to pop out on her forehead. He deflected, moving to a personal slight against himself. It was an old psychology tactic. "If I buy a stock, it will tank, guaranteed. I could bankrupt Amazon if I started buying their stuff."

"Dad was a genius. He turned his disability pension into a fortune."

"That must be nice."

Marybeth looked like she might punch him. "I would give all the money in the world for my parents to be alive instead of dead."

Abe said nothing. He didn't feel like anything he might say would bring comfort or take back the idea that he questioned her parents' wealth.

Like a fat, sweatshirted savior, Duff chose that moment to kick open the screen door and step out into the day. He was carrying a box of Swiss Cake Rolls. "Hey, Rico. I'm done if you are."

"I'm not going to answer to Rico." Abe moved a few steps away from Marybeth. He wanted to give her some space to calm down a bit.

"How about Spider?"

"Gross. No."

"Venom?"

Shelby Ree stepped out onto the little concrete porch behind Duff. "He looks more like an Ace to me. Try Ace."

"How about Ace?" Duff waggled his eyebrows.

"No."

Duff's face fell like a failed soufflé. "Damn it." He opened another pack of Swiss Cake Rolls and shoved half of one into his mouth.

"Ma'am, I'd recommend you let the crime scene cleaners take care of that house before you go back in there. It's not a pretty sight." Ree handed one of her business cards to Marybeth. "My personal cell phone number is on that. Feel free to call me if you need anything or have any questions."

"Thank you." Marybeth tilted her head at Duff. "Is he eating my dead parents' snack cakes?"

Abe's mouth opened and closed like a landed carp. "Yes. Yes, he is."

"Why?"

"I try not to ask questions like that. The answers are always disappointing."

Without a word to Marybeth or the deputy, Duff walked to the passenger side of *The Bad Luck Charm* and dropped himself into the shotgun seat before closing the door.

"Well, I think that's Duff's way of declaring we're done." Abe apologized to Marybeth about the Swiss Cake Rolls and nodded at Ree. "I'll give you a call later."

"Where are you guys staying?"

"A hotel in Verona."

"I'll find you." Ree's tone was confident.

Abe pointed at the battered van. "It's because of...that, right?"

"It does stand out."

Marybeth began to look distressed. "Wait! That's it? You're just going?"

Abe tried to apologize again. "Duff's just a little brusque when—"

Marybeth wasn't listening. She strode around to the passenger side of Abe's van and yanked open the door. If Duff was surprised, he didn't show it. He was calmly polishing off a Swiss Cake Roll.

"I let you in the house. What happened?"

Duff continued to chew, staring straight ahead.

"Answer me! What happened to my parents?"

Duff swallowed his treat and licked his fingertips calmly, deliberately. He wiped his wet fingers on his jeans. "They were murdered."

Marybeth collapsed as if someone had removed all her bones and began crying again.

SHELBY REE HELPED Marybeth Collier back into her van and gave the boys a wave as Abe piloted *The Bad Luck Charm* away from the Laskeys' home.

"Murder, then? You're one-hundred-percent certain?"

"I'm ninety-nine-point-nine-percent certain. I suppose it could still be a murder-suicide, but I'm not buying that as the official story. Feels like something's off about this whole thing."

"What'd you find in the house?"

Duff rattled off the finding in the dishwasher, the fact that the murder happened in the middle of the room, and the relative size and weight differences in the two victims. "I think someone made a stupid mistake. If whoever did this put the gun in Art's hand instead of Michelle's, I probably don't even get a hinky feeling about it. I don't understand the logic of trying to make us believe Michelle was the killer."

Abe said, "Marybeth seems to believe her parents' money came from wise investing. She made out her father to be some sort of financial genius."

Duff said nothing for a moment. He closed his eyes. Abe knew he was retreating into his thoughts, something he called a memory palace, which was a place where he could build with perfect detail a replica of any room which he had inspected. It was a powerful gift, but not without its downsides. The memory construct had great limits. If Duff didn't open a drawer in that room, for example, that drawer would remain closed forever. He could never know what was in it. It was a memory tool, not divination.

Duff's eyes snapped open. "I found no letters or forms from investing houses. No Fidelity. No Edward Jones. No nothing. Maybe the Laskeys had something on their computer, but it was PIN locked, so I couldn't get in."

"You couldn't do that trick where you guess the number?"

"No. I didn't see enough info around the house. I might have been able to muddle through it with Marybeth's help, but I don't know if she's in the right state for it at the moment."

"You're probably right." Abe brought the van back into Mount Horeb, slowing down as they broached the edge of the town. A Mount Horeb patrol unit was sitting off the road on a little embankment tagging cars with radar. Abe was never going to be accused of being too heavy on the gas pedal without good reason, so he was not worried about the local cop suddenly coming after him.

"What's the next step?" They had reached the logical end of the day's investigation. They had seen the house, and the house had convinced Duff that it was a murder of some kind.

"Same step that we always take on a murder: we figure out who had the motive to do it."

"The kids will probably have a nice inheritance," said Abe.

"Didn't seem like Marybeth was the killing sort, did it? She looked pretty broken up over it."

Abe wavered on that. "I'm not so sure."

"Oh?" Duff perked up. "Do tell."

"There's a strange form of hysteria that can happen sometimes when some people are trying to hide a lack of sadness or a guilty feeling. It's part of the guilt complex. It can manifest by wild crying or manic episodes. When I was with Marybeth outside, I saw her run a wild gamut of emotions from sadness to anger to rage to distrust. She was barely keeping herself from flying off the handle. That whole flop-crying episode after you said her parents were murdered, that's right there in line with that sort of hysteria. I don't know if she's a little bipolar to begin with, but she was definitely on the edge of something."

"That was more than normal sadness and grief, then?"

"Maybe." Abe couldn't tell. He didn't know Marybeth. He didn't know how she functioned on a normal day, so judging her during one of the worst weeks in her life was unfair. "I'm not certain."

"What's your gut say?"

"I don't fully buy her act."

"Then she's on the list."

"But I might be wrong."

"She's still on the list. It never hurts to put people on the list. We can always take them off later. Hell, you look at me wrong, and I'm gonna put you on the list."

"Who else can be on the list?" Abe hit the roundabout in the center of town and guided the van around the circle.

"I want to know about whatever they were storing in the barn. Someone must know something, and my gut tells me that whoever knows something about what was getting stored in the barn knows something about why the Laskeys had to die."

"It does seem suspicious, doesn't it?"

"I remember back when I was a kid, Buddy Olson ran a drug bust on this farm out in Waukesha. Now, this was 1989, right? So, he hits the farm with his team, they arrest a bunch of fools for growing weed in a cornfield. While they're doing their preliminary search of the joint, they find this little detached one-car garage on the property. They open the door, and the goddamned thing is filled—and I mean *filled*—floor to ceiling, back to front, with VCRs, good ones too, all the same model, all factory sealed."

Abe was confused. "A bunch of hicks growing weed had a garage full of VCRs? Were they really big movie buffs?"

"Turns out, the VCRs had been the cargo of some truck that got stolen in Chicago by someone who was mobbed up. They were storing the VCRs at the hicks' place until they could be sold in a few months after the heat died down."

"That makes sense."

"Maybe that's how the Laskeys were making money. Maybe they were storing stolen goods for the mob."

Abe was impressed by that jump in logic. "It would make sense, wouldn't it? No cop is going to go sniffing around another cop's property, even a former cop. No thieves would dare hit a cop's property."

"Plus, the Laskeys' place was remote. Secure. You aren't going there unless you need to go there. They're not getting looky-loos or passersby. If you're on the road, it's because you live there or you need to deliver something."

"It's a good operating theory," said Abe. "What do you want me to do, put the mob on the list of suspects like a big coverall?"

"Might as well. If they were murdered, it looked like a pro hit. Mob's got a lot of pro hitters."

"Fine. The ghost of Al Capone and the Chicago Outfit is on the list. Who else?"

"We haven't heard from Marcus Laskey, yet. I have no idea what his story is. He goes on the list. And we have to look at the medical examiner for Dane County. Buddy said he was slippery. He might have had a hand in something. He goes on the list."

"Anyone else?"

"Until we have a better list of suspects, everyone could be a potential suspect. But let's start with who we have and narrow it down from there."

Abe nodded. He pointed at a Culver's restaurant a half-mile down the road. "Lunch?"

"Definitely."

Abe guided the van into the crowded parking lot. Culver's was a busy place for lunch any day of the week, but the Sunday crowds were constant. Everyone loves a Bacon Double-Deluxe on a fine early spring day.

Abe parked and they walked inside a noisy, crowded lobby. They ordered their food after a short wait and got cups for the self-serve fountain drinks. Then, when it was time to find a table, Abe surveyed the restaurant. It was remarkably crowded, save for a circular table in the back corner where a white-haired man was sitting alone with a cup of coffee. Abe recognized him instantly. So did Duff.

Buddy Olson was reading one of Craig Johnson's Longmire novels while he waited for them. Abe and Duff walked to the table and sat down. "Waiting long?" asked Duff.

Buddy looked up from his book, sliding a folded Post-It note into it as a bookmark. "I've been here since they opened at ten."

"How'd you know we'd be here?" asked Abe.

"I know how the chubby guy's brain works. When it's time for lunch, he really only goes to one of three places, and I'm betting he already had Mexican food for breakfast."

"I was supposed to get McDonald's, but we opted for ease of access."

Buddy cut to the chase. "What'd you find out?"

"I'm betting it was a double murder." Duff sipped his diet soda through a straw.

"That's why I'm here. What hotel are you jokers staying at?"

"The Super 8 in Verona."

"Sounds like a plan."

"You're going to hang out for the investigation?" asked Duff. "What happened to being in another sheriff's jurisdiction?"

"Yeah, that shit's out the window now. I got work to do." Buddy waved down one of the teenagers working the Sunday shift and held up his cup of coffee in the universal sign for a refill. "What's the next step?"

"We're waiting on Shelby Ree to get us some info."

"Who?"

"Dane County deputy. Seems nice. She knew the Laskeys. She doesn't believe Michelle could pull a trigger, either."

"I like her already. What else?" Buddy popped the plastic lid off his coffee as the girl from Culver's approached with the pot. She filled it smartly and asked if he'd need cream or sugar, but Buddy shook his head and thanked her.

"Well, we've already started a list of suspects," said Duff.

"Who?"

Abe rattled them off. "The Laskeys' kids, the medical examiner, and the ghost of Al Capone."

"Perfect. I've been meaning to get Capone booked on something better than tax evasion for years."

4

SHELBY REE WAS lost in thought. She was parked on the entrance ramp to Highway 151 on the western edge of Mount Horeb. She was supposed to be doing speed checks, but she did not have the heart to ruin anyone's day. Instead, she was contemplating the Laskeys and wondering how much she could trust the two out-of-staters who showed up that morning.

She used her cell phone to run a check on them online and found they were who they said they were, but outside of that, they kept a very low public profile. No website. No social media. No nothing. It appeared they were capable detectives because their business had been operating for more than two decades without much advertising, but that was it. Their names weren't in the papers. They didn't have criminal records. Their licenses checked out and were current, but they were largely ghosts. Was that by coincidence or design? They looked like guys whose names would never be remembered minutes after meeting them. They were the definition of nondescript, Midwestern, pasty white, middle-aged guys. She dealt with those sorts of guys every day. They were usually respectful, sometimes quick to anger, and largely forgettable. They were the plain yogurt of human beings.

At least they helped confirm her suspicions about the Laskeys. The Laskeys were good people. They needed the record about them to be set straight. She remembered the first day she met them. She had been doing a routine traffic watch near Barneveld when she noticed a pickup truck pull to the side of the road opposite her and come to a stop. Art Laskey had stepped out, all six-foot-three of him, broad in the shoulders and barrel-chested. He looked like trouble. She leapt out of the car ready to rumble as she'd been trained, but he just stuck out a big bear paw of a hand and introduced himself. He said he used to be a county deputy until he was injured, he pointed out his house, and said if she needed anything just ask. Then he slipped her a piece of paper with his phone number on it. When she asked the other deputies back at the station about him, they all vouched for him. Salt of the earth kind of guy, they all said. The Laskeys were loved by all the deputies.

About a week after that, Michelle Laskey pulled up alongside Ree at the Kwik Trip parking lot in her little blue car. She handed Ree a little stack of homemade brownies in a Ziploc bag and introduced herself as Art's wife. She invited Ree to the house for dinner that night. Shelby had gone, figuring she needed all the police-friendly contacts she could get. They had been lovely dinner companions, funny and charming, and they treated her like family. In the year or so she knew them, they had always been delighted to see her, and she had gotten nothing but the warmest, friendliest vibes from them. If she was parked somewhere fixing the paperwork and the Laskeys drove by, they would always slow down and talk to her from the window of their car, make sure she was okay with the work, and make sure she didn't need anything. People like that deserved better than what they got.

Ree decided since Andruzzi didn't do a good job on the crime scene, and Bob Benedict, the medical examiner, didn't do a good job on the forensic examination, and since it took the fat guy less than five minutes to give her more than enough evidence to think the Laskeys were murdered, she knew she was going to help the detectives, and if she ruffled Andruzzi's or Benedict's feathers while she was at it, she would just ride out whatever hell it brought her. The more she thought about it, the simpler her decision became.

Shelby's grandfather had been a county sheriff for almost forty years. He lived by one edict: get the investigation right. Following her grandfather's words was the least she could do.

Someone had been in that house with the Laskeys just before they died. Something had been stored on their property. Ree needed answers.

SHELBY KNEW DETECTIVE Paul Andruzzi often worked out of the Verona substation on Madison's far west side. She did not want to accidentally run into him. The next-closest substation was the office in the village of Black Earth. That was only thirteen miles north of Mount Horeb, a straight shot up a winding road through the valley along Highway 78. With nothing else going on during that lazy Sunday morning, Ree decided to head up to the substation and see what she could dig out through the network up there.

On a Sunday, the substation was closed to general visitors. Since Black Earth was too small to afford its own police force, the village contracted with the Dane County Sheriff's Office for coverage. There were only two deputies assigned to the village on a full-time basis, one for first shift, and one for second shift. The remainder of coverage was provided by patrol deputies assigned to cover the area west of Madison like Ree. The station would be dark, but she had the key to get in when she needed.

Ree pulled up to the building and slipped in through the side door. As predicted, the tiny office was dark, but there were two computers available, both in sleep mode. She woke one of them with a nudge of the mouse and entered her credentials to access the network.

Andruzzi's work would be locked to her, she knew that. She wasn't high enough on the ladder to get info on the big cases. But she also knew she could get a considerable amount of information because the department had already officially closed the case. Some information would already be accessible to the public under the Freedom of Information Act. That was all fair game. Shelby downloaded the .pdfs and printed them out, gathering them in a neat file. She made a second copy of the sheets to give to Abe & Duff. They would need it. Then, she logged off the computer, let herself out of the station, and locked the door behind her.

She parked in a conspicuous spot just outside of Black Earth along Highway 14. It was a painfully obvious spot, one that was so brazen and obtuse that speeders could not help but see her. She set up so it looked like she was looking for speeders. Sometimes, the best deterrent to speeding was just seeing the big brown-and-white Chevy with the roof lights. She just wanted time to go over the files she'd just printed. Still, it was a delight to watch people come over the little hill in the distance, see the big SUV with the telltale lightbar on the roof, and watch them tromp the brake pedal in hopes of avoiding a well-deserved ticket.

The files Andruzzi and Bob Benedict filled out gave a cursory examination of the scene, detailed how they believe the murder went down, and gave an explanation of the wounds suffered by both victims. Their hypothesis was that Michelle Laskey snuck up behind her husband, Art, put a gun to the side of his head, and pulled the trigger. Then she laid down next to Art, put the gun to the side of her own head, and ended her life. The first bullet pierced Art's skull cleanly and lodged in the far wall. The bullet rendered Art unconscious and brain-dead, but his heart continued to beat until he bled out. The official cause of death for Art Laskey was exsanguination by GSW. The second shot didn't fully pierce Michelle's skull, so it ended up ricocheting around inside, did a tremendous amount of damage, and caused instantaneous death. Her heart stopped beating almost immediately, no exsanguination.

Benedict believed that the time of death was sometime around 8:00 PM on Wednesday night. The couple had laid on the floor for almost a full day before a FedEx delivery driver had stopped by the house to deliver a package late Thursday afternoon. He happened to look through the window of the door as he was dropping off a box and saw the bodies on the floor. He called 911 immediately and waited for deputies to arrive. The scene was searched and cleared in less than ten hours, and it had been cordoned off with police tape since.

Benedict declared the case a clear-cut case of murder-suicide, pointing to the fact Michelle Laskey had traces of donepezil in her system.

Ree had to use her phone to look up donepezil. It was a prescription drug used for treating early stages of Alzheimer's-related dementia. The common name for the drug was Aricept.

Ree dropped the folder on the passenger seat. She was stunned. Did Michelle have Alzheimer's? Why hadn't she or Art mentioned it? Ree felt a chill creep up her back. Did the Laskeys' kids know? Maybe they were hiding it from the kids until they couldn't. Ree knew there were any number of reasons for a couple like Art and Michelle to hide their medical issues from the public, but this seemed like a big deal.

It occurred to her that Michelle being on Aricept might change Duff's mind about the investigation. Hell, it might change her mind about the investigation. She put her unit in drive and slipped her sunglasses on her face. She left Black Earth, heading east on Highway 14 toward Madison. It would take her around thirty minutes to get to the hotel in Verona.

5

ABE AND DUFF checked into their room at the Super 8 in Verona. Buddy booked his own room next to theirs. Abe was no stranger to Super 8 hotels. He was even a member of their frequent guests club, although he would not consider himself a frequent guest. He and Duff used Super 8 hotels maybe twice a year, max. Their business did not often call them away from Chicago for more than a day or two, and sometimes they would even sleep in the van at a roadside rest stop for a couple of hours rather than spend hard-earned simoleons on a hotel room.

There was something comforting about Super 8 hotels. They were all basically the same, nothing fancy, no frills. Abe liked simple. He only needed a bed, a shower, and a TV. And the TV was optional. Simple was better. Abe once stayed in a really nice hotel room back when he and Katherine had first married. On their first vacation as a married couple, they had splurged for a really nice hotel room even though they really couldn't afford it. It felt strange, like it was a world to which they weren't supposed to witness. It made them uncomfortable, like they didn't deserve it. After that, they always made sure to get rooms at the lower end of the chain-quality hotel spectrum. Super 8. Motel 6. Red Roof Inn. Maybe the occasional Best Western. Abe knew his place, and his place was in low-cost, no-frills places.

Duff took the bed closest to the window. He sprawled across it like a failed skydiving attempt, face pressed into the Poly-rayon comforter spread across the bed. His voice was muffled by the mattress. "This smells like death and Fritos."

"You like Fritos." Abe tossed his bag onto the other bed.

"I wasn't complaining; just pointing out facts."

Abe sat on his bed and checked his watch. They'd left Culver's near two in the afternoon. With Buddy in the van, they'd toured around the roads near the Laskeys' house, moving out in a circular pattern until they had a good feel of the land. While they drove, Duff detailed his take on the murder scene for their benefit. The drive over the winding, twisting county roads had made Duff a little carsick, but he hadn't ralphed up his double ButterBurger with cheese, so that was a win. "Do we call it a day? Go strong at it tomorrow?"

"Unless you can think of something better to do tonight."

There was a knock at the door. Abe thought it was Buddy, so he opened it. To his surprise, Deputy Shelby Ree was there with a stack of papers in a manila folder in her hand. "What does Aricept mean to you?"

"Gesundheit." Duff did not bother to lift his face from the mattress.

"Sounds like either a prescription drug or an Egyptian pharaoh." Abe stepped aside to let Ree into the room.

"It's a drug." Ree walked in and took a seat at the only chair in the room, a standard hotel desk chair at the little desk along the wall opposite Abe's bed. She tossed the folder onto the desk. "I got the released coroner's report from the investigation. It said Michelle had Aricept in her blood at the time of the autopsy."

"I have cholesterol in my blood." Duff's voice was still muffled by the mattress and comforter on his bed. He had not moved an inch since Ree entered the room. "What's Aricept?"

"It's the brand name of a drug called donepezil."

That caused Duff to pop to his feet. "Seriously?"

"Why would I lie about that?"

Abe searched his own memory banks. His recall was perfect, like Duff's, but it was nowhere near as fast. "Alzheimer's?"

Duff looked incredulous. "Michelle had dementia?"

"That's what the report says." Ree nodded toward the folder. "Read it yourself."

Abe picked up the sheets and began leafing through them, skimming the text while he did.

"Well, fuck." Duff sat down on the bed. "Might as well go home, then."

"Alzheimer's doesn't mean Michelle Laskey did this." Abe continued to leaf through the sheets. "Donepezil is for treatment in the early stages. Dementia can take years to fully set into someone."

"Yeah, or it can take days or weeks or months." Duff fell backwards on the bed, arms sprawling straight out from his sides. "I guess maybe I might be wrong about it being a double murder. Maybe it was a murder-suicide."

"What was a murder-suicide?" Buddy appeared in the door that Abe had not shut after Ree entered the room.

"Michelle Laskey had anti-dementia drugs in her system at the autopsy," said Ree.

Buddy looked surprised at the deputy's appearance. "Oh, my. You must be that girl the boys told me about. Was it Shelly?"

"Shelby," she corrected. "Shelby Ree."

Buddy stuck out his hand. "Buddy Olson."

Ree shook it. "The Buddy Olson? From Waukesha?"

"The same."

"You're something of a legend around these parts. You got a lot of cases closed under your watch."

"I hired good detectives. It wasn't me."

"How many of those did I close?" Duff was still flopped on the bed staring at the ceiling.

"In the nine months you wouldn't stop pestering me and my guys? Probably twenty."

"You never paid me for those, by the way."

"And I'm not going to."

Abe was scanning the file Shelby Ree brought them. From the looks of the medical examiner's report, it was a clear-cut case of murder-suicide caused by a dementia-related break from reality. Michelle, under a spell of dementia, shot and killed her husband, then laid next to him and killed herself. From the evidence as it was presented by the ME, it was plain as day. Anyone with two brain cells to rub together would have jumped to the same conclusion. But it wasn't sitting right with Abe. What were the Laskeys storing in the barn? Who was the third person who was worthy of the fine china? "Hey, Deputy—"

She held up a finger. "Call me Ree. Or Shelby. Not Deputy."

"Sorry, Ree. When you went to the Laskeys for dinner or coffee, did Michelle and Art ever use that fine china for you?"

Ree thought for a moment. "No. Not once."

"Buddy, in all the times you ate with the Laskeys, did they ever use that fine china?"

Buddy huffed through his mustache while he thought. "You know, I'd probably guess that most of the time I ate with them, it was something off Art's grill, so we ate off of paper plates."

"But no china."

Buddy thought for a second longer. "No china."

"Who was so important they broke out the fancy plates?" Abe looked around the room. "And where did they get all their money? If it was investing, we should be able to figure that out pretty easily. If it wasn't, we should also be able to figure that out pretty easily. Either way, it's not a completely cut-and-dried mystery."

Duff sat up again. "Trace the money. Always trace the money."

"Whoever profits from someone's death is always suspect number one. That's the first thing I taught you when you started hanging out at the station," said Buddy.

"We need to see what's on that computer." Duff stood. "We're going back to the house."

"We need to find financial statements." Abe turned to Ree. "Did the investigators take anything like that from the home?"

"I can go downtown and look."

"Please do." Abe grabbed the van keys off the nightstand. "Buddy, you want to come along for the ride?"

"Might as well." The old sheriff pushed himself to his feet with a grunt.

Ree stood, too. She headed toward the door. "I'll give you a call if I find something."

Duff and Abe started walking toward the door, but Buddy stopped them. "You boys forgetting anything?"

They started feeling their pockets. "Wallet and phone are present, boss," said Duff.

Buddy nodded toward Duff's bed where the plastic grocery bag was haphazardly tossed, the Walther PPK inside it clearly visible.

Duff gave a gritted-teeth wince. "Do I have to?"

"Do you have to wear a life vest on a sailboat? No. But if you fall overboard, will you want one? Yes. But then it's too fuckin' late. Get my drift?"

"But guns are so loud, and they make people permanently stop breathing."

"That's kind of the idea. Get it, dummy."

"Aye, Cap'n." Duff snapped a cartoonish salute and started digging out his gun and holster.

Buddy eyeballed Abe. "You too, Stretch."

Abe did not argue with the sheriff. He fetched his Smith and Wesson from his suitcase and slipped it onto his belt in a holster.

Duff struggled into his shoulder holster, which he insisted on because of James Bond, but such a device was not the most serviceable of holsters for a large man. He pulled his Carhartt sweatshirt on over the gun to hide it from view.

"If you start catching gunfire, you're going to have to pull up that shirt to get the gun out. Those are three seconds you might not have." Buddy did not play when it came to weapons.

"If I don't have those three seconds, I'm already dead," said Duff. "I'll take my chances. Besides, with you and ol' Deadeye to cover me, I'll be fine."

Abe shook his head. "Still no on the nickname."

"Killjoy." Duff's face suddenly brightened. "That should be your nickname!"

"No."

Duff scowled. "But it fits your personality."

THE LASKEYS' FARMHOUSE seemed smaller when they arrived. The thick woods on the western edge of the property blocked some of the late afternoon sun, and the giant mound that was Blue Mounds State Park blocked some of it, as well. The house was cast into premature evening shadows by this phenomenon. It made the place look darker and more foreboding.

When the group arrived, a trio of whitetail deer were in the taller grass of the field next to the house just beyond the edge of the trimmed lawn area. The deer had been grazing, but when Abe turned down the long gravel driveway all three simultaneously jerked their heads up, turned, and bounded toward the safety of the woods in the distance, their fluffy white tails standing straight up like warning flags.

"There's something you don't get to see in Chicago," said Abe.

Duff was unimpressed. "I once saw a group of rats act out the death scene from *Carmen*, so I think the city wins this one."

Buddy grunted in disgust. "Deer are basically hundred-and-fifty-pound pigeons. They're dumb as hell and cause a lot of trouble. If I had a nickel for every call-out we got over the years because of car versus deer, I would have retired to California twenty years ago and started banging lingerie models."

"As if they'd have you." Duff slid open the side door to the van and stepped out into the little turnabout in front of the garage. "Did Ree lock the house?"

"Not to my knowledge." Abe stepped out of the van, as well. He sniffed the air. It was crisp and clean. Whatever manure smells had been on the wind earlier had dissipated. The temperature was dropping and would bottom out around thirty-five degrees that night. He could see his breath. The winds that had been up earlier had also died down to a gentle breeze. It was eerily quiet.

Abe walked to the door of the house and tried it. It was locked. "Someone locked it. Maybe Ree twisted the lock before she walked out."

"Maybe." Duff reached into his back pocket and pulled out a slim leather case with lock-picking tools. Duff was an accomplished lock-picker. An old farmhouse lock worn down by years of keying was no challenge for his skills. Duff used a hook to pop the tumblers and swept the lock with a pick a second later. The door opened as if by magic. Duff waved his hands in a magician's flourish. "Ta-da!"

"I didn't see that." Buddy stepped past Duff and into the house. He made a line for the crime scene. The dried bloodstain was no less gruesome than it was that morning. If anything, the lower level of ambient light made it look worse.

"Damned shame." Buddy stood over the blood and closed his eyes as if in prayer. "Damned, damned shame."

Duff made for the stairs, taking the old farmhouse steps two at a time which was a trial given how steep old farmhouse steps were. He ascended the steps in four bounds and hooked left toward the office. At the door of the office, he froze. The computer was gone. "Curiouser and curiouser."

Duff looked around the room, the desk drawer that contained files was open, but it did not look like any of them were taken. Duff retreated into his memory. His eyes became distant and glazed. In his head, he reconstructed the room as he had seen it earlier that day. He walked through the scene as if it was a video playback. He saw himself and Ree enter the room. He saw the computer; the screen was still locked in his memory. He opened the desk drawer. Everything froze. Duff quickly counted the file folders present in his memory. Fifteen.

Duff's eyes snapped back to focus. He squatted at the drawer and flipped through the folders counting as he did. Fifteen. None of them were empty, though. Was nothing taken, or was one sheet taken from one of them? Duff would never know since he did not bother to examine all the papers in the folders earlier. He had only noted there were various documents and news clippings, mostly related to Art's time as a deputy. Anything beyond that would be locked out of his memories. He cursed his own laziness.

Duff called down the stairs. "Hey, fellas—funny story. The computer is gone."

Buddy and Abe tromped up the stairs to the office. Buddy was in the lead. "What do you mean the computer is gone?"

"I can't say it any clearer than that. It's gone. As in, someone took it." Duff flicked his fingers in a gesture meant to mimic a puff of smoke. "Poof."

Buddy leaned against the door frame in the office. "Well, who took it?"

"I don't have any proof of the matter, but I think it was that damned Sasquatch. You know how Bigfoots are, always sneaking into crime scenes and stealing the high-end computing equipment of the newly deceased."

"You're not helpful. Has anyone ever told you that?"

Duff nodded enthusiastically. "It was written on pretty much every report card I ever got."

Abe walked to the window in the office and looked out across the yard. "The front door wasn't damaged, and I didn't feel any drafts that would indicate a broken window, so let's assume someone had a key." The office window faced the woods behind the house which were growing into a dense, black mass from the oncoming nightfall. The woods were ominous and bathed in shadow. Leaves had yet to bud, so the tall maples and oaks were all bare, spindly branches.

"Marybeth had a key." Duff sat in the desk chair and leaned back. "I have to assume Marcus probably did, too. Maybe a neighbor, as well."

"Out here in the sticks, a lot of people hide a spare key in the garage or the barn for emergencies. Someone might have used that. Often, a family will let close friends know where the spare key is, just in case the neighbor needs to get in the house to feed a cat or something," said Buddy.

"The Laskeys had no pets," said Duff.

"Remember, Spanky—the country is a lot different from the city. People are more trusting out here. I could probably go down the road and within five houses I could find someone who just leaves their back door unlocked all the time just in case someone needs to borrow something."

"Well, that's insanity. In Chicago, that's just an invite for someone to take your stuff." Duff turned to Abe. "Although, I do like the Little Rascals nickname. Abe, can I call you Froggy? Or Alfalfa? What about Darla?"

"No."

"See, you're a killjoy."

Abe ignored Duff. He was an expert at ignoring his partner considering how often he had to do it. "Does the computer getting taken change anything? Could it just be harmless? Maybe Marybeth came and got it to get pictures off it or something?"

"Or maybe someone picked the lock like Duff did and took the laptop because they knew something on it was important to an investigation." Buddy huffed through his bushy mustache.

"You look like Doctor Zoidberg from *Futurama* when you do that," said Duff.

"We could go to Marybeth's and ask her." Buddy jabbed a thumb over his shoulder. "She lives a few miles south of here."

"We'll give Marcus another call on the way." Abe wanted to talk to the man and get his take on his parents' situation.

Duff pointed to the ceiling. "Before we do that, I'd like to get into the attic."

"You think there might be something up there?"

"It's the best place to hide your collection of dirty magazines." Duff waggled an eyebrow at Abe. "It's also out of sight and out of mind. I didn't even consider it this morning because I'm so used to apartment life. I forgot old farmhouses like this have weird attics and limestone basements, sometimes with clay-packed floors instead of poured cement slabs."

The door to the attic was at the far end of the short second floor hall. It was a small square cutaway blocked off by a push-up tile painted to match the rest of the ceiling. Abe looked at the size of the cutaway, and then looked at his two compatriots. "I take it I'm going through the ceiling?"

"Well, me and Chubbs sure ain't," said Buddy. "C'mon, we'll give you a boost."

Buddy and Duff each took a half-squat position beneath the hole to the attic. Abe took their hands for balance and stepped onto each of their thighs. He pushed the ceiling tile away from the hole, and Buddy and Duff grabbed his legs and pushed him into the attic.

"Less Chick-fil-A for you, big guy." Duff was gritting his teeth and straining to lift.

"Hey, now. No need to be rude. I don't see you minimizing your daily taco orders so you can do this kind of high-wire work." Abe used his hands to grab at a ceiling joist and pull himself into the attic. It was nearly pitch black up there, with no windows to the exterior world. It smelled musty and cold, with a prevailing odor of dust and dry, brittle wood. Cobwebs hung from most of the surfaces. Abe used the light from his cell phone as a flashlight and shone it around the attic. Big layers of pink Fiberglass insulation were dropped along most of the attic space, and thinner, less energy efficient black Thermacel insulation was stapled to all the vertical parts of the roof. In one corner of the attic, someone long ago had laid down four sheets of plywood on top of some insulation to create a storage space. It was easy to step onto from the attic entrance. Four cardboard banker's boxes were in that corner. They had all been emptied and piles of papers were scattered around them haphazardly. Someone had been looking for something.

"I've got something." Abe stepped to the platform and knelt. He scanned the papers and folders. "I've got land maps for the area. Is that anything? Someone was looking through them. Left them in a mess."

Duff called through the access hole, "Maybe something. Maybe nothing. If it's in a mess, then it's probably something. But if it's something, and it's important, why store them in the attic? Is it a hobby? Curiosity? I don't know."

Abe sifted through the papers. He found a small paperback book from the 1950s about spelunking and a stack of newspaper clippings about the Blue Mounds Area. Abe leafed through them. There were a couple of manila file folders with articles about farms around Blue Mounds, and a few articles about Blue Mounds State Park and the Cave of the Mounds, a natural limestone cave discovered in 1939 when some blasting for roads opened a gaping wound in the cave which happened to be located on the property once owned by Ebenezer Brigham. "Looks like Art was a fan of Blue Mounds."

"Who isn't?" Duff called back. "You know what? We can just take those boxes if it's just nonsensical stuff. Maybe it pans out later, maybe it doesn't."

"What if it doesn't?"

"We'll throw them back in the garage on a moonless night."

Abe put the papers and maps back together as best he could in his limited space. He stuffed them into the boxes, closed them, and carried the first one to the hole in the attic floor. "Bombs away." Duff caught the box and tossed it to the side. The second followed shortly thereafter.

Abe sat on the edge of the hole, dangling his legs through. He had to steel himself before he dropped through. At one point in his life, a seven-foot drop wouldn't have given him a second thought; he just would have done it. He was in his mid-forties now, and he could see fifty looming on the horizon. Despite working out, he was at that age where he no longer jumped down the last three steps of a staircase or even stepped off a curb without thinking about his knee popping to the side or rolling his ankle. Abe grabbed the joist next to the hole and began to lower himself through. Halfway down, Abe was struck with the terrifying notion that he was not going to be able to support his weight given the weird angle his arms were in, and he had no choice but to fall.

Abe landed hard on the heels of his feet, and he sprawled backward. A pair of big hands caught him before he went all the way to the ground. He looked up to see Buddy Olson looking down at him. "Easy there, Hopalong. You're a little past your jumping-down days."

"Hopalong! That's a great nickname." Duff was holding the stacked boxes in front of him. "I'm taking this out to the van."

Buddy tossed Abe back to his feet. Abe was impressed. For an older man who anchored a desk for most of the last three decades, Buddy still had a lot of cop strength in those old arms. Buddy pointed at the floor at his feet. "Hopalong and I are going to go down to the basement to see what we can find there."

"If you find a demon clown who feasts on the fear of children, tell him he still owes me six bucks." Duff began a slow clatter down the stairs. Buddy carried the other two boxes to the kitchen table.

The evening was coming on like a freight train. Despite moving into the longer days of the year, it was only mid-March, and Daylight Savings Time not until the coming weekend so it was still getting dark before six. The house was awash in twilight and Abe had to continue to use his phone's light to guide them since they did not want to risk turning on lights inside the house.

The basement door was off the kitchen, hidden in a little corner which wrapped around the narrow hall in the back of the house. A lot of old farmhouses, even renovated ones like the Laskeys' home, had strange angles and weird halls as if the original construction crew built the home without blueprints or even a sketch of how to do it. The houses had been built over time, an addition here, an extra room here, indoor plumbing when it came available. This led to a lot of odd construction choices. A hall behind the kitchen that leads to the basement door? Sure, why not? It was likely the basement had once had an exterior entrance like the root cellar where Dorothy Gale might have hidden from a Kansas tornado, but somewhere over the years, some owner decided to wall it inside the house so they would no longer have to put on a coat and boots and hike through snow to access their preserves and canned goods stored in the basement during long Wisconsin winters.

The basement was surprisingly dry, but it had the strong smell of stone and age. The foundation was fieldstone stacked and held with a primitive mortar of mud and clay. The weight of the house kept the foundation in place, but it was showing its advanced age. There were cracks all over the place plastered up with haphazard concrete patches, and some of those patches were so old they had been patched multiple times over the decades. The freeze and thaw of the seasons is hard on foundations in the Midwest.

The basement was also surprisingly empty. It looked like a little handyman's workshop, not much stuff stored down there other than some tools around a woodworker's workbench.

Buddy was crouched halfway down the stairs. The basement was less than half the area of the house above it. It was easy to see the entirety of it from his vantage point. "They don't have a lot of stuff, do they?"

Abe wiped some cobwebs off the wall. "Must be practicing that *döstädning* thing I keep reading about."

"What?"

"*Döstädning*. Swedish death cleaning."

"Swedish death cleaning?"

"It's an exercise practiced all over the world, but I think the Swedes get the most credit for it. Basically, once a couple hits middle age and the kids have left the nest, and they look around at the stuff they've accumulated over the years and just purge it all so their loved ones don't have to do it when they die."

"Make sense." Buddy lowered himself to a sitting position on the stairs. "I've been called out to mortality events in some homes that were floor-to-ceiling with junk. One lady, I swear she had some deep-seated mental issue, I got to her house, and she just had one whole room that was basically a pile of yarn. She had balls of yarn stacked in baskets, on shelves, in piles—skeins and skeins of it everywhere. I think her kids ended up donating it all to a nursing home or something."

There was a stack of tools leaning against the wall in one corner of the basement, all long-handled gardening implements: a hoe, an old-fashioned double-ended miner's pick, an assortment of spades and shovels. Abe walked over to them and scanned them with his phone light. Any dirt or mud on them had long dried. "Why would they keep these down here and not out in the outbuildings?"

"Theft? Maybe they're being stored for the winter? Maybe they put them down here when they moved in and never used them? Doesn't look like they're doing a lot of gardening out in the yard. Just mowing."

Abe moved away from the tools and looked at the workbench. It was clean and tidy. There were a few chisels and other tools for woodworking, but none of them looked like they had seen much use. "Was this a hobby of Art's or Michelle's?"

Buddy shrugged. "Don't know. They never spoke about it to me. I guess it might be one of those things Art thought he'd take up in retirement, but never really got into like he thought he would."

Abe understood that. When he and Katherine first bought their house, he tried out a lot of hobbies. Turns out, he didn't like any of them. He liked watching old movies or listening to the records he liked to listen to when he was in college. Those were his hobbies. The ten-speed touring bike he bought was still in Katherine's garage collecting dust. He gave away the cross-country skis he'd bought. He had even tried painting with watercolors, but realized he was not artistic and did not enjoy the process. He was happy to stick with 1950s detective noir films and Pink Floyd.

"See anything down here that I'm missing?" Abe scanned the basement with his flashlight one more time.

"Nope. Looks basic to me. If there's anything important down here, it's hidden well."

Abe turned and surveyed the room. Duff had the weird sort of vision that allowed him to size up a room in an instant and see things no one else would notice. Abe had tried to cultivate that gift over the years, and with some of Duff's tutelage, he had learned how to do it to a small degree, but he was nowhere near Duff's league. Still, there wasn't a place to hide anything. It was a small room with no real storage. There were floor joists above their heads thick with dust and cobwebs. "How long have they lived here?"

Buddy thought for a moment, his thumb counting the years on his fingertips as he added it up. "Twenty years, I think. Moved out here after Art's accident and retirement."

Abe looked under the stairs, but they were skeleton steps, open to the rest of the basement. Nothing behind them but a healthy collection of spiderwebs. "I guess we're done here."

The kitchen door opened and slammed shut. Duff's footsteps made it to the top of the basement stairs, and the big man clattered down to the step behind Buddy. He bent over, hands on his knees, to look under the joists at the basement. "Not much down here."

"I didn't find anything," said Abe. "Doesn't look like they used the basement much."

"Art was a big guy. I bet it hurt his knees to go down up and down these steps. Getting up to his bed every night was probably more than enough of a challenge." Duff scanned the room one more time and huffed a strained breath through pursed lips. He stood and looped his thumbs into the pocket of his sweatshirt. "Well, as long as you've looked behind that patch on the wall, I guess we're done here."

Abe's head whipped around, and he scanned the wall. "What patch? Where?"

Duff pointed to a crag in the fieldstone foundation on the far wall. "That one. It's loose."

"How can you tell?"

"The shadow. It's different from the rest of the shadows on the wall. The patch is just hanging in place, which means there's probably a little space behind it."

Abe ventured over to the wall. When he shone his phone's light over the patch, it did have a shadow that made it look like it was floating off the wall ever so slightly. He never noticed it until Duff pointed it out. Angry at himself for missing it, Abe pulled the patch off the wall with a little too much force. The time-weakened slab patch cracked in half in his hands. There was a small recess carved into the fieldstone wall behind the patch. It was smaller than a coffee mug, but it was clear that someone had worked at the limestone with tools specifically to carve out that little spot. A small glass jar was sitting in the little alcove.

Abe pulled out the jar and held it up for Duff and Buddy to see. It was a little baby food jar, the same kind he'd used to feed Matilda so many years ago. The label had been peeled off, so only the glass and metal lid remained. The lid was rusty. It looked like a relic. Inside the jar were several curious objects. Abe held up his phone light to the jar so he could see them better. "Looks like a trio of finishing nails welded together at odd angles, a decaying bit of ribbon, a lock of hair, and some sort of dark brown liquid."

"Turpentine." Duff wasn't guessing; he was certain. "Pop the lid and smell it."

Abe did as he was told. The sharp, stinging scene of turpentine assaulted his nose the second the lid was free of the glass. Abe screwed the lid back down quickly. "Yep. Turpentine."

Buddy looked up at Duff. "How'd you know?"

"It's a witchball."

Buddy snorted. "I thought you called them a warlock if they had balls."

"Not those kinds of balls. Witchballs are old folk magic. They date back to the Eighteenth Century, maybe older, but this one is modernized. A lot of weird fringe religions and cultural practices used them. German Pow-wow, for instance. The hill folk of the Appalachians. Early American Puritan settlers, especially around the whole hubbub in Salem."

Abe had never heard of a witchball, but he tended to stick more to scientific reading or crime and literary fiction. Duff's interests were everywhere, especially when it came to the strange and the paranormal. Abe figured his partner's hobbyist embracing of the supernatural was probably born from a rebellious rejection of Duff's parents' insistence on purely ivory tower academic pursuits. Abe turned the little glass jar over in his hands. He brushed his thumb over the lid to clean off the dust coating. The jar's expiration date stamp was still barely readable. June of 1977. That was well before the Laskeys purchased the property. "Think this has anything to do with the murder?"

Duff shook his head, his eyes sad. "Highly unlikely. That one probably belonged to a previous owner. There is nothing in the house to indicate the Laskeys had any beliefs in that sort of thing. There's not even a crucifix on the walls. Witchballs are put into the foundations of homes to prevent witches from scrying into them and seeing what you're doing, or they're put there to repel evil." Duff turned and started walking up the stairs. "In light of recent events, I think it's safe to say this one clearly didn't work."

6

THE COLLIER FAMILY lived in a small farmhouse south of Blue Mounds. The house was situated down a lonely country road, down an even lonelier single-lane driveway, and set deep in a valley. It was isolated and quiet. Deep in the valley, no sounds that weren't made by nature could reach them. Any passing trucks on the distant county road were silenced by a half-mile of trees and hillside. The sun hit the home hard in the mornings, but by the late afternoon it would drop below the hill to the west and plunge the valley in shadow. "Looks like the setting for a horror movie," said Buddy.

The Bad Luck Charm descended the steep driveway at a crawl with Abe riding the brake the whole way down. No dogs came out to greet them as would be typical for a country home. They saw no cats or other animals.

The little, boxy National-style farmhouse looked as though the exterior had been recently refinished with a light gray vinyl siding to make it look newer than it truly was. It was a house that dated to the 1920s. A large stone slab was exposed to the world a hundred feet from the house to mark where a barn had once stood. It had been torn down and either burned or hauled away long ago. The cement was cracking and being reclaimed by nature. Grass shoots were thick and tall in the many open crags. Another couple of years and the slab foundation would be completely hidden from view, swallowed by grass and bushes. A few sad, rotting wooden posts dotted the edge of the yard where a pasture was once cordoned off for cattle.

There was no garage, so the Colliers' vehicles were parked on a large area of packed gravel next to the house. Marybeth's black minivan was standing next to a black Dodge Ram pickup, presumably her husband's truck. Abe parked behind the minivan.

Abe and Duff made their way to the wraparound porch of the Collier home. The front door was large and stately. The windows on the first floor of the home glowed with warmth and light. Abe rapped on the front door with his knuckles. Faintly, muffled by the door, an excited small voice declared there was someone visiting the house. Over the years, living on a densely populated street and being the father to a very popular young lady with many friends, Abe had gotten used to frequent knocks on the door. However, it was plain to see that visitors were a novelty when the house was as remote as the one in which the Colliers lived.

A shadow approached the door, face obscured by the lights behind his head. The shape was male, tall and broad-shouldered. Marybeth Collier must have married a man who reminded her of her father. When the man spoke, his voice was low and tense. "Who is it?"

Abe launched into his well-rehearsed patter. "I'm Abe. This is Duff. We're private investigators. We'd like to ask you some questions." He held his license folio to the window.

"I didn't hire any detectives."

"I did." Buddy pulled his retired LEO badge from his pocket and slapped it on the window next to Abe's folio. "Tell Marybeth that Buddy Olson is here."

There was a series of muffled footfalls. Marybeth ripped open the heavy door and threw herself at Buddy. He caught her in his arms and held her for a moment, her feet dangling just above the porch deck. "Thank you for coming." Her voice was muffled, her face buried in his chest.

Buddy blushed and eased her to the ground. "How you holding together, Sprite?"

Marybeth Collier stepped back from Buddy, but she clung to his forearms with her hands. Her eyes were red-rimmed, and her face was peaked. She was trying to keep things together for the sake of her kids, but it was taking a toll on her. "I'm okay. Abe and Duff think Mom and Dad were murdered."

"Well, I trust these guys. If that's what they say, then that's what happened."

"Come in, all of you." Marybeth turned and indicated a large man blocking the threshold of the home. "This is my husband, Chris."

Chris Collier stepped forward. He was thick-necked and showed the evidence of a lot of gym time. He looked like a professional wrestler with big arms and a buzz-cut. He offered a hand to Abe. The second Abe grasped it, Collier did the alpha male squeeze to display power, a deliberate crushing of Abe's hand meant to show dominance and intimidate. Abe felt his knees buckle slightly from pain.

Duff was quick to defend his partner. "Hey, Bruno—if you're going to show off how much creatine you eat every day, maybe do it to someone whose idea of lifting weights didn't mean picking up an algebra textbook in college. Abe's no threat to you."

Collier's head snapped around. Abe saw a brief flash of rage in his eyes. "And you are, is that what you're saying?"

"Fuck, no. I'm a pacifist. The only thing I like to hit is the salad bar, and that's only because it's where they keep the chocolate pudding."

"Chris, they're friends." Marybeth pushed her husband to the side.

Collier flicked his gaze toward Buddy and then his wife. He stepped back, slightly chastened. His eyes dropped to the porch floor. "Sorry. I'm not like that. I mean, I used to be once upon a time. I purposely changed because I didn't like being that kind of guy. I apologize. It's been a trying week."

Abe flicked his right hand up and down to regain some circulation. "It's fine. I understand."

Buddy stepped up to Chris. "I'll shake your hand if you promise not to crush it. My old bones can't take it."

They shook, but Collier was much more accommodating to the old man. He held out a hand toward Duff, but Duff pretended not to see it. He was not a big shaker of hands. Collier gestured toward the door. "Please, come inside."

They stepped into the house. Like the Laskeys' place, it was renovated inside so that it looked modern. Hardwood floors ran through the whole place, except for strategically placed area rugs. The front door opened into a sprawling living room. A large TV on one wall was playing a cartoon. Since Matilda had stopped watching cartoons a few years back, Abe was out of touch with what small kids liked. It looked like something on PBS, though. A small girl, perhaps five years old, was glued to it, standing in front of the wide-screened monstrosity in total television hypnosis. A boy of nine or ten was curled up on a chair in the corner playing a handheld video game. The boy looked like a miniature, less-muscled version of his father right down to the buzz-cut. The girl was a replica of her mother with a tiny frame and eyes so large they made her look like a Disney animator's best attempt as drawing a child.

"We won't take up much of your evening," said Abe. "We were just over at your parents' house, and we noticed someone was in there today after we left earlier. Someone took their laptop computer from the office. If you have it, we'd like to take a look at it."

Marybeth and Chris exchanged a look. Marybeth said, "Well, maybe my brother took it, then."

"Have you seen him recently?"

"Not in the last day or so." Marybeth thought for a moment. "No. Not since Thursday, I think. It's been a few days."

"I'm trying to call him, but he's not returning my calls."

Marybeth shrugged that off. "Marcus has his own agenda. He does things on his schedule, always has. He...has made some poor choices in life."

Abe caught Marybeth flicking her eyes toward her husband, an involuntary movement. It meant regret. It was a subconscious acknowledgment that she was also not happy with some of her choices. Abe let that moment lie. "And Marcus lives near here?"

"Sort of. He lives down near Monroe, which is like an hour south of here."

"Go Cheesemakers." Duff had an incredible, if pointless ability to recall every high school mascot in the state of Wisconsin.

"Could you give him a call? Maybe he'll answer your call."

Marybeth pulled her phone from the back pocket of her jeans and started calling.

Duff walked over and sat on the couch. He looked over the boy playing video games. "What're you playing?"

The kid didn't look up from his Nintendo Switch. "*Breath of the Wild.*"

"Outstanding. You tame the Giant Horse, yet?"

The kid shook his head, eyes never leaving the screen. "Not yet."

"All he does is play those stupid games," said Chris. "When I was his age, all I cared about was football and baseball. Real football and real baseball. That kid will sit and play Madden all day, but he won't throw a real ball with me in the yard. What the hell is wrong with these kids?"

Duff arched an eyebrow. He could see the contempt in the boy's father's face. "You can't get hurt playing Madden. You also don't get teased at school for being bad at it during recess." Duff saw the kid pause the game and look up at him. That told him all he needed to know on whether he was right or not. He'd been an undersized, uncoordinated nerd once, too.

Marybeth's call got sent to voicemail after several rings. She did not bother to leave a message. "He's not answering. Like I said, Marcus does his own thing. He's kind of a black sheep."

"Well, if he calls back, please have him get in touch with me as soon as he can," said Abe.

Duff stood up from the couch and slapped his hands against his thighs as he did. "We'll leave you to your evening, then. We didn't mean to interrupt. We just wanted to know if you had the computer."

The trio moved toward the door. Marybeth offered them cake and coffee. "You've only just gotten here."

Buddy patted her on the shoulder. "We'll be around for the next day or three. I'll take you up on that offer, later." Duff strode out of the house and to the van without even a glance in Chris Collier's direction. Abe followed. Buddy tapped his index and middle fingers against his brow in a salute. "Have a good night."

As they climbed the steep driveway out of the valley, Abe looked over his shoulder at Duff, who was in the center of the middle seat in the van. "What was up with that?"

"I don't like that Collier guy."

"He's definitely shady," confirmed Buddy. "He has a couple of small-time misdemeanors on his record from when he was a teenager. I looked him up. Nothing over the last decade, though."

"Small-time teenage indiscretions don't mean much if he's been clean for a decade," Abe reminded them.

"Has he, though?" Duff wasn't sold. "He drives a fifty-thousand-dollar pickup truck. He put his wife in a forty-thousand-dollar minivan. He owns a house and land worth what, maybe five-hundred-grand, and he's had that house renovated to look new within the last couple of years, probably to the tune of twenty grand, at least. What does he do for a living? Because a guy in his early thirties like he is should not be rolling that large, especially not with two kids."

"Art told me his son-in-law was in something to do with real estate. Not sure what, though," said Buddy.

"That sounds sketchy. Might be worth looking into."

Abe made a mental note to do some background digging on the man once he got back to the hotel room.

Duff clamped a hand to his side as if he remembered something. "And, hey! We didn't need our guns."

Buddy turned in the passenger seat to look behind him at Duff. "We didn't need our guns *yet*. The night's still young." He turned forward again. "What's our next move, Nestor Burma?"

"Nestor Burma? Pulled that one out of left field." That was not a fictional detective Abe thought he'd hear referenced ever in his life.

"I figured you'd appreciate it. You look a little like Guy Marchand, you know."

"Very little," said Abe.

"My next move is dinner." Duff slapped the back of Abe's seat twice. "To the nearest house of swill and dining, Jeeves."

Abe knew his role here. He did his very best Stephen Fry imitation. "Very good, sir."

7

SHELBY REE MADE sure Paul Andruzzi's personal vehicle wasn't at the west side station before she got out of her SUV. The detective drove a rebuilt 1988 Chevy Monte Carlo, black, with T-tops. It was the sort of car he probably coveted while he was in high school and now that he was on a detective's salary, he could afford to own a halfway decent resto model.

The car was nowhere to be seen which was expected for a Sunday night. Unless the proverbial shit hit a fan and he was needed, Andruzzi was home with his family. Ree knew the man lived somewhere in Verona, but she had never bothered to learn where. It wasn't like she was close with him, nor he with her. They were distant colleagues who knew each other's names, but that was the extent of their relationship. They had different jobs, different roles. There was at least a twenty-year gap between their ages. Ree knew Andruzzi to be a bit prickly and quick to anger. She knew he was at least halfway decent at his job and closed a fair number of cases. She also had respect for the fact that he shunned the spotlight. Some detectives seemed to really enjoy it when the local news vans gathered for juicy live shots, but Andruzzi was content to be a detective, not a celebrity.

Still, she had seen him pull up to the station on more than one occasion with the T-tops down last summer, some horrible '80s metal band blasting on the stereo. Andruzzi was the kind of guy who still unironically listened to Warrant's *Cherry Pie* album. That was the sort of guy whom she tended to avoid. She knew his type. She wanted nothing to do with that.

Ree parked and radioed in her position to dispatch. She left the squad and walked into the nearly empty west side station. Only Lonnie Rostenbach was in the place. He was already in his civvies and carrying a knapsack on one shoulder. He was freshly showered and smelled like too much Old Spice.

Lonnie was a couple years older than Shelby, but he had gotten a college degree in Criminal Justice and worked a few odd jobs for a couple of years before getting into policework. He had joined the sheriff's office only a few months before Shelby, so like her he got a lot of the shit shifts and weekend work. Ree liked him. Lonnie was short, but wiry. He was leather-tough, with a surprisingly strong upper body in such a small frame. The week after he'd been promoted to solo patrols, he'd gotten into a tangle with a belligerent drunk who outweighed him by at least a buck-fifty and had more than six inches of height on him. It took him a bit, and Lonnie caught more than his fair share of punches during the incident, but he managed to corral and cuff the drunk before backup arrived. Lonnie had earned a considerable amount of respect from the Lifers that day. Ree had yet to earn her stripes in such a manner, and she questioned whether or not she wanted to do so. It would be nice to get some of the boys' club credibility for taking a beating like that and still securing the attacker, but it was also nice to have a smooth, straight nose—something Lonnie no longer possessed.

Lonnie's attitude was always upbeat, always positive. He greeted everyone the same way and flashed his ever-present smile. "Hey, hey! It's Shelby Ree!"

"What's up, troop?" Ree knew that Lonnie didn't mind the many nicknames that came with being an LEO.

"Oh, I was just calling it a night. I've been at it since before dawn."

"Those twelve-hour weekend shifts will get you." Ree slipped past Lonnie in the narrow entryway.

"Truth." Lonnie paused, a confused look on his face. He pointed to the northeast. "Don't you usually work out of the Mazo office?"

"Most days. Today I'm here."

If Lonnie suspected anything, he didn't show it. "Hey, sounds good. I'm heading home. I got frozen pizza and Miller Lite in case you feel like stopping by. You know you're always welcome."

Ree shot him a smile. He always invited her over. She got the notion that he was hoping for a relationship, especially after her recent breakup, but she wasn't feeling it. "I'm busy tonight, sadly. Thanks, though."

Lonnie's smile did not dim. "Your loss. It's a stuffed-crust pizza. I'm not low-balling the offer with some sort of cheap-ass pizza. I got the good stuff."

"You know, you keep telling me about how you're such a good cook, and how your grandparents had a restaurant, but when you invite me over, you always offer frozen pizza."

"After a twelve-hour shift, frozen pizza is all I have the energy to make. You know how it goes." He winked at her and pushed open the precinct door. Lonnie walked out to the parking lot whistling a song.

The door shut and plunged the precinct into silence. Only the hum of computer cooling fans could be heard. Without turning on extra lights, Ree wandered over to the detectives' room and found the desk where Andruzzi liked to work. Ree would have liked to know Andruzzi's password for the computer system. She could have easily slipped into his work, figured out what he knew, and left without anyone knowing anything.

Ree sat at the desk and looked at the items on it. The detectives shared desks since they were often roaming around the county, and they all had laptops with 5G wireless service now, but Andruzzi favored this desk heavily. He stored things in it, and Ree knew that most of the other detectives just assumed it was Andruzzi's desk. Because of that, Andruzzi had placed a few personal mementos on it, including a Maynard Mallard bobblehead and a Robin Yount bobblehead. The cartoonish duck bobblehead was wearing a jersey with the number 18 on it, presumably for the year 2018. The Kid was of course wearing the iconic 19 he wore all those years in Brewers' pinstripes and powder blue.

It couldn't be that simple, right?

Ree clicked the mouse to wake the computer from sleep mode. She typed in Andruzzi's login name, which was the same for everyone in the department: first initial, last name. Then, she tried 1819 as a password. That failed. She tried 1918. Another fail.

Ree stopped typing and got angry for being stupid. The password had to be at least eight characters long. There were no rules about capital letters or special characters, so Ree tried Andruzzi's badge number, 8347 followed by 1819. That failed, as well. So, she tried 18198347.

Bingo.

People made passwords easy to remember for a reason. Despite all the warnings that cybersecurity experts put out there, the human brain is only capable of remembering a certain number of codes or sequences. Overly complicated passwords were just password resets waiting to happen. Hacking was not difficult when social engineering was so simple.

Andruzzi's desktop appeared on her monitor. He had taken the time to personalize it, and the backdrop picture was of him and another deputy, Lewis Symdon, holding up a massive fish on a boat. It looked like they were in ocean waters off the coast of Florida. They had hooked into some sleek sportfish and had taken a picture to commemorate the battle before chucking it back into the drink. Ree didn't understand that mentality. She had done more than her fair share of fishing over the years, but that had been for food, not memories. Why anyone would go fishing for fun was beyond her. She didn't understand hunting for anything other than sustenance, either. And she didn't understand why people wanted the dead-eyed heads of things they'd shot mounted on their walls. She felt guilty enough when her family had to hunt deer for food back when she was young and growing up on the reservation, before her mother reconnected with her father and moved to Madison. She didn't need it staring at her reminding her of what she'd done.

Ree dove into Andruzzi's personal files first, the ones stored in the documents folder. They wouldn't be on the community server, accessible by all members of the department. They would be for Andruzzi's eyes only. She sorted the folders by the ones most recently accessed and found the cases Andruzzi was currently working. He had a couple of thefts, nothing major. The files for the Laskeys were down a few. He hadn't touched them in five days. He'd given his final determination on Wednesday. His files were reviewed Thursday. The higher-ups made the final presentation on Friday. Case closed. Andruzzi had moved on to more pressing issues.

Ree went into the Laskey folder. It was empty. The folder itself was still in Andruzzi's files, but no documents were within it. Usually there were .pdfs of notes and write-ups and .jpgs of the crime scene. There were text documents of transcriptions of witness statements. There were any number of other forms and files, but the folder was completely empty, and had been since last Wednesday. Every alarm bell in Ree's head began clanging. Why? Where had the files gone?

She clicked into Andruzzi's other closed case files from months ago. There were still documents in all of them. Why was the Laskey file empty?

Ree went into the community drives with Laskey's account privileges. It allowed her to get into files that would otherwise be locked to her since regular patrol deputies weren't expected to solve high profile crimes. She clicked through the files as high as Andruzzi's privileges would allow. She only found basic summary reports, including a printout of the medical examiner's report stating the cause of death to be single GSWs to the head, and the most likely cause of violence was a dementia-related break from reality by Michelle Laskey. Simple. Direct. No one was going to argue with it. No alarm bells there; that was an easy case to solve.

But if it was so easy, where were the rest of the files and scans? Any murder case usually has a mountain of evidence. For complex murder cases, there might be dozens of gigabytes of data. That was why the IT guys were so important in keeping the computers running and the cloud storage systems error-free. The days of gumshoe policing and gut hunches were long gone. It was all done with digital notebooks and files, now. Adobe Acrobat was as important to police work as a badge, gun, and sensible shoes.

Ree logged out of the computer. Any physical evidence would be downtown at the main station. That was where they kept most case-related materials, but there might be some at the west side precinct in the temporary evidence room.

The evidence room was a dim, cramped space the size of a wealthy man's walk-in closet. It was lined with tall utility shelves that held cardboard file boxes filled with manila folders, forms and papers, and occasionally plastic bags with necessary items. Once the boxes were shipped downtown, they'd be wrapped with red tape and labeled. They'd be kept in a locked room and anyone handling them would be made to fill out a requisition form and any additions or removals from the boxes would be strictly recorded so there was a constant paper trail. However, given the nature of this case, the quick conclusion, and the simplicity of the findings, there had not been the strict adherence to formality with this evidence box. It was tossed on the shelf casually and sat waiting to be shipped downtown. It would be sealed there and held for the attorneys for Dane County to decide whether any sort of charges would or could be filed in this case. It was unlikely that any charges would ever progress, so the evidence box would be held downtown for a year. Anything that could be digitally scanned and stored would be. Anything physical that needed to be kept would be shipped to offsite storage and held until the Rapture. With this case, it was highly unlikely that anything physical would be saved, outside of the gun used to commit the actual crime, and even then, if the children of the heirs of the decedents petitioned for the gun to be returned or destroyed, it would be.

Ree slid the evidence box off the shelf. It was surprisingly light. There was no way there was a gun in the box. There should be. Another alarm bell went off in Ree's head. She set the box on the floor and lifted the lid. Inside were only a half-dozen folders and one sealed plastic envelope. The plastic envelope was clear, so Ree could see a vial of pills in the bag. It was a standard brown prescription bottle with a white lid. Michelle Laskey's name was printed on it. The pills were donepezil. The prescription date was only a few weeks ago. The bottle was still nearly full.

Was that the first time she'd been prescribed these pills? There was no doctor's name on the bottle in the spot where the prescribing physician's name was usually printed. There was also no issuing pharmacy. Another warning bell. It was a generic bottle of pills that any detective worth his salt should have thought was a little hinky.

The files were crime scene forms and printouts of digital photos. Ree doubted they'd help the two strange detectives from Chicago, but she gathered up the files and took them to the copier anyhow. She zipped off copies of all the papers and stacked them into a pile. Then she put all the files and folders back into the box and back on the shelf.

Ree was getting a sick feeling deep in her gut. Something was amiss within the department. Was it Andruzzi? Was it the coroner? Was it someone else entirely? Something was rotten in the county of Dane. This only reaffirmed her belief the Laskeys were murdered, but she needed to discover the reason why. What was the motive? Money was the logical guess. The Laskeys had it, but was it legal or suspect? And where were they getting it from?

Ree made sure everything in the precinct looked the way it did when she entered. She left the building with her files and headed to her vehicle. She would go home and really go over the photocopies. Then, the next day was her day off. She'd go find Abe and Duff and make a new plan.

8

ABE WAS AWAKE before the alarm on his phone could start beeping. He was usually up early, but he slept even more lightly than normal in a hotel. The beds never felt right. The sheets were laundered within an inch of their life. The duvet was cheap and thin. The pillows were never right, always too soft so he needed to fold them in half or use multiple pillows stacked on top of each other to get the support he got from his pillow at home. And, obviously, it took a superhuman mental effort to try not to think about everything people had done in that room, in that very bed over the years. Sure, most of them just slept or watched TV, but there were enough recreational activities performed in those beds to give Abe serious pause. He wasn't a prude, but he also did not like to think about those who had used this mattress before him and how many naked rears had found their way to those sheets. No matter how much bleach and detergent the laundry crew used, it could never be enough to make his mind not ponder the possibilities. It was a side effect from using cheap motels as stakeout rooms or seeing crime scenes in cheap motels over the years. It was also why he never went barefoot in a hotel room. They rarely, if ever, scrubbed the floors. The housekeepers would run a cursory vacuum over them, but that was about it. Abe shuddered to consider what manner of food, drink, and extraneous filth had been ground into hotel carpets over the years.

The hotel had a simple exercise room. There was a stationary bike that looked to be out of service, a cheap treadmill, and a small stack of dumbbells with a single weight bench. A TV in the corner of the room was playing Fox News with the sound muted, but the captions up. Abe ignored the TV and ran a mile on the treadmill. The machine sounded unhappy the whole time, so he stopped before he hit his daily three-mile goal. He did some basic calisthenics and a few sets of curls and presses with the dumbbells. It wasn't a great workout, but it would have to suffice. He never liked working out. He only did it because he was officially middle-aged and knew it was the only way to stave off some of the infirmities that come with that advancement. When he started using the gym in his apartment complex a few months after his divorce, one of the guys he met there told him he would become addicted to working out. That still had not happened. Abe was confident he could quit running and lifting weights cold turkey and never look back.

He showered and dressed without waking Duff, which was not difficult. Duff could sleep through warfare. It was still not even seven in the morning. The hotel was adjacent to a McDonald's. Abe decided to walk over and get Duff and Buddy some Sausage McMuffins and hash browns. He'd get coffees for himself and Buddy, even though he did not particularly enjoy coffee, and a diet Coke for Duff, who never drank coffee.

Abe strode out into another glorious blue-sky morning. Birds were singing. The sun was low on the horizon but still bright enough to see everything. There was a low din of engine noise and the drone of tires against pavement on the Monday morning commute. The main road through Verona was busy. A long line of cars was stacked up in the drive-thru at the McDonald's.

Abe grabbed three value meals and a cardboard holder for the drinks. Then he walked back to the Super 8. As he was nearing the door, he flicked his eyes toward *The Bad Luck Charm* in the lot. Immediately he realized something was not right. He deviated from his path to the hotel and walked closer to the van. It was leaning oddly. Upon closer inspection, it was evident someone had slashed the two driver's side tires at some point in the night. Someone had jammed a knife into the two tires leaving a nasty-looking gaping wound in the sides. They would not be repairable. They would have to be replaced. At that moment Abe was grateful he had not let Duff talk him into canceling his Triple-A membership. The roadside assistance was about to come in very handy. He looked around at the light posts and the building façade. There were no cameras anywhere. Whoever did it got away without leaving any evidence of the crime.

Abe walked back to the room and keyed into the door. "Get up. Someone slashed the van's tires."

Duff remained motionless in the bed, turtled in a covered ball, only his face exposed, his eyes closed. "I would have been disappointed if they hadn't."

"You know who did it, then?"

"Pretty obvious, isn't it? Only two suspects so far. Three if you count Marybeth, but I don't think this was her deal. She didn't strike me as the type."

"Chris Collier and who else?"

"Marcus Laskey."

"You think he knew what we drove, though?"

"I'll agree that Chris Collier is my first suspect, but c'mon. Most people who use hotels check out on Sunday night. We're one of what? Five, ten cars in the lot? And we're probably the only Illinois plates. Most people from the Chicago area would have just driven home and saved the price of a hotel." Duff emerged from his cocoon, rumpled and sleepy-eyed in black boxer-briefs and an ancient blue Pink Floyd shirt that looked stained and moth-bitten.

"I brought you food." Abe thrust one of the bags of breakfast at Duff and set the diet Coke on Duff's bedside table.

"My man." Duff gratefully accepted the bag. "I knew you were a good dude, regardless of what people are writing about you in bathroom stalls."

Abe walked to the room next door and knocked on Buddy's door. The door opened and revealed the old sheriff in a white V-neck t-shirt and boxer shorts. He did not have Abe's aversion to bare feet in hotel rooms. He was skin-footing the carpet like a pro. "I'm awake."

Abe held out the bag and coffee. "I brought you breakfast."

"My guy." Buddy took the coffee and sniffed it. "Black?"

"As Duff's soul."

"Perfect."

"My van tires are slashed."

"That sucks."

"Duff thinks Collier or Marcus Laskey might have done it."

Buddy considered it. "Maybe. But why?"

"Because Collier was a little touchy last night?"

"Married guy probably didn't abandon his family to drive ten miles to slash tires in the middle of the night."

"So who did it, then?"

Buddy gestured at the world around him. "You realize this is Green Bay Packer territory, right? And you've got FIB plates."

"So?"

"Some random drunkass could have slashed it just because you've got Illinois tags. I've seen it happened before."

Abe went back to his room and sat at the little circular table in the corner to choke down his sandwich and hash brown before they lost any more heat. Duff ate sitting on the edge of his bed. "Tires are gonna cost some money."

"Yup."

"Still got Triple-A?"

"Yup."

"Well, at least you and I won't have to change them, then. That'd be a safety issue at highway speeds. I wouldn't trust a vehicle where our inept asses had to make major repairs."

Abe wasn't sure if he would, either. "Buddy said we can ride in his truck."

"Fair enough, but I call shotgun. You have to ride bitch. Enjoy the floor hump."

"What is riding bitch?"

"It's the middle seat on the bench. Buddy's truck is a regular cab. No backseat. Sits three across."

"Why is it called riding bitch?"

"Because that's where the driver's bitch sits. I mean, if he has a bitch, which I don't think Buddy does anymore. At least, not without the help of magic blue pills."

"You have shorter legs than I do. Shouldn't you sit in the middle with your feet on the hump?"

"I probably should, but I already called shotgun, and the law of shotgun is absolute. You don't fuck with shotgun. The second somebody calls shotgun, they get shotgun. That's just how it goes. This is a fundamental truth. The second we start to ignore the rules of shotgun, our society descends into madness and anarchy. Everyone thinks Rome fell because its military forces took too much damage in skirmishes against the Goths. That's not true. It's because Emperor Nepos called shotgun and Romulus Augustulus chose to ignore it. Historians won't tell you that directly, but that's what happened."

Abe sipped his coffee. "A gun called the fowling piece, which is considered to be the first true shotgun, wasn't invented until 1722 AD. Rome fell in 476 AD."

"That's how powerful the law of shotgun is; it preceded history. Everyone saw what Nepos did, and they were like, *Oh, shit! Dude invoked the Rite of Shotgun. Someday, they're going to name a weapon after this!*"

"If shotgun was so important that it preceded time and space, then why didn't Romulus Augustulus heed it?"

"Because he was a little bitch, that's why."

"Full circle," said Abe.

Duff nodded and shoved his hash brown into his mouth. "Full circle."

ABE PLACED THE call to Triple-A and let them know what happened. They dispatched a wrecker to take the van to a tire shop and get the problem fixed. Then, Abe and Duff climbed into Buddy's truck. Abe rode bitch, as discussed. His knees were pulled high, and it was uncomfortable, but Abe chose to suffer in silence.

Buddy drove like he was still chasing bad guys. Everything was done at a minimum of ten miles over the speed limit. The fact his truck was decked out with stickers that made it pretty clear that he was a retired LEO probably helped with keeping him from getting pulled over twice a day. Buddy did not curse at other drivers, as Duff would, nor would he simply let them be slow in front of him, as Abe would. Buddy drove like there was a checkered flag in the distance and he needed a new sponsorship deal. The Dodge Ram's eight-cylinder engine roared, and the single-cab, short-bed pickup felt almost sporty, even with three grown men weighing it down. Buddy wove through the sparse traffic headed out of Verona to all points west on Highway 151. "Where to, Slim?"

Duff had thought about it all night. "We need to talk to the Laskeys' neighbors, particularly the ones who live along that lonely little road where they lived."

"If anything sketchy was afoot they would have noticed it, right?" said Abe.

"That's my hunch," said Duff.

Buddy nodded. "Seems like a solid start. Anyone heard from the gal?"

Abe and Duff shook their heads. Abe pulled out his phone. "I'll text her, let her know where we are. She can come find us when she's ready."

"A fine day for adventure, isn't it?" said Buddy.

"I'm still not down with you making us bring our guns." Duff refused to wear his shoulder holster, so Buddy acquiesced by making him bring it, but letting him stash the Walther and holster under the passenger seat unless they needed it. Abe's .38 was in the glove box. Only Buddy was truly carrying, his intimidating long-barreled .44 Special was in a shoulder holster beneath his left arm.

"They might be necessary."

"Yes, I'm sure some farmer will want to go all OK Corral on us over a couple of questions."

"You never know. Besides, you don't want to leave your sidearms unattended in the hotel room or your van."

For once, Duff conceded to Buddy's wisdom. "Fair point."

Buddy made the jaunt from Verona's east side to Mount Horeb's east side in record time. A normal drive time of fifteen minutes was done in less than ten. Buddy bypassed the Mount Horeb exits and flew to the exit for Blue Mounds. Since he was riding bitch, Abe had an unfettered view of the speedometer, and Buddy was regularly bouncing between seventy-five and eighty miles per hour, despite the posted limit of sixty-five. Buddy hit the corner where County F branched off the highway and hardly slowed down. The Ram took a precarious lean as it cornered, and for an instant Abe would have sworn they were on two wheels. In another five minutes, they were whizzing past Brigham Park and approaching the Laskeys' home. Then, and only then, did Buddy bother with the brakes. "Who's first?"

Duff pointed to the very first house on the road. It was a house that had been built sometime in the 1990s, and it looked the part. It did not blend in with the older farmhouses. It had brown clay-colored siding with a darker clay-colored trim. The two-car garage door and the front door of the house were a tasteful green. The house was right off Highway F, not too far down the lane near the turn-off for Sanders Way, the road where the Laskey house stood.

They looked like an odd trio: two big guys with a tall, skinny guy between them. Duff with his ever-present Milwaukee Brewers cap, Abe, bald pate glinting in the sun, and Buddy, with a cowboy hat, thick white mustache, and beer gut bulging out from his tan blazer. Abe approached the door and rang the bell. A dog began barking inside the house. "I hope they're home."

Duff was standing back from the concrete porch. He pointed at a window. "I see a light on. Someone is probably home."

It took more than a minute for someone to reach the door, but eventually the green interior door opened. A woman in her late fifties was there. She was hurriedly trying to hush an excited pointer dog, mostly white with a dark brown head and dark spots flecking its body. The woman was dressed casually, jeans and an orange sweatshirt with UW-Platteville Mom in blue letters on the front. She was preoccupied with the dog but froze when she saw three strangers on her porch. "Can I help you?"

Abe read her body language. All fear. Her hand was on the doorknob, ready to slam the door closed in an instant. He could see her tensed, ready to move. Her eyes were flicking to the right. Her phone, maybe? Maybe a gun? Something was there, something she knew she might need. Abe did his best to assuage her fears. "We're very sorry to bother you. I'm Abe, this is Duff. We're private investigators." Abe flashed his folio and stepped toward the door with a business card. "We'd like to ask you a couple questions about Art and Michelle Laskey, if we could."

The woman relaxed slightly. She looked to Buddy. "Who's the cowboy?"

Buddy pulled his badge from his pocket and held it so it caught the sun and flashed the golden light at her. "Buddy Olson, former sheriff of Waukesha County, retired."

The woman relaxed further. "Aren't you a little out of your jurisdiction, Sheriff?"

"Art Laskey was one of my deputies once upon a time. I'm looking into his death. Could we come in? Or would you mind stepping out to talk to us for a bit? It won't take long."

The woman thought about things for a moment. "Let me put on my coat and some shoes, and I'll come out."

The door closed for a moment, and then reopened. The woman stepped out into the day wrapped in a Columbia winter coat with a pair of bright blue Crocs on her feet. The pointer dog burst past her legs and into the yard like a fifty-pound rocket. It wheeled in a circle around the trio barking and wiggling excitedly, as if torn between wanting attention from the men and wanting to attack the men. "Don't mind him," the woman said. "He's a chicken dog. He talks a big game, but when it comes down to it, he's scared of everyone and everything. He really fears strangers at first, especially men. He'll calm down in a few seconds."

"He's a lovely dog," said Abe. "What's his name?"

"Ripley," said the woman. "My husband named him after Sigourney Weaver in *Alien*."

"Good name." Duff lowered himself to one knee on the gravel, not an easy move for a man his size with his knees. He held out a hand. "C'mere, Ripley."

The woman started to tell him, "Oh, he won't go for that—"

The dog immediately moved to Duff's outstretched hand, sniffed his fingers, and then flopped down to his side and rolled on his back. Duff started rubbing the dog's belly as if they were old friends.

The woman was dumbfounded. "Now, how in the hell did you do that? He normally hates men."

"I barely qualify as a man."

"He's not wrong," said Abe. "We've taken a poll."

"He's a Braque Français Pyrenean, isn't he?" Duff continued to shuffle his hands along the dog's belly. The dog's face was a mask of unfiltered joy, its tongue lolling.

The woman was shocked. "He is! Purebred! How'd you know?"

Abe was also impressed. The closest indication he'd ever had toward Duff being an animal lover was that he typically refrained from kicking at pigeons that wandered too close to his feet. "Yeah, how'd you know?"

"I watch a lot of dog shows on TV on the weekends when you're not around. I've learned things. Pyreneans were originally bred to be gun dogs."

The woman nodded, impressed. "My husband bought him because he wanted a pheasant-hunting companion. Ripley turned out to be scared of loud noises." As an afterthought, she added, "And pheasants."

"He's still a good boy." Duff flopped down on his side in the gravel and spooned the dog. The dog had a new best friend. "Dogs are better than people any day."

The woman said, "I'm Birgit, by the way. Birgit Huseth."

Abe handed her his business card. "That's a very Norwegian name."

Birgit shrugged, reading the card. "Yeah, well, this is Mount Horeb. Pretty much anyone who has lived here for more than forty years is probably Norwegian. There's a reason you see Norwegian flags flying around these parts. It's like Oslo West."

"And you've lived here a long time?"

"In Mount Horeb? My whole life. Viking born and raised. My husband Jerry and I built this house just after we got married—he's in construction—and we've been here ever since."

"And when did you get married?"

"Ninety-six. That was only eight years after we graduated from high school and six years after we got married. Boy, it's been a while. The years just sort of flew by."

"And you obviously like it out here," said Abe.

"Oh, very much. It's been a lovely place. Nice and quiet most days. No neighbors poking around. I can go tanning out on our back deck in the summer and nobody can see."

"Did you know the Laskeys well?"

Birgit cast a glance down the road toward the house in the distance. "Not well, no. They had us over for dinner once a few years back, and I'd occasionally bake them some cookies if Art plowed out our driveway with his four-wheeler while we were gone. If me or my husband was out mowing the lawn, Art or Michelle might pull over and chat from the window of their truck for a minute before heading on their way, but we weren't kindred spirits. Country friendly, is all. They were nice enough folks, though."

"So, you didn't notice anything odd about Michelle lately?"

"No, not a thing. Was she the one who pulled the trigger?"

Abe arched an eyebrow. "What would make you say that?"

"We don't know what happened. Just heard murder-suicide, so one of them had to be the shooter, right?"

"You assumed it was Art that pulled the trigger?" asked Buddy.

"Isn't that how it usually goes? Big guy. Anger issues."

Buddy and Abe exchanged a glance. Buddy said, "Anger issues? Did you witness him have an exchange with someone? In my experience, Art was as good-natured as they come."

"Well, once in a while we'd hear him yelling about something, but it was rare. And we could never make out what he was actually saying from up here, you know. He was too far away. It was just noise, but it was definitely coming from their place, and it was definitely Art."

"And you could only hear Art's voice?" asked Abe.

"Just one voice," Birgit confirmed. "Never heard anyone else hollering down there."

"Have you noticed anything unusual lately?"

Birgit looked off into the sky and chewed on her lip. "I don't know. What do you call unusual?"

"Well, this isn't a highly traveled road over here. And Sanders Way is even less traveled. I mean, have you seen more traffic? Less traffic? Any weird cars or trucks?"

"How do you mean weird?"

"Like, a car or a truck you haven't seen before, or a car that looks out of place out here?"

Birgit thought hard for a long moment. "You know, a few months back, my husband mentioned the Laskeys must have been doing a project because he saw a couple of box trucks at their house."

"Box trucks. Like delivery vans?" asked Abe.

"Bigger. Like those day rentals you can get from U-Haul, but these didn't have markings on the side. They were plain, white trucks. Fleet vehicles, my husband said."

"And you have no idea what they might have been carrying or who drove them?"

"I could ask my husband tonight, but I don't think he knows. They were trucks. He saw them at a distance. Might have been delivering new furniture or appliances for all I know."

"Boxes." Duff was still sprawled on the gravel driveway cuddling the deliriously happy pooch. "Had to be the boxes being stored in the barn and shed."

"Yeah, but what was in 'em?" said Buddy.

"That's the kicker, ain't it?"

Abe poised his pen over his little notebook. "And how long ago was this? You said a few months?"

"Did I?" Birgit's lips pursed in thought. "I guess I said months, but it might have been more than a year ago, already. Time sort of blends together, you know? Months, weeks, years—it all kind of takes on its own shape after a while."

"Did you see anything else out of the ordinary?" Abe asked. "Anything besides trucks and the yelling?"

The woman shook her head. "No. But out here, you can miss a lot. I mean, it's not like I sit at the window watching the road. Our TV room is in the basement. We spend most of our free time down there. A tornado could run through the backyard, and we wouldn't know."

"Thank you for your time, Ms. Huseth. If you think of anything else, or even see something sketchy in the next few days, please call me and let me know." Abe nudged Duff with his foot. "Say goodbye to your friend."

Duff pouted like a petulant child. "No. Ripley wants to be a detective dog. He can come with us and help us track the bad guys. We'll teach him to attack on command and make sarcastic comments about people's outfits."

"If he catches sight of a gun, he won't be friends for much longer." Birgit gave a short, shrill whistle. The dog, with protest on his face, rolled to his feet and trotted to her side. Duff looked disappointed, but he stood and brushed off the dust and gravel from the driveway.

They walked to Buddy's truck while Birgit and Ripley went back into the house. Buddy backed out of the driveway.

Duff said, "Well, we knew they were storing something in the barn and the shed. This proves I wasn't crazy. They took delivery of something, and later had it taken away."

"That's not a crime in and of itself," said Abe.

"Depends on what they're taking possession of," said Buddy.

"I'd be willing to put money on whatever it was they were taking possession of is what got them killed." Duff pointed down the road past the Laskey's house. There was a small dairy farm. "Head down to that place. Let's see what they know."

The farm was as typical as Wisconsin dairy farms could be. There was a small farmhouse painted white with black trim. There was a red barn with white trim. There were a few outbuildings between the house and the barn. A big pickup truck was in the driveway next to a Jeep Grand Cherokee. Thirty cows were standing in a mud-and-manure-covered pasture near the door to the barn. A faded red Case International tractor was parked in front of a spill where a machine was dumping manure from the barn gutters into a manure spreader hooked behind it. The tractor looked to be fifty years old, but it seemed to be no worse for wear.

A pair of mixed-breed dogs ran out to greet Buddy's truck as it entered the driveway. One was predominantly some sort of heeler, the other predominantly Labrador Retriever, but both had enough of something else in them to look like brand new breeds of dogs never before seen by man. When Buddy parked the truck, both dogs happily set about claiming all four tires with enthusiastic urination.

The second Duff was out of the truck, both dogs swarmed his legs. They danced on their back feet, pawing at Duff's thighs. They ignored Abe and Buddy entirely, and Duff gave the dogs plenty of attention.

Buddy frowned at the dogs and jabbed a thumb toward Duff. "Do you think they like him because he smells like a cheeseburger ninety-five percent of the time?"

"I have to say, I've never seen this side of you," said Abe. "It's...different."

"That's because you've only ever seen me deal with city dogs before. City dogs suck. They forgot how to be dogs. Country dogs still remember."

An older man in Red Kap denim bib overalls and a Carhartt winter jacket emerged from a side door in the barn to see what the commotion was. He wore a faded and stained ball cap with a Case IH logo on it, and his clothes were showing the wear and tear of years of hard work in the barn and the fields. He was shabbily dressed, but out on the farm there were no fashion critics. The man was overweight and waddled as he walked. He had bad knees and probably had a bad back and bad hips, the physical toll of a life spent crouching beneath cows and countless hours of manual labor. He called to them as he walked. "Can I help you fellas?"

Abe was ready with the business card and license folio, as usual. "I'm Abe. That's Duff. We're private investigators. That's Buddy Olson."

Buddy flashed his badge at the man. "Retired sheriff."

"Not of Dane County."

"Waukesha."

"Ah. Well, then. Name's Tom Hefty. What can I do for you gents?"

"We're looking into the Laskeys and their deaths," said Abe. "Can you tell us what you know of them?"

"Art and Michelle? Good people. Damn shame about what happened."

"What do you know about what happened?"

"Not much. They were killed, I know that. Read in the paper that it was murder-suicide, but beyond that I don't know much. I know Art had guns in the house. He and I used to hunt deer together occasionally."

"So, you knew the Laskeys well?" Duff was on his knees roughhousing with the dogs who seemed to enjoy being thrown around by the big man.

"Well enough, I guess." Hefty stuck his hands in his coat pockets and rocked back on his heels. He squinted at them through his thick glasses. "Me and Art got on alright. He'd stop by some nights when I was milking, and we'd shoot the shit while I worked. Michelle and my missus didn't have much in common, though. They were friendly, but not friends. We'd get together for fish fry down in Hollandale occasionally."

"Did you notice anything odd in the weeks leading up to their deaths?" asked Abe.

Hefty sniffed and spat something awful on the ground behind him. "Odd? Not really. Just life as normal, more or less. Of course, the cows keep me pretty occupied."

"We talked to Birgit Huseth up the road." Buddy gestured toward the Huseth residence, a tiny lump on a hill in the distance. "She said she noticed a few box trucks making deliveries or pickups at the Laskeys' in the last couple of weeks."

That triggered a little light in Hefty's eyes. "Oh, yeah. Now that you mention it, I have seen a few of them in the last few months." Hefty's thick Wisconsin accent sounded like he said *a few-ah dem in-dah lass few munts.* It reminded Abe of hanging with some of the guys who were local back in grad school in Madison, not that the Chicago accent was any better or even that much different. He did not carry much of an accent, himself. Neither did Duff, but Duff was something of a mimic and would unconsciously slip into one here and there, especially when talking to someone who spoke with a thick Chicago accent.

"Did you know what the trucks were doing?"

"Nah. They showed up occasionally. That's all I knew. Figured Art was getting a new fridge or something. I know they had some real nice furniture in that house."

"But you said you saw more than one box truck?"

Hefty seemed confused for a moment. He scratched at his chin before shoving his hand back in his pocket. "Well, yeah. I guess I did. I probably saw a couple of them over the last few weeks. Maybe four, maybe five. I guess I didn't count. I mean, you see one and you forget it. I wouldn't have thought it odd until you mentioned it, but yeah—I guess I seen a few of them. That's a little strange, I suppose. Not nothin' I would have called the cops about, but it's a little strange for out here."

Abe decided to press further. "What about other cars? Did you see any cars you didn't recognize? I mean, this is a pretty isolated little road. You don't really have to come down this road unless you live on it, right?"

"I suppose that's right."

"Do you know your neighbors' cars?"

"Most of them, probably. I mean, I know what Birgit and Jerry Huseth drive. And Art's always got a nice pickup. Michelle liked them little sporty cars. The Bergs over there, they got a minivan and a little pickup, and they got a nice boat they take up to the lakes in the summer."

"So, you know most of them. Have you seen any cars that you couldn't place? Anything that stuck out in your mind?"

"How about license plates?" Duff had the heeler-mix in a headlock and was scruffing the Lab-mix and keeping him at arm's length. Both dogs were trying to lick Duff's face like it was made out of goose liver pâté. "Wisconsin plates are white with black lettering. Standard Illinois plates are mostly blue with red lettering. Iowa plates are blue-and-white, and so are Minnesota plates. Maybe you saw any of them?"

Hefty's shoulders bobbed up to his ears. "Aw, hell, I don't pay that kind of attention. I hardly notice that sort of thing."

"What about car makes, then? Any sports cars or luxury cars, maybe a big SUV you didn't recognize?"

That triggered another light in Hefty's eyes. "Now that you mention it, I saw a big-ass SUV come down the lane the other day. I was on the tractor out in that field over there spreading manure." Hefty indicated a field that was two hundred yards down the road, but adjacent to the blacktop. "I seen this big SUV with tinted side windows. Might have been a Cadillac, I'm not sure. Anyhow, I waves at the guy driving, but he didn't wave back or nothing. Figured he wasn't nobody I knew, then."

This might be a big piece of the puzzle. Duff stopped playing with the dogs. "What color was it? Black?"

"No, more like a really deep gray."

Duff pressed the man. "What about the tires? Black rims? Silver?"

"I don't know. I was looking at the driver, not the wheels."

"What about the plates?"

"I didn't look."

"Anything on the back window? Anything on the sides? Any detailing?"

"Not that I remember. It was just a dark gray SUV. Really big." Hefty thought for another moment and snapped his fingers. "You know what? It was a Lincoln Navigator; I just remembered that. I remember thinking it was a Cadillac, at first, but when it passed me, I glanced at the back and saw the word Lincoln across the back. You don't see too many Lincolns anymore. Maybe that's why it stuck in my head."

"You don't see too many because they're Ford's luxury offshoot. They only make like four types of Lincolns anymore, and they're all big-ass SUVs."

"My wife had a really nice Lincoln Town Car back in the Eighties. That was a nice car."

"I'm sure it was," said Duff. "This Lincoln, it was new? It looked new?"

Hefty nodded. "Oh, hell yeah. It looked like it rolled off the lot last week. Couldn't have been more than a year or two old, tops. Maybe less than that. I'm not all that up on my Lincolns anymore."

"When was the last time you talked to Michelle Laskey?" asked Abe.

"Oh, a week or two ago, I guess. She came by to drop off a pie she made."

"Did she seem alright to you?"

Hefty shrugged again. "Sure, of course. Same as always."

"Did she walk over?"

"Nope, she came over in that snazzy little blue number she drives."

"What about Art?"

"Probably saw him Monday or Tuesday last week, I guess. He was coming home as I was heading to town. We stopped to say hello at the end of the road, up there, and talked about the Badgers playing in the tourney."

"And he seemed fine to you, nothing odd or different about him?"

"Yeah, nothing unusual. We both groused about the Badgers, but that's not unusual this time of year. They always manage to screw up the tournament, don't they?"

Abe looked at his compatriots. "Any other questions?"

Duff thought for a moment. "When you went hunting with Art, did he ever mention plat maps to you?"

"Plat maps?"

"Maps of land in the area that show the topography and property boundaries."

Hefty shook his head slowly. "No, can't say I ever heard those words come out of his mouth. I know he loved the land, though. He was always walking in the woods." He pointed down toward the woods that backed the edge of the Laskeys' property. "He was always out walking the tree line. He loved the woods. He liked watching the deer and turkeys."

"Can't blame him," said Duff. "Who doesn't love deer?"

"They're goddamned pests. Fun to hunt, but they'll fuck up a car for sure. That's what happened to my wife's old Lincoln. She came over a hill and hit three of the sumbitches."

Abe put his notebook away. "Well, we won't keep you from the chores. I appreciate your time, Mr. Hefty. If you think of anything else, or if you see anything sketchy or odd in the next few days, please let me know."

Hefty nodded. He slotted Abe's business card into the pocket on the front of his overalls. "Will do, sir. Pleasure to meet you all. Careful of the dogs on your way out."

In the cone of silence that was Buddy's pickup, Buddy waited for the dogs to retreat to their master's call before he started to back out of the driveway. "Well, Mr. Nadgett, what do you make of that?"

Abe bristled. "I think I prefer to be called Nestor Burma."

"I know, but I was feeling Charles Dickens at the moment."

"At least you went with a classic. Nadgett is considered the first private investigator to be mentioned in fiction." Duff stared at the cows in the pasture yard outside the barn. "Let's piece together what we know so far: The Laskeys were taking deliveries over the last few weeks. Someone in an expensive SUV drove down this road recently. Michelle Laskey was allegedly on anti-dementia pills that led her to shoot her husband. One of these things doesn't fit."

"If Michelle was on anti-dementia drugs, she wouldn't be driving, would she?" said Abe. The flaw in the coroner's report was large. If she had those drugs in her system, she must have started them the day of the murder, in which case it was extremely unlikely she was so far gone from dementia that she would have committed the murder in the first place.

"You'd hope she wouldn't. Hell, Buddy doesn't have dementia that we know about, and I'm barely comfortable letting him drive."

"Shaddup, Chubbs, or you'll be walking." Buddy hit the brake. "Someone's at the Laskeys' place."

They all looked to the lonely little cabin as they passed. An older Jeep

Cherokee was in the driveway, green with some body rust and a roof rack.

"Marcus Laskey?" Abe thought out loud what the other two were thinking.

Buddy pulled into the driveway and blocked the Cherokee's escape path like a cop would have. Old habits die hard.

The door to the Cherokee popped open and Shelby Ree stepped out to face the three men. Duff was disappointed. "Oh, it's only the lady cop. That's no fun." He rolled down the window and shouted, "You were supposed to be Marcus Laskey."

"I was supposed to be rich and famous, but that didn't work out too well for me. Where have you degenerates been? I went to the Super 8 in Verona, and your van was there, but you weren't. Shame about the tires. Was it Collier?"

"Maybe." Abe eased out of the truck behind Duff.

Ree nodded toward Duff. "Why does the guy with the shorter legs make you ride bitch?"

"Because he called shotgun," said Abe.

"Makes sense," said Ree. "You don't fuck with the rules of shotgun."

"I know. That's how Rome fell."

Ree nodded like whatever Abe said made perfect sense. "One warm night in June of 1876, Custer's second-in-command called shotgun and Custer ignored the declaration and took it for himself rather than ride in the back of the wagon. I guess we all know what happened the next day at the Battle of Greasy Grass."

"Little Bighorn," said Duff.

"You can call it the White name. I'm half-Ojibwe, so I'll call it by the Lakota name. Either way, the rules of shotgun are absolute."

"See? I'm not making this stuff up." Duff jabbed a thumb at the little house at the far end of the road, a lump of brown on the horizon. "We talked to a lady who lives in that house, and a farmer who lives down the other way. Both of them noticed multiple box trucks at the Laskeys' over the last few weeks."

Ree filled the fellows in on what she'd found at the west precinct: the missing murder weapon, the pills, the lack of files on Andruzzi's computer, and the missing files in the case box. "It's sketchy as hell. The pills they bagged look fake, like they weren't issued by a real doctor. I'd be shocked if Michelle Laskey had even seen a specialist about dementia."

Buddy sighed and stroked his mustache with his hand. "That means there's a high-level conspiracy. Someone in the department is in this, too. I hate that."

"But who? Andruzzi? Bob Benedict? Both? More? Someone else? Does it go as high as the current sheriff?" Ree's mouth was set in a thin line. It appeared she was as unhappy with corruption as Buddy.

"Art Laskey was a cop once," said Duff.

"I don't need to be reminded of that." Buddy cast a look at the house. He looked over to the pickup truck and Jeep in the garage. "They definitely had money. But how? They didn't get it from the settlement after Art's accident, I know that much. And an injured cop's pension is just enough to get by. There's no evidence of any sort of windfall from financial investments, unless it's on the missing computer, and even then, it's a little suspect not to have physical investment statements, especially for an older guy like Art."

"I have a hunch that whoever was driving the Lincoln Tom Hefty saw was the guy who got treated to the good china," said Duff. "If that's true, then there's a better-than-average chance he's the guy who killed the Laskeys."

"That means we're looking for someone with money, someone involved in some sort of illegal activity that makes a lot of money, someone who has managed to get sworn LEOs into the proverbial bed with him, and someone who wouldn't hesitate to murder a lovely couple in their sixties," said Buddy.

"Well, that narrows it down to most of gangland Chicago," said Abe.

"And gangland Minneapolis," said Duff.

"Does Minneapolis even have a gangland?" asked Ree.

"Someone has to control the underground hotdish market." Duff turned to Abe. "Have you heard from Marcus Laskey, yet?"

Abe checked his phone. "No." Abe saw Duff's face wrinkle into a mask he knew well. It was the face Duff made when something was bothering him. "You think something has happened to Marcus Laskey, don't you?"

"I do. It's only a gut feeling, though. I hate gut feelings. Gut feelings don't solve cases; evidence solves cases."

"If something happened to Marcus, then maybe there's a bigger conspiracy afoot than we thought." Buddy leaned against his truck, setting his cowboy hat crown-down on the hood as he did. He ran his fingers through his thick mop of white hair.

"There's a lot of annoying things about this case," said Duff. "Lots of pieces to the puzzle, and I have a good idea of what the puzzle is about, but it's not complete. It's not whole. I lack the proof I need to say what I'm really thinking about it."

"One of us needs to go to Marcus Laskey's house." Abe used his phone to find an address for Marcus's residence. It was a lonely little house on a plot of land out in the sticks near the Illinois/Wisconsin border less than an hour south of their current location.

"One of us needs to go to Chris Collier's house and see if we can find the missing computer. Either Marybeth or her brother has it. They're the only two people who would have taken it." Duff looked at the time on his phone. "It's mid-morning on a Monday. If Collier has a real job, he should be at it. If two of us go, maybe one of us can distract Marybeth while the other sneaks through the house quickly."

"How about we call Marybeth and get her over here under some pretense while one of us goes to her house?" said Buddy.

At that moment, an unmarked white cargo van pulled into the driveway. Two guys were in the front seat. One of them was Caucasian, middle-aged. The other was a younger Latino male. They were stuck behind Buddy's truck. The guy driving rolled down his window and stuck his head out. "Is there a problem? We were called in to clean this house." It was the crime scene cleaners.

"There's a good pretense if I ever saw one," said Ree. "I will call Marybeth over here. I can't be sneaking around her house, though. I'll be illegal-adjacent for this case, but I can't be the one breaking any laws."

Duff flashed the lockpick kit he kept in his back pocket for such occasions. "I'll do it, but you'll have to loan me your keys."

"You drive?"

"I do. Not well, mind you, but well enough. It's only a few miles in the country, so I think I can manage it."

Ree shrugged and flipped Duff the keys to her car.

"What if Marybeth asks about why you're there without a car?" asked Abe.

"I'll tell her I had car trouble and got a ride with a deputy." It was as simple an answer as any. "What about you guys?"

Buddy reached out and smacked Abe's shoulder. "C'mon, Slim. Me and you will take a road trip to Monroe. I'll treat you to a Limburger sandwich at Baumgartner's."

"Limburger sandwich? The kind of cheese that gets made by rubbing it with the same bacteria that causes body odor?"

"That's the stuff. Monroe has the only cheese factory in the world that still makes Limburger. A Limburger sandwich is a delicacy."

"I'm not sure if you know what that word means."

"Regroup at the hotel when we're done." Duff started to head to Ree's Jeep.

"Hey, Tex—you're forgettin' something." Buddy opened his jacket and pointed at the .44 hanging at his side.

"I'm already doing a B-and-E. If I have a gun on me while I'm doing it, doesn't that make the jail time worse?"

"Take it. If you need it, you'll be glad you have it."

With the put-upon huffing and posturing of a teenager being asked to pick up laundry from the floor, Duff stomped over to the truck, flung open the passenger door, and pulled out his Walther from its spot under the passenger seat.

"And put it on." Buddy's tone was stern and fatherly.

"But it chafes."

"Build up some calluses." Buddy saw the crime scene cleaners gawking at the sudden appearance of a pistol. He pulled out his badge and jabbed a thumb at Ree. "Relax. I'm LEO, retired. She's an active-duty LEO."

"Don't make me use my badge," said Ree.

"I'll move my pickup and you guys can get to work." Buddy nodded toward Abe. "Let's roll."

DUFF WAS NOT used to driving. It had been at least five years since the last time he had sat behind the wheel of a car, and that had been Abe's rickety old Volvo which Duff had glossed with the handle of *The Fucking Embarrassment*. It wasn't that Duff couldn't drive; it was that he did not have the temperament needed to drive in Chicago traffic. Everything everyone else did set him on edge. There was too much responsibility, too much to be aware of, and too much he could not control. It was really the lack of control that got to him. It made him angry. Duff fully believed humanity was not worth saving at the best of times, and in the middle of hectic traffic, he would frequently call out for God, Krishna, Zeus, Odin, or any other deity that happened to be listening to immediately deliver the apocalypse asteroid just to thin out the number of cars on the Dan Ryan Expressway.

It was a different event driving a car through lonely rural roads. The only traffic was usually oncoming, and they stayed in their own lane. There was no one in front of him tapping their brakes too much, and no one tailgating behind him and filling his rearview mirror. Duff could appreciate the thrill of driving when there was no danger of causing a catastrophic accident that might maim thirty people, however it would never be something he would ever fully enjoy.

Duff sat behind the driver's seat of the Cherokee gripping the steering wheel so tightly at ten-and-two that his knuckles had gone fish belly white. He was backed into a recessed entrance to a field road, a place where hunters might park their trucks for the day while they hiked out to tree stands in the nearby woods. The skeletal trees around him obscured him from the road. He had shut the car down and was content to watch the road, waiting for the Colliers' black Town and Country to roar past him. If Marybeth was home alone, she would have had to get the kids into the car before she could get to her parents' home. That would take a bit of time. It had taken Duff less than ten minutes to get to the road where the Colliers lived, and maybe another minute to decide where to wait. He'd found the little field road entrance and backed the car into place. It had been a long time since he'd needed to use reverse in a car. He wasn't good at it. It took a couple tries to get it parked so it hadn't looked like a drunk pulled off the road to take a rest.

He estimated it might take Marybeth anywhere from fifteen to twenty minutes to get both kids ready, strapped into car seats, and on the road. That was a generous estimate, too. He knew from his limited experience with the Allards when Matilda was small that it might take longer depending on the moods of the children and their desires to be combative on that particular morning. Everything was a gamble with kids.

Seventeen minutes elapsed from the time he left the Laskeys' driveway to the time Marybeth Collier rocketed past him. It was nice to see that, like her mother, she was also a fan of speeding. A Chrysler minivan was hardly as fast and nimble as a WRX, but Marybeth was not hurting for haste.

Duff turned the key to start the Cherokee and wasted no time getting down the road and down the long driveway to the Collier home. As he had hoped, there were no vehicles in front of the house. No one was home.

Duff pulled up to the house and estimated he had at least twenty minutes to get in and out of the house and back on the road without getting busted. If Ree was smart, she'd buy him another ten or twenty minutes. He didn't want to take that chance. Twenty minutes was more than enough.

Duff was good with lockpicks. Spending his formative years at Bensonhurst amidst teenage psychopaths and burgeoning career criminals taught him more than most college degrees could ever offer. Some of it was not great, like learning to take a beating without crying or showing fear or pain. Some of it, like learning to sweep a lock and turn it over for a clean, no mess break-in had ended up being surprisingly helpful over the years.

Duff pulled open the screen door and used his body to block it. He tested the doorknob just to make sure it was locked. It was. The Colliers had nice stuff and their house was hidden from the road. It wasn't a shock that they took the time to lock their doors.

Duff tried one of his trustiest hooks in the door. It didn't want to take. Most old country houses used a standard five-pin tumbler lock. In their renovations, the Colliers must have updated their security. The new one was a little fancier than a standard door lock. Duff tried three more hooks, each more elaborate than the last until he found one that felt like it was holding up the tumblers. Then, he started trying to sweep through the tumblers with a pick and turn over the lock. He felt himself start to sweat despite the relatively cool temperatures. As a fat guy, anything over freezing could get him sweating if the exercise caused enough worry and tension.

The lock wasn't turning over. Duff cursed under his breath. He pulled the pick from the lock and used his forearm to wipe the sweat from his head and face. Then, he tried again. Anytime there was pressure, it felt like minutes were slipping away instead of seconds. He swept the lock and found it stuck. Something was wrong. He felt the tumblers again. They were all up. Was there something blocking the door? He started to try to force the sweep which was the fastest way to break or bend a pick so that he would not be able to pull it from the lock. "Turn, you motherfu—"

The door suddenly opened and ripped the picks from Duff's hands. The boy who had been playing *Breath of the Wild* the night before was standing in front of him. They looked at each other for a long moment. The boy wasn't scared or worried. His Nintendo Switch was clutched in his right hand.

"Shouldn't you be in school?" Duff finally said.

The kid shrugged. "Mom has let me skip school until after the funeral because I miss my grandpa."

"Really looks like it." Duff stood and pulled the picks from the lock. "I'm Duff. I'm a detective."

The kid shrugged, wholly unimpressed. "Yeah, my dad said you're probably more concerned with investigating Taco Bell's menu than anything else."

Duff accepted that jibe. "He's probably not wrong."

"Why are you at my house?"

If the kid had been a little older, Duff probably wouldn't have been bothered to pull his verbal punch, but little kids and dogs were his Achilles Heel, and this kid just made the cut for kindness. He phrased his statement with as much sensitivity as he could muster. "I'm looking for something that might help us better understand what happened to your grandparents."

"You mean why my grandma killed my grandpa."

"That's precisely it. How'd you know that?"

"I heard my dad telling one of his friends on the phone."

"Ah. Rough way to learn. Does your mom know you know the details?"

The kid winced and tilted his head slightly to the side in one of the most lackadaisical responses ever given. Duff assumed it meant no.

"I'm sorry about your grandparents, kid."

"My name's Maverick."

"Maverick?"

"Yeah."

"Like Tom Cruise, *Top Gun*, Maverick?"

"I don't know what that means."

"Your parents call you Maverick?"

"They call me Mav most of the time. Sometimes Mom calls me Snuggerbottom, but I hate that."

"I can understand why. That sort of name gets out to your friends and you're going to be spending every recess knocking people's teeth loose."

"You get it." Maverick looked from Duff to the door and back to Duff. "I'm not supposed to let strangers in the house."

"Wise policy. I recommend that as well, but I'm not really a stranger, am I? I mean, I was here last night. We met once before."

The kid shrugged. "What are you looking for?"

"Your grandparents had a computer. Did your dad bring it home?"

"My mom did."

That was interesting. Duff wondered immediately if it was a conscious act because she knew something important was on it, or if she just knew she didn't want the crime scene cleaners taking it. Why did she lie about it the night before, then? "Can I see it? It might help us understand why your grandparents died."

Maverick thought for a moment and then shrugged. "I don't care." He turned and walked into the house leaving the door open. "It's this way."

He walked Duff to an office in the rear of the house. The door was closed. "Mom and Dad tell me I'm not allowed to go in here, but whenever they're not home, I usually go in. That's where Mom keeps the peanut butter cups we're not supposed to have because Mayzee is allergic to nuts."

"Your sister's name is Mayzee?"

"Yep." Maverick spelled out the girl's name for Duff. "I think it's a stupid name, but then again so is Maverick."

The kid was beginning to grow on Duff. He felt like a kindred spirit. "My real name is Clive. I always hated it. When you get to be an adult, you don't have to answer to names you don't like, so start thinking about what you might want to be called now."

The laptop was sitting out on a desk. It was plugged in and fully charged, but the lid was closed. Duff sat at the elegant wooden wing chair in front of the desk and opened the lid. He was confronted by the password screen. "I don't suppose—"

"It's Michelle." The kid already knew. "Eight characters and one capital letter. That's what all their passwords are. Grandma and Grandpa were pretty easy to hack."

The kid was correct. The desktop revealed the generic blue Windows background with a handful of icons on the left-hand side of the screen. A dozen files were saved to the desktop, but none looked important. Duff highlighted them all with the mouse and opened them all at once. The first three files were Word documents. One was a recipe file, one was an unimportant letter to someone named Leslie, and the last one took forever to open and contained a large collection of cut-and-pasted .jpgs of the grandchildren, as if Michelle Laskey didn't understand the photos could just be saved as .jpgs in a folder.

The .pdfs on the desktop were more interesting. The first one was the loan document for Art Laskey's new pickup. It had been financed, but Art and Michelle had put down $25,000 in cash to start the deal. Duff scanned the fine print. The Laskeys had a decent, but not excellent credit score. The truck's sale price was $59,000, which was a really good deal for that truck. The loan was also stretched to 72 months, which Duff considered excessive. The monthly payment for the thing was almost $600 a month. What sort of pensioners had that kind of jing to throw at a car payment for six years?

The second .pdf was for the pontoon boat. It was brand new and had a sale price of $80,000. Like the truck, the loan payment was spread out over six years and the Laskeys had ponied up thirty large as a down payment. How did this couple have that sort of cash lying around? Alarm bells were playing Westminster Quarters in Duff's head.

Duff looked at the web browser. The Laskeys had not even bothered to download Google Chrome or Mozilla's Firefox. They were using the basic Microsoft Edge browser that came installed on the computer. Duff opened the browser and looked at the bookmarked files. There were only a few pages in the folder and most of them were home improvement or recipe blogs. Duff rummaged through the browser history and found nothing important, nothing telling. He went through the Documents folder and the Downloads folder but came up snake-eyes. There were certainly no financial documents. There wasn't even a financial website bookmarked. Maybe there was something on Art or Michelle's phone? But where were their phones?

"Did your mom ever bring your grandparents' phones to the house?"

Maverick shook his head. "I never saw them. She might have them in her purse or something. I haven't looked there."

Duff pondered this for a moment. Everything was on cell phones now. A smart killer would have taken their phones and chucked them in the nearest river just in case.

Duff checked his watch. He was exceeding his twenty-minute window. Time to go. Duff stood and looked at Maverick. "How much will it cost me to make you forget I was ever here?"

"Fifty."

"Fair and shrewd." Duff pulled his wallet and peeled off two twenties and a ten. He held them out and the kid grabbed them. Duff walked to the door and paused. "You know, you might hate school now, but let me tell you something: I think you're going to do alright for yourself someday."

"School's dull."

"That's because you're smarter than everyone around you."

Duff beat feet back to the Cherokee. He gunned it up the driveway and was on the road long before he would ever see the black Town and Country returning home. If the kid kept his word and never mentioned Duff's presence, everything was golden. Duff felt certain the kid would keep his word.

THE DRIVE FROM Blue Mounds to Monroe would take an average driver roughly a little under an hour. If they had a bit of a lead foot, maybe they could do it in forty minutes. Buddy Olson managed to exceed Abe's expectations by almost ten minutes and got near Monroe in just over half an hour. The big pickup's tires kept a roaring drone as Buddy put it through its paces, wheeling down the road and wailing past slower cars whenever the mood struck him and not always when the stripes in the center of the road said he could pass another car. It was both a terrifying and exhilarating experience for Abe who tended to drive like someone's grandfather out for a lazy Sunday afternoon excursion.

"You're going to get pulled over." Abe's warning did little good.

Buddy wasn't worried. "Out here on this county road? Doubtful. I know the sheriff of Green County pretty well. He doesn't have the manpower for regular patrols on side roads. He keeps his guys on the bigger highways."

Abe's GPS app guided their mission to Marcus Laskey's place. Buddy had taken Highway 78 south of Blue Mounds to Highway 39 east, and then clipped down County Road J to Monroe. The road had been a picturesque journey through Wisconsin farmland, even at Buddy's breakneck speed. The road passed through valleys and hills and even ran beside a creek for a time. It was the sort of road that Wisconsin used to lure tourists to visit the state.

Marcus Laskey's place lay on a nearly hidden road off County J, on Budman's Court, an offshoot of a rather worryingly named one-road lane called Bad Turkey Road.

The house was hidden completely from Highway J, and Bad Turkey Road ended as a dead end. Budman's Court was listed as a court, but Laskey's place was the only house on it. There might have been another farm at one time, but it had long ago gone to seed and been torn down. The stone foundation where a house once stood was still visible, but judging by the tree growth within the foundation, it had to have been demolished forty years ago, at least.

Marcus Laskey's place was nowhere near as nice as the homes of his parents or his sister. It was a battered, broken-down farmhouse that had to have been built in the 1920s, maybe the '30s. It was a little one-and-a-half-story square farmhouse with a decrepit front porch. The house had once been white, but time and weather had beaten it down over the years so weather-worn gray boards with traces of paint clinging to them were all that was left. The roof had been shingled and patched several times so there were a mottled assortment of shades of black and green and gray shingles. An empty, single car, detached garage stood off the side of the house. The garage no longer had a door. A haphazard stack of lumber to the side of the garage looked like it might have been a door once. The yard of the house was mostly overgrown. An area around the front of the porch had been mowed before the winter set in months ago, but the rest of the yard was shaggy with long brown grass matted down by winter snow. A broken riding mower sat rusting away alongside the garage. A pair of old ten-speed bicycles were next to it, also in various stages of rusting and decay.

"Looks like the set for a biopic about Ed Gein." Buddy threw the truck into park. Before he stepped out of the vehicle, his hand dropped to the gun at his hip, the barrel running alongside his leg.

Abe felt his own hip for the snub-nose. He knew why Buddy had checked the weapon; the place was giving off all the wrong vibes. Despite the sunny skies overhead and relatively mild temperatures for mid-March, the place felt off, foreboding. Maybe Duff was right. Maybe something bad had happened to Marcus Laskey. Abe checked the safety on his pistol. It was still engaged, as it should be. He made a mental note of that fact in case he needed the weapon. He figured he wouldn't pull it unless Buddy pulled his gun. In which case, he'd let Buddy start shooting, and he'd take that second to thumb the safety.

A chill wind was blowing. It made Abe's head cold. He should have brought a beanie or wool cap. Sometimes he wished he wore a baseball cap like Duff, but he did not have the head shape to pull off a ball cap. With his tall, oval head, a hat just made him look like someone with a towering Frankenstein forehead. It wasn't flattering. Abe wrapped his jacket more tightly around his body and gave his scalp a quick rub.

Abe and Buddy walked up to the porch. The boards creaked with each step. Buddy rapped on the door. When Buddy's knuckles hit wood, they meant business. The knock was louder than most people's knocks. Abe wondered if they taught door-knocking like that at the police academy. There was no response from inside. Given the lack of a car on the property, they should have expected that. Buddy peeked into the large front window. A gauzy white curtain blocked it, but there was enough of a crack at the edge of the curtain to spy into the large living room beyond. "The man is a pig."

Abe walked to the narrow, drop-sash window on the other side. There was no curtain on that window. The panes of glass were ancient and clouded with dust and age. Paint smears were dried on the glass from the last time someone had bothered to touch up the trim. Abe rubbed one of the panes with his forearm and peered into the house. Unlike the man's parents or sister, Marcus Laskey did not appear to enjoy a renovated interior, and he was also not much of a housekeeper. Boxes, clothing, and trash were scattered everywhere. Next to a filthy, matted couch was a stack of pizza boxes four feet high. Abe had been inside homes like that before. He knew what they smelled like. His brain made him relive that smell in that moment despite being outside. It made him gag. "Try the doorknob. Something tells me he's not big on locking up."

Buddy twisted the handle and the door opened. "I guess not." Buddy stepped into the house. His right hand dropped to the handle of his gun. It was a habit trained into him over decades of law enforcement. Abe knew that Buddy did that subconsciously even when he wasn't wearing a sidearm. "Anyone home? This is the sheriff!"

"You're not the sheriff."

"I'm *a* sheriff. Maybe not *the* sheriff." Buddy took two more steps into the house. "Jesus, it stinks in here like old cheese and ass."

"I get the feeling that Marcus is something of a black sheep." Abe followed Buddy into the house. The smell was not as bad as he feared it would be, but it was still assaultive. There was a heavy smell of time and age mixed with rotting food and body odor.

The house was chilly, but not cold. Buddy walked to the box on the wall and thumbed the dial. "Thermostat is set low."

"I always turn down my thermostat if I'm not going to be home for hours."

"I'm always home now. Goddamned retirement. I don't futz much with it. Keep it at sixty-seven in the winter, and seventy-three in the summer."

"Sixty-seven is a little chilly for the winter, isn't it?"

"I'm fat, and I wear sweatshirts."

Abe looked at the cluttered coffee table in front of the couch. Nothing looked fresh. Nothing looked recent. Any food that was there was congealed or covered in mold. "It doesn't look like anyone's been here in a few days."

Abe pushed deeper into the home. The kitchen, like the living room, was filthy. Plates and silverware were piled up in the sink. The garbage can was overflowing, a mountain of rubbish and garbage spilling onto the floor from the rim.

Abe knew from experience garbage told you a lot about people. Sometimes what someone threw out was a lot more telling than what they kept. For instance, if someone had a binge eating disorder, you never looked in their cabinets to figure that out, you always looked for the wrappers in the garbage. Marcus Laskey's garbage was mostly food waste. He did not separate out recyclables, which Abe found strangely barbaric in this day and age. Cans, plastic bottles, paper, and whatever else he deemed he no longer needed got chucked into the corner to molder and rot.

Abe went to the pile and started sorting through it with the tip of his foot. "Should have brought plastic gloves."

"Should've brought hazmat suits." Buddy walked to the stairs around the corner from the living room. Like most old houses the stairs were steep and narrow compared to modern stairs. These particular ones went up four steps to a landing and took a sharp left turn. "How the hell do you get a mattress upstairs? Or furniture?"

Buddy disappeared as he ascended the stairs. A few seconds later he called down, "Got a pretty nasty-looking futon mat up here, and a few piles of garbage, but Marcus isn't up here."

"He might be at work," said Abe.

Buddy called back, "I got a feeling he's not really into the whole punch-a-clock, nine-to-five thing."

Abe was finding a lot of gross things but mixed in with the gross things were an excessive number of silver-foil packages with empty plastic bubbles on the other side. Pills. Abe reached down and plucked one of them up by the corner with just the tip of his thumb and forefinger. He did not want to think about the germs crawling on that package. The package was for something called Proin Chewable Tablets. Abe dropped the package and wiped his fingers on his slacks. He punched that name into his phone and looked over the results that popped up. "Is there any evidence Laskey had a dog in here?"

Buddy looked at the floor and then at the bottoms of his boots. "I think we'd have stepped in piles of dog shit by now if there was."

"Then why does he have a lot of pills for treating urinary incontinence in older dogs?"

Buddy abandoned the stairs and walked to the pile of garbage. With no squeamishness or hesitation, he reached into the filth and picked up a pill pack like the one Abe had just grabbed. He flipped it back and forth. "Phenylpropanolamine."

Abe knew what that meant. "Meth."

Buddy shrugged and chucked the pill pack back into the trash. "Look around us. Doesn't this scream meth? This place looks like the cover photo for *Better Homes and Tweakers.*"

"I guess it does." Abe had plenty of dealings with meth users over the years on Chicago's colorful streets and alleys, but he went out of his way not to go into their homes if he could help it in the least. "I don't see the paraphernalia, though. He might be making it, but I don't think he's using it. I mean, the pizza boxes alone say he's not smoking it." Heavy meth users tended to lose their appetites.

"You're probably right. Users tend to leave their kits out in plain sight; it takes too much work to hide them. With this many packets of ingredients, he's got to be cooking." Buddy sighed heavily. "Damn it."

"You knew Marcus Laskey."

"I knew him back when he was a kid. I haven't seen him in ten years, maybe. I knew the military didn't work out for him, and I knew he had a real rough go of it overseas and was dealing with some heavy PTSD issues and some legal scuffles, but Art and Michelle told me he landed on his feet. I think they were sugar-coating his situation for me."

"I think it's worse than you think." Abe flicked the garbage pile with his foot a few more times. "Look at the number of pills."

"You would need a lot of those tablets to make meth, yes."

Abe was already drawing the lines. "And Art and Michelle were storing a lot of boxes of something in their shed and barn, weren't they?"

"Well, hell." Buddy fit the puzzle pieces together for himself. "That would explain where their money was coming from, wouldn't it?"

"Meth is pretty brisk business."

"Think their son-in-law is in on it, too?"

Abe wasn't sure. "I want to say yes, because he seems like he's a royal pain, but we have nothing tying him to whatever the Laskeys were doing, other than the fact he's married to their daughter." Abe wanted to get away from all the filth in Marcus's house.

"So, where did all the pills come from?"

Abe started walking out of the house. "I couldn't tell you. I'm betting that's what those box trucks were picking up and dropping off, though."

Buddy was on Abe's heels. "And how's the Lincoln Navigator fit into this?"

"That says high-level kingpin or organized crime to me."

"If it's organized crime, then he has to be cooking meth on a large scale. They're not going to waste time with little trickles of product here and there. He's got to have some sort of intense operation going."

They broke into the fresh air, and Abe inhaled it deeply. The crisp, chill wind scrubbed the stale rot stench from his sinuses. "I think we have a bigger worry on our hands, though."

"Which cop is helping some high-level meth traffickers move pills and rocks through Dane County, you mean?"

"You're already ahead of me."

Buddy slid behind the driver's seat of his truck. "This ain't my first rodeo, cowboy." Buddy checked his watch. "It's almost noon. We'll hit Baumgartner's for lunch before we head back. Saddle up, it's Limburger time."

9

BACK IN VERONA, Duff and Shelby Ree regrouped over a diner lunch at a little Fifties-style throwback place called Gus's Diner. The place was built recently, but it was constructed to look like someplace Archie and Jughead would have patronized back in the day. Fifties memorabilia and photos were hung all over the walls. There was a heavy Marilyn Monroe and Elvis Presley representation along with a smattering of Wisconsin-related propaganda such as Packers photos, Brewers memorabilia, and Badgers sports plaques. A long lunch counter stood on one side of the restaurant with circular stools anchored to the floor in front of it. There was a considerable salad bar along one wall. Each booth along the outer wall was outfitted with a little Crosley jukebox, but sadly none of them worked. They were decoration-only.

Duff was most disappointed about that fact. "I could have really gone for some *Earth Angel* right about now." His finger pressed the numbers that would have keyed up the hit song by the Penguins if the machine had been working. He mournfully hummed the melody.

"You like Oldies?"

"I liked any music that annoyed my father, and that would have been all music except classical hymns and Fifteenth Century religious chant."

"Churchy kind of guy, was he?"

"The churchiest. He believed public crucifixion should be brought back as a crime deterrent."

"Where is he now?"

"Dead."

"So, he got to meet God in the end."

"If Heaven exists, I have strong doubts that he's there."

"Hell, then?"

"He was too churchy for Hell. He's probably out in Limbo protesting to get the Catholic Church to restore it to its former glory."

Ree ordered a simple platter of pancakes, bacon, and eggs. Duff went for a pure cholesterol bomb, a monstrosity called the Cheese Curd Burger, which was a standard double cheeseburger, but in addition to the second layer of cheese on top of the top patty, a layer of deep-fried cheese curds was slapped into place and held there by the miracle glue of melted cheddar.

"You eat like a man who doesn't want to be around much longer," said Ree.

"You observe like a woman who is accurate a lot." Duff lifted the burger to his face without hesitation.

"Death wish?"

"Not exactly. More like a really-tired-and-bored-of-life-complex."

"That's a shame."

"Living is for the wealthy. The rest of us are just killing time until the clock stops, lady."

Ree changed the subject before she could become more depressed by that statement. "Marybeth seemed to be in decent spirits today, at least."

Duff had already told Ree about the lack of information on the laptop save for the extravagant car payments on the drive to Verona. "Define *decent spirits.*"

"I mean, she wasn't all over the place emotionally. She seemed in control. Level."

"She named her kids Maverick and Mayzee. I don't know how level she can really be."

"She told me she would be glad when her parents' house was clean because that meant she could get in and get it ready to sell."

"Not going to keep it for herself? That seems like a prime spot of land to let go, especially considering where she currently lives. I mean, it's upland versus lowland properties. Her parents' place gets more sun. Her place is practically in a lowland fen."

Ree carved her pancakes into squares and drowned them with maple syrup. "Her parents' place is worth some coin. With how much property they have attached to that place, its location, and how nice the interior of the house is, it's probably worth six-hundred-grand, easy. If she lucks out and gets a bidding war over it, she might get six-and-a-half, maybe seven. Split that in half, subtract taxes, and she and her husband can probably pay off whatever they owe on their current home."

"What if her parents' place ends up as the center of an investigation?"

"Well, then she'll probably be SOL."

Duff took another bite of his burger. "I think she's gonna be SOL."

"The money?"

"The money. Where the hell is it coming from? I wish we could get access to their bank records—" Duff stopped short. An idea popped into his mind. "What was their bank?"

"I have no idea. I never saw anything."

"They're locals, right? What's the most local bank in Mount Horeb?"

Ree shrugged. "State Bank of Cross Plains?"

"No. That's a different town. Is there a State Bank of Mount Horeb?"

"Not anymore."

"Give me another name?"

Ree's face scrunched in confusion. "I don't know what you're looking for." She spit out some names. "Summit Credit Union? UW Credit Union? Old National Bank? Farmers Savings Bank?"

Duff snapped his fingers. "That's it." Something about the name of the place rang out as the sort of institution Art and Michelle would have chosen for holding onto their money. It was simple, rural, and easy to remember. Duff grabbed his own phone and went to the Farmers Savings Bank website. They had a login for their online banking. Duff retreated into his memory palace. Mentally, he reconstructed everything he saw on the laptop. When he had clicked into the start menu, he'd seen an email address referenced: *art.laskey@farmernet*.

He entered that as the login ID and typed in Michelle as the password. No dice. The login needed a number and a special character, too. He knew what year the Laskeys married: 1989. He had known them then. As a password, he tried the simplest combo he could think of for a couple in their sixties: *Michelle1989!* He hit send. If there was a two-stage authentication protocol, he knew he'd be screwed. Duff held his breath.

The website opened for him immediately. He exhaled in disgust. "Well, that wasn't exactly like hacking into the national defense grid, was it? It's no wonder the Nigerian princes are scamming the elderly all the time."

Ree craned her neck to see the phone screen. She shook her head in disgust. "We ought to be giving Boomers a mandatory Internet safety course."

"I think they were technically the first-wave of Gen X."

"Either way—they didn't grow up with computers like everyone under the age of fifty."

Art and Michelle's finances were on display. Everything looked legit at first blush, with both Art and Michelle getting regular, humble payouts from their pensions, but it certainly was not buy-an-expensive-truck money, and it sure as hell wasn't half-a-million-dollar-property money. The only outgoing payments were for their mortgage and a few miscellaneous purchases like gas and groceries. There were no cash withdrawals. Duff scrolled back through the accounts. Their savings account had a healthy amount of cash in it, almost fifty grand. There had been some minimal deposits to it in the last year, but nothing shocking. Their checking account was far more liquid, with the deposits from the pensions being the bulk of the income, and a little extra here and there. However, at the end of every month, if the amount in the account started to get a little thin, there was always a miraculous cash deposit to cover the difference. It was never grandiose. It was never extravagant. It was three hundred bucks here, or six hundred there. It was never enough to draw attention. It was just enough to make sure they didn't dip into the red, whatever that might be.

Duff showed Ree the deposits. "Sketchy."

Ree agreed. "That means Art and Michelle were doing a lot of cash buying, weren't they?"

"There are no truck payments on this. No car payments. No boat payments. No motorcycle payments. Those were all getting done in another fashion. I'm betting money orders. They would take the cash to a place, get the money order, and send that in instead of a check or paying online."

Ree connected the dots. "Laundering?"

"Got to be."

"That's a lot of cash to launder. If they're getting a money order from the same place every time, that's going to raise alarm bells."

Duff already had that part figured out. "That's why they were always driving places. Their daughter said Art loved riding that motorcycle, right? He wasn't joyriding; he was on a mission. He was off getting money orders from different places all over southern Wisconsin, and probably Iowa and Illinois, too. Maybe even Minnesota. You could be in four different states from here in under two hours. You could be in Indiana inside of five hours, and Michigan in six. Hell, if you really wanted to get away for a day, you can be in Canada in less than eight hours from Madison."

"There are a lot of places to get money orders in Madison alone. Probably half the convenience stores in this state will do it for you, half of the pharmacies, too. Probably all of the liquor stores. Walmart will do it, even."

"If a guy shows up a few times a month and hands over a fat stack of cash for a money order, that's going to alert people. If he shows up once a year with small stack of cash, no one will notice."

"The feds would notice," said Ree. "That'd eventually trace back to him."

"Not if he was using fake IDs."

"Where was he getting fake IDs?"

"Probably from the same mobsters that were storing shit in their barn.

106

That'd be my guess."

Ree dropped her fork and threw up her hands. "That's a big piece to this puzzle."

"Not big enough. We still don't know where the money is coming from, and why it's getting laundered."

Ree said, "Mob money, probably."

Duff agreed. "Which mob, though? We know it doesn't take a lot of money to gin up the motivation for someone to put a bullet in someone's head."

Duff shoved a handful of fries into his mouth. They had gotten cold, but he ate them anyway. "We're still not close to home plate, but at least we're on base."

"Can't score if you don't get to base."

"We need to show this to Gumby and Pokey whenever they get back." Duff took a monumental bite of his burger, chewing quickly. "Finish eating. We'll go back to the hotel room to wait."

Ree shoved food into her mouth and spoke while she chewed. "Before I go into any hotel room with you, just let me remind you that I think you're old and gross, and I have a gun."

Duff snorted. "I think it's cute you think I could give two shits about you in that way."

"You're a guy, all guys give two shits about that."

"Nope, not all guys. Trust me on this one: I have zero time or desire for women, particularly those of the law enforcement persuasion."

"Gay?"

"I have even less time or desire for men."

"Isaac Newton?"

Duff wavered for a second, and then said, "Sure, let's go with that. That's close enough. I'm Newtonian."

"Fair enough." Ree did not press the issue again.

IN THE HOTEL room, Duff sorted through the boxes they had taken from the Laskeys' attic. He pulled out the plat maps and started spreading them around his and Abe's respective beds. With hands on hips, Ree stood and watched him. "What are you doing?"

"It's called looking for more clues." Duff spread out another map. "Why did he have all these plat maps? Was he a collector? Was it something else? It doesn't make sense. And why were they in his attic? Why were they scattered around? Someone dug through them." Duff unfolded another map. "And look at this one—it's a topographic map. Why does he have so many friggin' maps?"

Ree couldn't answer that. "Hobby? Maybe he was collecting them for a craft project? People do all sorts of weird things with maps."

Duff was moving maps around the bed. He was squinting at edges, reading numbers, and turning them in ninety-degree increments. "He's got maps for most of the greater Blue Mounds area here. Most of them are property border plat maps which are public domain if you got the money to get copies, but then he's got these larger topographic maps which you have to order from geological survey companies, but he doesn't have any general reference maps like a normal person would. No road maps at all."

Ree held up her cell phone. "We already have reference maps on our phones at our disposal. Why would we need general reference maps on paper?"

Duff peeled his cap from his head and scratched his scalp. He squinted at the maps in frustration. "It feels like he's doing something with these maps, but damned if I know what it is at this point."

"Do you think it's relevant to the investigation?"

"I think everything is relevant until it isn't."

There was a noise at the door to the room. Abe keyed in with Buddy on his heels. He looked at the mess spread over the beds and frowned. "What did you find out?"

Duff didn't look up from his maps. "The Laskeys were funneling a lot of cash through money orders, and we have no idea where they were getting it from, but we think it probably has something to do with whoever was driving the Lincoln, and it's probably mob-connected. Did you find Marcus?"

"No, but we found evidence that shows he's cooking meth, and we think whatever the Laskeys were holding had something to do with his meth cooking."

"Dog incontinence meds." Buddy flopped into the chair in the corner of the room and tossed his hat onto the table.

"Dog incontinence meds?" Duff was confused enough to look away from his plat maps.

Abe said, "One of the primary ingredients is phenylpropanolamine."

"What's that?" asked Ree.

The three men answered in unison: "Meth."

Ree understood. She'd seen the damage that particularly insidious drug inflicted firsthand many nights. "The scourge of rural communities."

"That explains what the box trucks were bringing them, and what was being stored in the shed," said Duff. "It would have taken a hell of a lot of leaky dog wang drugs to make enough meth to pay for all those vehicles and stuff."

Ree grimaced at Duff's description. "Leaky dog wang? Really?"

"What else would you call it when a dog can't stop dribbling when he drops his leg?"

"A Labrador Pee-triever."

Duff sat on a bit of clear space on the edge of his bed. "Recap what we know: the Laskeys were probably filtering money and storing meth ingredients. Marcus is a likely meth cook. The Laskeys were getting deliveries of puppy drugs. Someone in a Lincoln is a suspect in their murder. We're not sure if Marybeth and Chris Collier know anything."

"And it's probably likely someone, if not several someones, in the Dane County law enforcement is in on it, too," said Buddy. "Might be local PD. Might be the sheriff's office or the state patrol. Maybe someone from all three."

"Well, hell." Ree leaned against the wall and put a hand over her eyes. "This is going to be a lousy week, isn't it?"

"It's not going to be an award-winner," said Duff.

"I don't think Art and Michelle were connected enough to arrange massive drop-shipments of veterinary meds on their own," said Buddy. "I imagine there has to be some sort of larger player involved."

"Organized crime," said Duff. "It would make sense. And that would probably be whoever was driving the Lincoln and getting served on the good china, I imagine."

"You have to put out the good china for the organized crime guys," said Ree.

"Goes without saying," said Abe. "That's rule number one of getting in bed with the mob: their guys get good china."

"And homemade pie," said Duff. "You don't bother with any of that crap from Walmart."

Buddy asked Duff, "You boys got any contacts in the OC world in Chicago? Maybe we can find out who's moving the doggy pills."

"We have several. I'll give one of them a call." Duff turned his attention back to the maps on the bed.

"Who do we go to about rooting out a rat in the sheriff's department, that's a better question," said Ree. "I've barely got a year on solo patrols, and there ain't no way those guys will let me into a boys' club area like that."

"I got somebody I can talk to." Buddy's jaw was set. "I know the old sheriff. He's recently retired. He'll let me know what's up."

"I can go over to Lonnie Rostenbach's place. He's another deputy in the department a little longer than me. Maybe he knows something."

"Good kid?" asked Buddy.

Ree replied with a tilt of her hand. "Seems alright. Good attitude. Everyone seems to like him."

Abe said, "If people like him, then maybe they let something slip around him."

"After I talk to Lonnie, I'm going to talk to Bob Benedict. If he falsified his report, I want to look him in the eye when he lies to me."

"I guess we should add Detective Andruzzi to the list of people who we need to see, as well," said Abe.

"Those are the logical next steps," said Ree. "Although, I doubt Andruzzi would talk to us about an investigation he got wrong."

"I feel like these maps are important to this whole deal, but why?" Duff started shuffling the maps. "This one has a little mark on it, but why? It seems deliberate in a way, but it might be a stray pencil touch. It's really tiny. It's it important? Is it a mistake?" Duff pointed to a pencil line barely more than a little tick of graphite. It was easy to miss amongst all the other lines and notations on the maps.

"This one has a line on it, too." Ree pointed at another map on the corner of the bed. She jabbed her finger at a simple pencil mark barely three millimeters long. The mark was the same on the second map. "One of the maps is topographic, and the other is a plat map that shows the property boundary. Does that make a difference?"

Duff shrugged. He looked at one map, and then the other. He tilted his head in an odd angle. He tilted his head the other way. Something dawned on him. "I have no idea." He held up one map to the light streaming in from the window and examined the map on the bed. "They seem like they're in nearly the same location, though." His voice trailed off and he turned his head to look at the maps in back-and-forth succession.

Duff grabbed the plat map from the bed and swept it to the window. He held up the plat map with his right hand. The light from the window made it almost transparent. He stuck the topographic map on top of it and adjusted it until the land they represented lined up with each other, not their edges. The topographic map was off kilter to the plat map, which was adjusted to be laid out at squared angles. The topographic map also representing a larger land mass, so the maps did not properly line up edge-to-edge. Duff readjusted the maps using the location of the Laskeys' home as the anchor point to each map. The two pencil marks lined up to cross each other and make a small *X*.

Duff looked to the three surprised faces staring back at him. "I'm no pirate, but something tells me we should dig here."

A PLAN WAS formulated with all due haste. Abe and Duff would go back out to the farm and see where the X would lead them. The respectable law enforcement people would deal with the police interviews.

Buddy looked at the young deputy with a serious eye. "You know that rubbing the cat the wrong way might get you scratched." It was a warning, a chance to back out if she didn't want this going south on her. Buddy knew well what could happen in the hierarchy of law enforcement if someone stepped on the wrong toes. He'd seen it early in his career, and he'd worked to prevent it from happening to others later in his career. Navigating the internal politics of any organization is a little like ballet with boxing gloves on your feet. You had to try your best to stay graceful, but if the situation called for it you had to be ready to kick someone in the mouth as hard as you could.

Ree knew what the old sheriff was asking. "I don't want to be in a department that turns a blind eye to this sort of thing. If I don't get to be a deputy anymore, so be it."

"Fair enough."

Ree tossed Abe the keys to her car. "Take my ride. I'll go in Cowboy Bob's truck."

Buddy picked up his cowboy hat from the table. "C'mon, flatfoot. Lead the way."

"You should talk. Your feet are flatter than mine." Ree stalked out of the hotel room. She called over her shoulder, "Let me know what you find."

"Take your guns." Buddy pointed a finger at Abe and Duff and gave them a steely-eyed glare. "I'm not kidding."

"Aye, Cap'n." Duff saluted him palm-out in the British fashion. Buddy closed the door behind him as he left.

Duff was scanning through the other maps on the bed. "Another mark." He pulled that plat map up and held it against the window with the others. "It's farther into the Laskeys' property."

Abe came and looked over Duff's shoulder at the maps. "You think that's why the Laskeys had digging tools in their basement?"

"Maybe. It seems like you'd make an X where you buried something, doesn't it?"

It all felt fishy to Abe. "Why would you make one mark on one map and another mark on another map? Seems like overkill, doesn't it?"

"Not if you don't want someone to know what you're doing. Let's face it, I lucked into this one. It was a random chance thing. The marks are small. There are only one or two tiny marks per map. None of the maps are perfect overlays for each other; they have to be lined up on property lines or landmarks, not edges. This makes those marks look like accidents. Whoever did this made sure that no one else would figure it out without stupid luck or amazing skill. They had to know the process. That means Art Laskey was hiding something from someone."

"Why were they hiding it in the first place?"

"I'm not certain, but I think it kept them valuable," said Duff. "They had something hidden, and the big hitters, the guy in the Lincoln, for instance, he had to pay them to keep it going. I'm not sure what they had hidden, but I'm betting it was integral to moving meth around the county. That's probably why the maps were all scattered around. Someone wanted to know what they knew."

"Seems extreme," said Abe.

"If an ex-cop got into bed with the mob, you'd think he knew enough to protect himself as best he could, didn't he?"

"So why were the Laskeys killed, then?"

Duff looked back at the maps. "I guess whatever they knew stopped being important to the money men, or maybe they had made enough money and were trying to get out. Trying to end that sort of a relationship before the money men were ready to end it is a good way to catch lead upside your dome."

"What about the Colliers?"

"Seems likely they knew something, right? Marybeth was close with her parents. She must have known, especially if Marcus was doing something with them."

"We don't have proof."

Duff's face fell. "No. No, we don't. We have maps, though. These might tell us something now that we know their secrets."

Abe and Duff pored over the maps with the proverbial fine-toothed comb. They found a half-dozen marks that made three distinct X marks deep in the Laskeys' four-hundred-acre property.

"That's a lot of land to search." Abe's feet were hurting just thinking about trying to find those sites. "That's more than a mile between the two marks furthest from each other, if I'm reading this map correctly."

"I guess we better get to it." Duff hopped to his feet. "Want me to drive?"

"Not in the least."

10

LONNIE ROSTENBACH'S FACE lit up like a kid seeing his birthday candles when he opened the door of his apartment and saw Shelby Ree standing before him. Ree could plainly read the hope in it; not joy, not arousal—hope. All his offers to go out for a drink after shifts, all those offers for lunch, in that split-second it looked to him like they had finally come true. That hope made him look even younger than he was; he looked like a teenager again. In that instant, she knew Lonnie's crush on her was far deeper than she realized, and she felt badly that she could not return his interest. She also did not like watching the hope in Lonnie's face be chased away when he saw the burly shape of Buddy Olson step into his view from beyond the edge of the door.

Lonnie could only register a confused look. "Shelb? What's going on?"

Shelby pointed at Buddy with her shoulder. "This is Buddy Olson. He used to be the sheriff of Waukesha County, now retired."

"How's it going, Deputy?" Buddy reached up to the brim of his cowboy hat and touched it with two fingers.

"Fine, Sheriff." Lonnie stood in stunned silence for several seconds before shaking himself out of it. "Uh, would you like to come in? Can I get you anything? Beer? Coffee?"

"Nothing for me." Ree stepped into the apartment. It was sparsely decorated. There was a couch, a TV, and a small coffee table in the living room. A small table sat beneath the wall-mounted TV, and that was where Lonnie's Playstation and a dozen or so framed pictures sat. There was no kitchen table, no chairs other than the couch. A pair of forty-pound dumbbells were next to the couch. "Nice place."

Lonnie blushed and rubbed the back of his head. "Yeah, I'm trying to save up for a house. I don't want to have to move too much stuff when I finally get there."

"It's a bachelor pad. Nothing wrong with that," said Buddy.

"Lonnie, I'll cut to the chase so you can get back to your day off. We need to know if you know of anyone dirty in the department."

"Dirty?" Lonnie was taken back. "I don't know anyone dirty."

"I know they wouldn't let you in on anything important, given how you're still a kid like me. But have you heard anything? Maybe heard someone talk about something that made you think twice?"

"Maybe there's just someone you don't like because they give off the wrong sort of vibes," said Buddy. "Trust your gut on this one."

Lonnie was shaking his head. "No, no one like that."

"Not even Bob Benedict?"

Lonnie's entire demeanor shifted. "Oh, him? Yeah, fuck that guy. He's weird as hell."

"Dirty, you mean?" asked Buddy.

"Nah, just weird. He's...he's..."

"Greasy?" said Ree.

"That's it. Greasy."

"What are your feelings toward Andruzzi?"

Lonnie looked at Ree with surprise. "Paul Andruzzi? Seems like a good dude. I haven't heard anything bad about him, other than some people think he slacks a little too much on the tougher cases, but I mean—it's not like we hang out a lot or anything. He calls me Lenny when he sees me. I don't think he knows my real name."

Ree knew that feeling well. "He calls me Toots."

"What do you think is going on in the department that has you out here grilling me for answers?"

Ree and Buddy exchanged a look. Buddy nodded slightly. The retired sheriff wandered deeper into Lonnie's apartment, busying himself with looking at a few of the pictures on display on the table below the television.

Ree took a deep breath. "We think someone might be trafficking drugs through the county. We think Art and Michelle Laskey were in on it, and Art's past as a cop is why people were looking the other way. We also think Art and Michelle were murdered by whoever is moving the drugs."

Lonnie's jaw dropped, and his eyes went wide. "Damn."

"Damn is right."

Lonnie shook off his initial shock. "Are you serious? I haven't heard anything about anything like that. That's crazy."

"Well, thanks for your time, Lonnie. We'll let you get back to your day off."

Ree moved to the door. Buddy lingered over the photos for a long moment, and then followed after her.

Lonnie moved to intercept. "Wait. If I can be of any help, you let me know, right?"

"If this goes sideways on me, it's going to hump my career. You don't want any part of that."

"I want to do what's right, not what's safe."

Buddy rubbed his hand over his face. "Well, that sounds like something what's-his-nuts would say in a shitty made-for-TV movie."

"What's-his-nuts?"

"You know, the douchebag."

Ree arched an eyebrow. "Chris Pratt?"

"No, the other douchebag. The one with all the brothers."

"Mark Wahlberg?"

"That's the one."

Lonnie was undeterred. "Hey, I mean it. You need something, just call. I'll be there."

Ree patted his shoulder. "Thanks, man. I appreciate that. I'll keep you in mind."

Buddy and Ree left Lonnie's apartment. They hit the sidewalk outside his building and headed to the truck waiting in a visitor's parking spot. Buddy couldn't help but state the obvious. "Kid's sweet on you."

"Yeah, I guess he is."

Buddy picked up on the change of tone. "Unrequited, then?"

"Very unrequited."

"Shame. Seems like a good kid."

"He is. Lonnie's going to be a good cop with a long career."

"So, we're not calling him if we need anything, are we?"

"Nope."

"Probably for the best," said Buddy.

"You think so?"

"I do. I also don't think he's going to have quite the career you think he is."

"Because we're not getting him involved?"

"Oh, us not getting him involved isn't going to be the reason he doesn't have a long career," said Buddy. "One of those pictures I saw on his table—it was him and Marcus Laskey together, real buddy-buddy. Looked recent. They were fishing."

"Really?"

Buddy nodded. "I think little Lonnie might know more about what's going on than he lets on."

THE COUNTY MEDICAL examiner's office where Bob Benedict worked was next on Ree and Buddy's agenda. Andruzzi would be tougher to track down. Unless he was in the precinct, he could be anywhere in the county. The dispatchers would know where he was, but Ree did not want to go through them if she could avoid it. The fewer people alerted to an unauthorized investigation going on within the department, the better.

Dane County once had an elected County Coroner position. They transitioned out of that political quagmire to having a hired position of professional medical examiner to eliminate some of the problems that come with having someone in that position who needed to make voters happy. As it often was with having these sorts of positions decided by the will of the people, the elected coroners' qualifications were frequently suspect. They were usually former police officers, not medical professionals or forensic researchers. Often, political favors could be bought off of these officials. Did someone commit suicide, but the family was depending on a big insurance policy? For a small kickback, a county coroner could change that death certificate to prevent the insurance company from denying the claim. For decades, elected coroners have been sources of great controversy for everything from protecting police against valid brutality complaints, to falsifying data, to hiring unqualified family members to high-paying, cushy positions within the department on the taxpayers' dime. A hired position with strict qualifications was supposed to eliminate much of that trouble.

The problem with Bob Benedict was not that he was unqualified to do the job, because he was highly qualified to do it. It was that Benedict came out of the old system where coroners used to have to play politics, and he treated every day like he was still out there shaking hands and kissing babies.

Benedict greeted Ree and Buddy with a big, fake smile, painfully white veneers flashing, and those handshakes where he enveloped their hands with both of his, pumping their arms enthusiastically. "Shelby Ree, good to see you again! You're looking well. What brings you down here to the depths of hell? Ha! Just a little joke. Who's your friend? Is this your grandfather? What news do you have of the surface world?"

That was prototypical Benedict. Active. Fast-talking. Ree wondered if he might be bumping some Peruvian marching powder because he was so jacked up all the time. He might just be excitable and active, though. It was hard to tell the difference sometimes. Benedict was tall and thin. He favored black suits and white shirts with crisp collars. He reminded Ree vaguely of the Australian singer Nick Cave, if Cave had gone into politics or sales instead of goth rock.

Ree introduced Buddy, and Benedict was off and running. "Waukesha is such a wonderful place. I love guitars, and all those Les Paul statues everywhere are such a wonderful addition to the town. I love to go there on Fridays in the summer and listen to everyone out busking on the streets. Absolutely magical, just magical! Oh, and those coffee shops!" He would not stop talking. Benedict came off initially as perfectly pleasant and agreeable, but there was something about him which rang false. It was a mask. It was a demeanor. There was something inhuman about him, possibly in the eyes, maybe in his lanky body and posture. He gave Ree the impression that everything he did and said was an act. Five minutes with Benedict made you feel like you were about to buy a lemon of a used car and couldn't stop yourself from doing it. If you didn't buy what Benedict was selling, he had no time or use for you. He would move on to the next mark.

Ree cut him off in the middle of his Waukesha rant. "Look, Bob, we're here because Buddy was good friends with Art and Michelle Laskey—"

Bob cut her off. "Oh, that's so terrible, isn't it? Just terrible. After all those years together, to go out like that. Absolute tragedy. Just awful. Her daughter came here for the identification of the bodies, and she was just inconsolable. She broke down in a pool of tears when she saw them. Wailing, weeping, screaming! It was just horrible."

Ree had to step into his rant again. "Yeah, that's why we're here. Buddy was good friends with them, and he would like to see your autopsy report."

"My report?" Benedict drew back, his hand going toward his neck as if clutching at invisible pearls. "My reports are flawless. They are one of the things I'm best at, let's be honest. I am a prurient T-crosser and relentless I-dotter."

"I know. We all know. We just need to see the report."

There was a momentary flash of something in Benedict's eyes. Disgust? Anger? Ree couldn't read it. It was something she did not like, but was it something she didn't like because Benedict was truly greasy, or was he just annoying as hell?

"Fine. I have a hard copy over here." Benedict went to a line of gray filing cabinets and opened the third drawer from the top. He flipped through several hanging files. Then, he huffed a breath through pursed lips and started flipping again. He issued a confused grunt that came from somewhere deep in his throat. He opened the drawer above that one and proceeded to flip through files furiously. Then he repeated this in the top drawer. Benedict turned away from the cabinets, leaving them open. He moved to his desk, crowded with files, papers, and started to shuffle through them. Benedict reached over to his phone and hit a button. He dialed four numbers. There was a short ring, and someone answered. Before they could speak, Benedict barked, "Meredith, did you move the Laskey file?"

There was a long beat. "The Laskey—what?"

"The Laskey file. The murder-suicide from last week, the one out in Blue Mounds. Did you move it? It's not in the cabinet anymore."

"I didn't touch it."

Benedict punched a finger at the phone to hang it up. He stood, a barely contained rage simmering behind his eyes. "I regret to inform you that I shall not be able to show you the file. Someone seems to have misplaced it. I can bring up the scans on the computer, though."

Ree felt Buddy poke her lightly in the back. She didn't need the prompt. She knew it was fishy.

Benedict sat at his desk and started punching keys on the thin, wireless keyboard in front of his expansive monitor. After a few moments, he seemed to relax slightly. "Here. Here is what you want." He swiveled his screen slightly and beckoned Buddy and Ree to come closer.

Ree stooped slightly to get a better view of the monitor. It was showing .pdfs of what looked like physical scans of a very simple, very routine coroner's report on two bodies. Ree reached over and took the mouse from Benedict's hand. She clicked through the reports scanning for any differences from the released report. She didn't see any, but she wondered if she knew it well enough to know if anything had changed.

"Michelle had Aricept in her system, right?" asked Buddy.

Benedict looked at Buddy. His jaw was set. He looked annoyed. "Donepezil and alcohol. Trace amounts, yes."

"Alcohol?"

"Some. Very faint. Ingested probably more than two or three hours before she died, and a very small, insignificant quantity. A half-glass of wine, most likely. Nothing important, but I am thorough, and I always make sure to note everything, especially in cases like this where it was a murder-suicide. The family will want answers, and I like to provide them if I'm able."

"Trace amounts of booze. How much Aricept?"

"Not much. Enough, though," said Benedict.

"Could the booze have magnified its effects?" asked Buddy.

"Certainly, if ingested in large enough amounts. The amount that Michelle Laskey had in her system, though? Unlikely, bordering on impossible."

"Does it have any side effects?"

"The usual assortment of drug side effects. Heart issues, vomiting, difficulty sleeping."

"Any chance Michelle had a break from reality because of the pills?"

Benedict shook his head. "No. If she had a break from reality, it wasn't the fault of the pills. The pills were there to stop that sort of thing."

"Michelle was still driving, you know. Days before her alleged suicide, she was still driving," said Ree.

Benedict shrugged. "That is something for you to take up with her primary care physician or the DMV, I guess. I know nothing about that."

118

"And the causes of death? Single GSW to the head?" asked Buddy.

"Indeed."

"Did you do any X-rays or scans?" asked Ree.

"Of course. X-rays in any perforating wound case is standard procedure. I did X-rays before even beginning the autopsies. They're in the report."

"They're not," said Ree.

Benedict's eyes flashed again. He inhaled sharply through his nose. Ree could tell he was barely containing some fiery burst of rage. She wondered how many times Meredith—whoever she was—had been subjected to that rage. She wondered how much she would enjoy it if Benedict tried to unleash some of that rage at her, and she replied with a palm-heel strike to his philtrum. Would it be worth the departmental suspension, write-up, and anger-management counseling? Ree wasn't sure. It would probably feel good, though.

Benedict stood up from his desk. "Someone has been messing with this case. I intend to speak with the sheriff about this. I am going to demand a full investigation and, rest assured, I shall not be resting until I find out exactly who has been going through my files and deleting pages from my case reports. This will not stand! I will go through—"

Ree had to step on his rant again. Jesus, the guy liked to hear himself get on a soapbox. "I get that. Definitely take it up with the sheriff. I'm sure he'll be concerned, and this definitely needs to be looked into. Now, do you have hard copies of the X-rays?"

"I do not, but there is a separate computer storage device that keeps those. I can print new ones, if need be." Benedict beckoned Ree and Buddy to follow him as he stalked out of his office.

The medical examiner's strides were long and purposeful. He walked to an X-ray room twenty feet down the other side of the hallway and opened the door. The X-ray room was divided into two parts: the scanning room and a control area. In the scanning room there was a large X-ray machine above a table. In the control room was the computer behind lead-lined glass. Benedict logged into the machine and brought up the scans. They were still intact in long-term storage on the hard drive. Benedict stepped aside from the monitor with a sniff of indignity. "Someone had to have interfered with my files in the other room."

There is something particularly horrific about a skull X-ray, and it's even more terrifying when it's a postmortem X-ray from someone who died from a gunshot wound. Ree had seen them a few times prior to seeing the Laskeys' scans, and Buddy had seen his fair share, and then some over the course of his career. The bullet sent shards of skull into the brain, and those slivers showed up like white pearls on an X-ray. In the X-ray for Michelle Laskey, a small, white blob showed where the bullet was when it failed to exit the other side of her skull.

"Is that unusual?" asked Ree. She pointed at the bullet. "How come it penetrated Art's skull, which is presumably much thicker than Michelle's, but not Michelle's?"

Benedict shrugged. "It's possible. If the angle was right, and if Art had a weak spot in his skull, anything's possible."

"What gun killed them?" asked Buddy.

"A .22 caliber handgun. A Taurus 942, a six-shot revolver."

"And you dug the bullet that killed Art out of the wall?"

"I tried to, but it had either pierced the house or fallen into the bays between the studs."

"So, you didn't bother to cut open the wall lower and snake it out?"

"No. Why would I do that?"

"And did you use calipers to measure the wounds on both Art and Michelle?"

Benedict started to speak but stopped. He inhaled sharply and shot daggers at Buddy with a narrow-eyed stare. His next words came out clipped and terse. "It was a cut-and-dried case, sir. Look at the evidence. Look at the situation. There was no mystery behind how they died, no matter how badly you're trying to create one."

Buddy's big mustache curled up slightly at either end. His lips were hidden, but he was smiling. "I guess you're right. Well, thank you for the help, Mr. Benedict. I imagine you're going to want to figure out who altered your files post-haste."

"You're welcome. And yes, I will be going to speak with the sheriff directly."

"If you find out why your files were altered, let me know, please." Ree handed Benedict a card with her department-issued cell number on it. "Just call me directly."

Benedict took the card and slipped it into his interior jacket pocket. "I will, Deputy Ree. Thank you. Now, if you'll excuse me." Benedict ushered them into the hallway. He closed and locked the door to the X-ray room and rushed away on his long-legged strides.

Buddy watched him go. He turned to Ree when he knew Benedict was out of earshot. "Five bucks says the hole in Art's head was from a bigger gun than the one that put the hole in Michelle's head. When I asked about measuring the wounds with calipers, Benedict got defensive instead of answering. That was a big misstep on his part. He saw a clear domestic situation, just like Andruzzi, and he decided to cut corners. He would never admit to making a mistake."

"How'd Michelle get killed by the smaller gun that the Laskeys owned, then?"

Buddy hesitated. He scrubbed at his mustache with his wrist for a second. "Well, I don't have proof, but this case isn't too different from some of the ones

I've read about over the years. Some of the Chicago ones, at least."

"How do you mean?"

"I think it's a professional hit."

"If they were in bed with organized crime over these drugs, that's entirely possible," said Ree.

"I think the killer put Michelle down in a different manner, maybe choked her out first, or maybe hit her with the butt of his bigger gun and then used the smaller gun after she was dead to mask it. I think Art was killed with the hitter's gun, which was bigger than the .22 in Michelle's hand. It also explains why it happened in the middle of the room instead of when Art would be sleeping, which makes a lot more sense."

"Head trauma like pistol whipping would be masked entirely by a gunshot wound."

"Might have even used something like an ice pick." Buddy said. "Even a small caliber gun would do enough damage to mask a small head wound; I've seen it before. A few of the professionals out there who have given up the bad guy life swear by it. A slim weapon to the temple incapacitates the victim so a suicide scene can be staged. It's a good way to make someone nice and mellow so you can take your time killing them. However, it's also a pretty nasty way to work. Really cold-blooded."

Ree knew what the next step was. "We have to get the bullet out of the wall, don't we?"

"We do."

"What about talking to your sheriff?"

"He can wait," said Buddy. "That old coot is going nowhere fast. Text the boys and let them know what they have to do when they get to the house."

Shelby started firing a text to Abe and Duff's phones but stopped. "There's not much cell signal out there, you know."

"Send it anyhow. We might get lucky."

11

ABE AND DUFF were at the edge of the woods on the Laskeys' property. The duo had walked from the back of the machine shed where they parked Shelby Ree's car well out of view of the road. They stumbled across the uneven ground, each of them carrying a shovel pilfered from the Laskeys' basement.

There was an art to walking on bumpy, rutted fields. It was an art city people were not always quick to learn. The terrain in farm fields was always changing. Small clumps of dirt, a rock, or even a gopher or badger hole might be hidden by shin-high, matted, winter grass. It was very easy for a person to think he was walking on flat and even ground one moment and then catch his toe on a fieldstone completely hidden from view by a cluster of brown, brittle alfalfa. It used leg muscles one could not work out in any other way. No treadmill or smooth, Chicago sidewalk could match the transitory muscle-and-ligament action needed to maintain balance over uneven ground like a Wisconsin farm field gone fallow. Duff had tripped and nearly fallen several times, and each time he screamed his finest string of obscenities at whatever inanimate object had dared to impede him. This caused Abe to remark that he did not believe rocks had mothers, let alone being capable of engaging in intercourse with them.

Abe was enjoying the walk. It was different. He had been to the country before. He had even been camping with his family once, long ago. He had even gone hiking on a gravel hiking trail, but this felt different. It was open and empty. There were no groomed trails. There were no mown paths in the grass. Abe found himself thinking about the westward expansion of America, and the settlers who first ventured out onto the plains of western Minnesota and South

Dakota. He imagined how it must have felt to look out onto that sea of endless grass barren of roads or trails. It must have felt intimidating, maybe even frightening. Abe was in southern Wisconsin. If he walked more than a mile or two, he would inevitably come across a paved road. If he turned around and looked behind him, he would see a farmhouse on the horizon. In the distance, he could see pinpricks of lights from halogen lamps hanging off someone's barn. It was not like he was in the barren wilderness, but he still found it exciting to dream about those vast, lonely plains with nothing but dreams to propel them.

"How many raccoons do you think pissed in this field over the centuries?"

Abe was snapped out of his reverie. "What?"

"Just thinking aloud, but, c'mon, gotta be a lotta raccoon piss in this field, right?"

"I have no idea."

"Deer, too. Tons of deer whizzing all over here, I bet. I mean, I bet this place is loaded with deer piss."

"What is it with you and urination?"

"Drank too much diet Coke in the van."

"It's a diuretic, you know."

"Tell me about it." Duff pointed at the trees a hundred yards from them. "As soon as we get past the edge of the woods, I'm going to water a tree like a sprung hydrant."

Duff did exactly as he promised, unzipping and pelting the first tree he walked past. When he was finished, after what felt like an extraordinarily long time, he zipped up and turned to face the woods.

The sun was still above the horizon, but the golden light of a late afternoon did not penetrate too far beyond the wall of the forest. The bare branches offered less shade than full leaves would have, but the skeletal twigs cast dark shadows that bobbed and weaved with every breeze. It gave the impression of constant motion around them. Abe's hand went to the handle of his gun on his hip, just to reassure himself it was still there. He touched it with the heel of his palm. The grip was cold from exposure.

Duff caught his partner's move. "You gonna put a bullet in a maple tree for the syrup?"

Abe felt himself blush. "I was just making sure the safety was engaged."

"There's nothing out here." Duff stopped and cupped hands to his mouth. "Hello!" He was loud, but his voice was swallowed up by the timber and the wind. He held a hand to his ear listening for a reply. "See? No one here."

"You got yours, right?"

Duff patted his left side with his left hand. "Right here, Dad. Geez, you're as bad as Buddy."

The woods were quiet and eerily still. The wind rattled the small branches in the tops of the trees, but very little of the breeze made it through the thick wall the trunks provided. Abe looked for signs of life, but aside from a couple of crows, he saw nothing, not even a stray squirrel. There were squirrel nests, big, bulky blobs of leaves crammed into the crotches of high branches, but none of the little rodents were scampering around. Did that mean something? Abe thought about how animals tended to be better barometers of the weather than science at times. The day had started sunny and relatively warm, but clouds had been steadily moving in throughout the afternoon, and the winds had kicked up carrying a chilly bite.

Abe tried to check the weather app on his phone. It refused to connect. There was no signal at all that far in the shadow of the mound to the west. "Don't get bitten by a rattlesnake. We're too far out to get service."

"Too early in the year for rattlesnakes to be awake. Besides, they're really rare around these parts." Duff checked his own phone to find a matching lack of cellular service and pocketed it in disgust. "We haven't figured out how to fully blanket an area with cell service, but yet we're dependent on these goddamn things. Reminds me of that spot at the end of the block back home, if you turn the corner too close to the building, you can lose the call you're on. Technology can land an SUV on Mars but can't figure out how to get consistent cell signal to the boonies."

They walked further into the woods, moving slowly through the dense forest scrub. Brambles and low bushes, the type that thrived in the shade of the overlord maples, ash, and oaks, clung at their pants. Burdock bushes, although still dead and dormant from the winter, still managed to get their brown and wilted burrs to stick to Duff's sweatshirt and shoelaces. Abe realized that his khaki Dockers probably weren't the smartest choice of outdoor wear. He did own a pair of jeans, but he did not care to wear them. He wasn't a jeans type of guy, and he knew it. At least he'd worn his New Balance sneakers that day, a smarter active footwear choice than the brown leather Rockports he favored around the office.

Duff folded the maps as small as he could get them. He paused, slowly lowering himself to a knee on the leaf-litter. He matched up two maps by landmarks and held them toward the fading sun. Then, he looked around them. He counted something silently, mouthing the numbers. He put the maps down on the ground in front of him and looked around the area. Then he stood and craned his neck, peering deeper into the woods.

"Well?" Abe asked.

Duff brushed his hands off, rubbing his palms together like cymbals. "I have no fucking idea what I'm doing. I was never a Boy Scout."

Abe was a little taken aback by this revelation. He'd known Duff had never been a Boy Scout, of course. That much was not news. However, Duff was so good with everything else academic, Abe had just assumed he knew how to read a map. "They didn't teach you orienteering at Bensonhurst?"

"Not in the least. If we knew how to read maps and find locations in the deep wilderness, we all probably would have escaped. I suppose Maps 101 was not a prerequisite for law school."

"No, I tested out by getting a 4.35 for my undergrad degree. I guess they assumed I'd be able to figure out maps or at least pay someone to do it for me."

Duff picked up the map. "Well, old chum, I guess we just found our mutual weakness."

"We have a lot of those; let's be fair." Abe looked at the map over Duff's shoulder. "We're men of above-average intelligence. We can read road maps just fine. We should be able to figure this out, right?"

Duff counted Abe's incorrect assumptions on his fingers. "One, we're hardly men. Two, we're book smart, not forest smart. Three, we get lost a lot, even in the city where we've lived and worked for more than twenty years."

"We can read road maps in theory," Abe corrected.

"There you go, Chief." Duff squinted at the map. He slashed out a hand and stuck it into Abe's jacket.

Abe could feel the man's meaty fist probing at his chest. "What are you doing?"

Duff pulled Abe's reading glasses from his breast pocket and shoved them onto his own face. "Not one word. Don't say a goddamned word, Aberforth."

Duff squinted at the map with Abe's reading glasses on his face. He looked back over his shoulder at the Laskeys' house in the distance. There were several prolonged moments of looking, squinting, and twisting and turning of the map. Finally, Duff pointed. "That way."

"Are you sure?"

"Seventy…maybe seventy-five-percent sure." Duff gestured broadly to his left. "I mean, that's west over there, right? Sun is setting and all." He gestured behind him. "The Laskeys' house is back there. So, if I am reading these maps right, the first X should be in a general direction that way." Duff pointed down a steep slope toward several trees in a clump. Duff handed Abe back his reading glasses.

"How far, though?"

"I don't know. I'm going to treat whatever it is that map is highlighting how Justice Potter Stewart treats pornography: I'll know it when I see it."

They waded further into the woods. The terrain began to become more treacherous as the ridge where the Laskeys' woods started began to slope downward into a narrow gully where a trickle of a creek ran through it, still icy cold from snowmelt and freezing temperatures at night. The trees were more numerous on the slopes. Abe and Duff moved carefully, sliding on the detritus and mud. The ground was thawing, so the winter permafrost had given way to sloppy conditions. At one point, Abe slipped and went down to one knee, sliding downhill for a few feet before he could right the ship. Wet mud soaked into his khakis immediately and he felt the cold creeping up his thigh.

Duff moved from tree to tree like a man rappelling from a tower. He more or less fell forward, taking a few hasty, unbalanced steps until he slammed into a tree trunk, throwing his free hand around it as though his life depended on it. He then found his next target, released himself from the tree, and slammed into the next-closest stopping point.

They made it to the bottom of the gully and had to leap over the creek which was now flowing freely with ice-cold water. Duff, with his girth, did not make the leap as gracefully as he might have wished and ended up planting his right foot fully into the mud and water. He somehow managed to pluck his foot from the creek with the shoe still on his foot, but he was drenched to mid-shin and his Nike was coated with a thick layer of foul-smelling bog mud. This might have thrown off other people, but Duff seemed to barely notice. He kicked the excess mud from his foot and just kept moving forward.

The climb up the other side of the gully was more difficult, and Abe's thighs were burning by the time the ground started to level out and become walkable again. He was sweating from the effort despite the chilly air and had to stop to rub his forearm over his head.

Abe paused to look around them. The Laskeys' home was no longer visible. As far as they could see all around them, there was only thick forest. If they kept walking for another half-mile or so, eventually they would cross a road or stumble into someone's barren fields or maybe even a backyard. But for now, they were as deeply into the countryside as Abe had ever been in his life. He couldn't hear any cars or see any houses. There was the noise of the wind and his own huffing. It was as alone as he had even been in the woods. It gave him a prickle of joy up his back and over his scalp. He liked it. He could get used to that sensation.

"This whole place should be burned to the ground." Duff was leaning heavily on a tree, fanning himself with one hand. "Build a strip mall or something useful. Maybe a Dave and Buster's."

Abe ignored him. He walked deeper into the quiet and the shadow. Then he stopped. Ahead of him, there was a considerable path through the trees, an old field road. It wasn't large enough for a pickup truck or a tractor like most field roads, but it could definitely fit a small four-wheeler or off-road motorcycle. Maybe it was a snowmobile track in the winter. Abe thought about the ATV stolen out of the Laskeys' shed. The road was showing winter wear but judging from the number of leaves and wear on the parallel paths where an ATV's tires would have fit, someone had been down that road within the last week or two. Abe knelt and touched his fingertips to the impression left in the mud by a rugged, off-road tire.

"What are you doing?"

"I don't know. They do this in the movies all the time."

"Yeah…because actors and directors are stupid as hell and don't have any clue how the world actually works. That's why MMA fights never look like martial arts in the movies." Duff walked across the field road. He pulled the maps from his pocket and oriented them to approximate where they were. He pulled a pen from his jeans pocket and traced a thin line where the road was. "Strange that this road isn't on the maps."

Abe looked at the map over Duff's shoulder. "We're close to the X, though."

"Should be right on the other side of this track somewhere."

"We still don't know what we'll find."

Duff shrugged. "I'm hoping it's gold. We could use the income."

They walked further into the woods beyond the field road with Duff leading the way. Like so much of the terrain in the Driftless region, it pitched suddenly and dropped into a deep gully, but the bottom of this one was dry, more of a place where snowmelt gathered than a creek.

Duff stopped and began to survey the area slowly. His eyes were squinting and focused. Abe was envious of Duff's preternatural observational skills. Duff could walk into a room and know what had been moved a centimeter out of place since the last time he was in there. When Matilda had been young, she quickly learned to refuse to play any sort of memory game with him because he would always win, win quickly, and refused to ever let her win. Abe was no slouch, but Duff somehow just knew when things were out of place. He could tell when something stuck out of a scene when no one else could, like with the witchball in the Laskeys' basement. Abe had not noticed the concrete patch was wrong. Neither had Buddy. But Duff knew. He always knew.

"There." Duff pointed at a spot on the rising hill. "It's there."

Abe followed Duff's finger. He had no idea where Duff was pointing. "I just see trees and scrub bushes."

"Look for an indentation in the land. It's just enough of a dip that it looks out of place."

When Duff told Abe what he was looking for, the land instantly seemed to scream out for him to see something was wrong. His eyes could not help but land on a dip in the side of the hill partially obscured by scrub and leaves which now seemed as though it was simply wrong for the rest of the hill. It had been utterly hidden moments before, and now it was as if there was a Las Vegas-style flashing arrow pointing to it.

Abe was impressed. "How do you do that?"

Duff brushed off the praise. "When I was a teen in Canada, a Cree shaman prayed over me and granted me the power of Sight Beyond Sight."

"That's one-hundred-percent false."

"Okay. How about this big fuckin' Cree kid who was in Bensonhurst with me used to hide behind shit like trees or doors and kick the crap outta me when I passed, so I got really good at seeing what's wrong before that could happen."

"That, I believe."

"Good, because it's true. C'mon, Gravedigger. Let's check it out."

Abe shouldered the shovel he was toting. "Was that a reference to the shovel, another weak nickname attempt, or were you making a Chester Himes reference?"

"Why not all three?"

Abe started following after Duff. "I don't know if we're allowed to call each other by the names of Harlem street detectives from the Thirties."

Duff gestured to the trees around them. "Who the hell is gonna know out here?"

THE DIVOT IN the side of the hill ended up being the mouth of a cave covered by a few thin sticks and a layer of leaves and moss. The cave was natural. The mouth of it was not. It had been dug out with an opening chipped into it through four inches of limestone. It looked as if it had been done with a combination of hand and power tools. Mud and dirt had been dug away from the mouth of the cave and replaced around it to mask it from the extremely unlikely chance someone would pass that area. It was hidden with purpose, expertly hidden. The only question was why.

"This explains the books on spelunking and the plat maps," said Duff. "Art Laskey used to love to rumble around the woods of his property, right? Imagine how much better it got when he accidentally stumbled on a hole in the ground that turned out to be a cave."

"Seems kind of weird, doesn't it?"

Duff gestured around them. "This whole part of the state is mostly sitting on limestone. That's the perfect breeding ground for caves. Look at Cave of the Mounds. I'm sure it'd be a lot weirder if that was the only cave in the area."

"I suppose." Abe looked around at the countryside. "I wonder how many undiscovered caves just under the surface of the earth there could be in this county? Hundreds? Thousands?"

"I guess we hauled these out here for nothing." Duff cocked an arm back and threw the shovel he carried like a javelin. It flew ten feet, clipped a low-hanging branch, and fell harmlessly in the detritus.

"Someone might need that some day."

"We won't."

"It's littering."

"It's wood and metal. Technically, I'm returning it to its rightful home." Duff looked at the mouth of the cave. He would fit, but just barely. "I guess we have to go in it, don't we?"

"I guess we do." Abe would have no trouble fitting, but he wasn't a fan of small spaces. He was not claustrophobic, exactly; he just listed toward that direction.

Duff lowered himself to a knee and flopped forward on his stomach like a beaching walrus. He pulled his phone from his pocket and flipped on the flashlight mode. He looked into the cave for a moment before looking up at Abe. "Not too bad, actually. Maybe six feet of space to stand. There's some stuff at the rear of it. Looks like metal and cardboard. We have to go take a look."

"Maybe one of us should stay out of the cave in case something happens, and we have to run for help."

"If you don't want to get in, just say that."

"I don't want to get in."

"Fine." Duff pocketed his phone. "This is gonna suck, isn't it?"

"Oh, most definitely."

"Well, give a fat man a hand."

Duff spun himself so his feet were at the cave mouth. "I suppose it would have been nice if we'd thought to bring rope."

"You know, we have never once needed to prepare for spelunking in Chicago. I would think you'd be enjoying this change."

Duff rocked himself backward, legs dropping into the cave. "I guess my heart just isn't in the right place."

Duff dropped into the hole. His head and shoulders stuck out of the opening before he ducked down and disappeared into the cave.

Abe stood in the woods alone. He gave a cursory glance around him. He spotted a lone tom turkey, puffed up and carefully picking a path through the scrub, thirty yards to his right. It made no noise, and its tail was not in display posture. With its bald head, stretched neck, and odd, head-forward gait, Abe felt like it looked a little too similar to the unfortunate face he saw in the mirror every morning.

Duff's voice echoed up from somewhere in the cave. "Guess what I found!"

"Jimmy Hoffa."

"He's here, too." A moment later an empty cardboard box, dampened and warped, popped out of the hole.

Abe plucked the box from the hole and looked at what was printed on it. It was a rugged cardboard box from a veterinary supply company. The brand name *Cystolamine* was printed on the side of the box. "Let me guess: The primary ingredient is phenylpropanolamine."

Duff's head popped out of the hole. "Pretty much the only ingredient. Looks like Art and Michelle Laskey were definitely in the meth business."

"That gives us the probable reason for why they died, just as we suspected. Is that all you found for this cave?"

"Pretty much the only thing worth finding. There's other meth ingredients in there, too. Iodine. Acetone. All the usual stuff from your average meth-making kit."

Abe fit the pieces together. "The mob moved ingredients to Art's barn. Art moved the ingredients to the hidden caves. Marcus used the ingredients to make meth. Art carted the finished product to the mob guys. The mob guys moved it to Chicago or Minneapolis."

"Exactly. Now, help me out of here, would you?"

Duff took a half-hearted jump to get his shoulders above the hole. Surprisingly strong, despite his obvious distaste for exercise, Duff managed to start lifting himself out of the cave mouth. Abe tossed the box aside and dropped to his knees. He grabbed the back of Duff's belt and pulled with everything he had in him. Duff barked out a strained squawk. "Oh, that's a wicked wedgie."

It took them a few seconds, but eventually Duff cleared his girth from the cave and rolled away from the mouth, rolling over onto his back to catch his breath.

The turkey in the distance watched them through cold, black, beady eyes, wholly unimpressed by the performance.

AT THE SECOND map location, they found the mouth to another well-hidden cave. As with the first one, Abe could not see it until Duff pointed it out. It was exquisitely hidden, blending into the forest seamlessly. The second cave was much smaller than the first, with a narrow opening barely big enough for a normal-sized man to squeeze through almost on the floor of the cave. Duff would never fit, and Abe only needed to get his head and shoulders wriggled inside before he could see the entirety of it. It was empty, but there had been something stored there once upon a time. The footprints in the mud on the cave floor confirmed that.

The third map location was a larger cave mouth than either of the previous two, again so well-hidden that only Duff could spot it because of his uncanny ability to see something that doesn't fit. For the average person, it was merely a leaf-covered spot on the ground. When Duff pulled away a cleverly built door, it revealed an entrance to almost three feet high with the mouth extending down to the floor of the cave so one would only have to duck under the lip and crawl for a couple of feet to be fully inside. Abe and Duff paused in front of it. "I'll stand guard," said Abe.

Duff rolled his eyes. "As you wish." He sat on the ground and lowered his legs into the cave mouth. "If I have to fight a bear in this one, I'm going to be very upset with you."

"I don't think there are bears this far south."

"Bigfoots, then. If I have to fight a sasquatch, that's on your ass."

"I'll take that chance."

Duff started to wiggle into the hole. "If I die in hand-to-hand combat with a Bigfoot, tell everyone I died doing what I loved."

Abe waited in the stock-still silence of the woods after Duff disappeared into the cave. There was only one more location to scout after that one. That was good; it was getting too dark to be bopping around the forest. They had been out among the trees for more than two hours. The sun had dropped fully below the horizon. The big hill of Blue Mounds State Park was somewhere west of them, and it served to block most of the ambient light still radiating in the western sky. It was getting on full dark rapidly; a blanket of black being laid over the countryside.

Duff was gone for more than a minute. That's not a long time, but when standing in the middle of an unfamiliar darkened woods, sixty seconds is an eternity. Abe's hand drifted to the grip of his pistol again. There was nothing to be concerned about. The worst thing in those woods would be a coyote or a raccoon, maybe a fox. At the very worst, maybe the animal could have rabies, but even if it did, it would still be unlikely to seek Abe out for any confrontation. Abe knew there was the occasional mountain lion or bobcat in Wisconsin, but they were extremely rare in the southern part of the state. It didn't make him feel better to know that, though. He scanned through the treetops looking for a lurking cat-shaped shadow, just in case.

The summer after Abe graduated from high school, he had worked at a summer camp as a counselor. It had been one of the best summers of his life. It had also been the longest he'd ever spent in the wilderness, if one could consider a summer camp with throngs of screaming elementary school-aged children as wilderness. He had been nervous about the wildlife at first, but one of the other counselors, a country boy from central Iowa called Randy, told him, *If you see anything bigger than a squirrel, it's because that thing wanted you to see it.* Randy had also told him that in all his years on the farm in Iowa, he had only ever seen coyotes as roadkill on the side of the road. He'd heard them howling at night on occasion, sure, but to actually see a coyote, that was rare.

Abe heard a snap of a twig in the distance. He couldn't tell what direction it came from, let alone what might have snapped it. Was it close or distant? The report of the twig was too fast to let him discern those details. Abe's pulse began to quicken. He crouched and hoped the shadows would hide him in case something was stalking him.

The light from Duff's phone began to illuminate the cave entrance. Another moment later and his round face poked out of the hole. "You're going to have to come see this."

Abe did not argue. He could see it on Duff's face: it was important. As much as his mind was screaming at him not to do it, Abe dropped to his knees and crawled into the cave. His pulse elevated to a rapid cadence.

There was an odd smell in the cave. Abe knew from past experience visiting various caves in national parks, back when Matilda was small, that caves had a damp, musty, aged smell. It was sterile. The smell in this cave was a strange mixture: oddly sweet mixed with something fetid, something chemical mixed with something acrid and acidic. It was not a proper cave smell.

Duff led the way through thirty feet of cave tunnel only four feet high. It was tall enough for them to comfortably walk bent over at the waist, but Abe still managed to bump his head against the ceiling twice. At the end of the thirty feet, the tunnel opened into an oblong space the size of the detectives' apartment office back in Chicago. The ceiling was a tad higher than Abe's height, so he could stand comfortably.

All the stalactites that had formed over the centuries had been broken off and scattered to the edges of the cavern. The room had several flimsy card tables at the edge of the room. On the tables, it looked like something out of Dr. Frankenstein's laboratory. There were beakers and glassware, propane torches and hot plates fueled by propane tanks. It was, without a doubt, a meth lab. It looked like it had not been used in a while, at least a week or more, which was understandable given why Abe and Duff were there in the first place.

"They went full Walter White." Duff shone his light over the lab. He saw a couple of twist-wraps with small, gray-white rocks in them. "And that's their own version of Blue Sky."

"Great place to hide a lab." Abe was using his own phone light to search around the cave. A vent pipe ran to the ceiling in the rear of the cave. He could feel cold air descending into the cave from it. When the cave was warmer than the outside air, the heat would rise and take the harmful vapors outside where they could be dissipated. Several cardboard boxes were broken down and shoved under one of the folding tables. There were a few of the Cystolamine boxes like they had found in the first cave, of course, but there were also boxes of pseudoephedrine and other chemical components related to the manufacturing of crystal methamphetamine. A couple of full-face gas masks were on one table. Abe knocked on the vent pipe. It made a dull, hollow sound. "At least we know why they had a rock auger, now."

"No one would have known they had this level of an operation going on out here. Even if they weren't home and some suspicious cop went to their house and started poking around without a warrant, at worst they would have found a few boxes of medicine for dogs who can't control their bladders. I imagine Art used that ATV of his to drive supplies out to the caves. Marcus cooked the product. They distributed out to whoever was getting the dog meds to them and got paid a lot. Then, they just laundered the cash through money orders and other purchases around the tri-state area. Genius."

Abe rubbed his face with his hand. "Why kill the Laskeys, though?"

"Probably because they had fixed whatever financial issues they were having, and they wanted out. Or they wanted a bigger cut. You know how the drug guys work: They will punk you out for as long as they can; the second you try getting too big for your britches, you gotta go." Duff sniffed back the start of a runny nose. "Especially if you know too much about them."

Duff wandered deeper into the cave, past the makeshift meth lab. He found a dirty Durostar generator and a few work lights. The generator no longer had any gas in it. A tube ran from the generator's exhaust to a heat-proof plastic connector, which ran to a piece of straight pipe which had been vented out of through the ceiling of the cave somewhere into the scrub above. "Hey! Free generator! This is a four-hundred-dollar piece of equipment. Seems a shame to just let it rot here."

"In more than two decades, we have never once needed a generator."

"But it's free."

"You carry it back to the van then, because I'm sure not going to."

Duff paused. "You know, now that I think about it, we've never once needed a generator in more than two decades. Maybe we're not living right."

"How would needing a generator indicate we're living right?"

"I dunno. Just seems manly, doesn't it?"

Duff pressed further into the cavern. It doglegged to the left, and Duff disappeared around the bend. Abe could see the light from his phone bouncing off the walls.

Abe followed and found Duff crouched at the mouth of a passageway about half the size of the one that led them to the meth room. There were scrapes in the dirt at the mouth that showed it had been in use in the recent past. Abe knew what the next step to the cave exploration was: they had to crawl through that section.

Duff dropped to his stomach. "Stiff upper lip, Aberforth. This cave has been here for millennia. It's not going to collapse now."

"That's not the argument you think you're making. If it hasn't collapsed yet, that just means it's closer to collapsing every second we're in there."

The crawl through the tunnel was not as bad as Abe feared. It was a short distance before the cave opened up again to a much larger room. The new cave was almost twice as big as the room where the cooking took place, and there were dozens of boxes of supplies stacked up against the edges of the room. Half the boxes were the canine incontinence drugs or other meth ingredients, and half were blank, unlabeled cardboard boxes sealed with packing tape. Abe used the edge of one of his car keys and slit the tape. Inside the box was about fifty little bags of packaged, crystalline pebbles. Abe knew crystal meth when he saw it. Next to alcohol, it was the most abused drug in Chicago. He held up a handful of the baggies for Duff to see.

Duff issued a low whistle. He counted the boxes and did the math in his head. "If this stuff is going for about a grand an ounce, we're looking at what? Three million dollars in product right in front of us? Maybe three-and-a-half?"

"At least."

"The Laskeys were in deep."

Abe knew nothing good could come from getting involved with any faction of organized crime over this much money. Most gangs were more than willing to kill someone over a few thousand dollars. Abe shuddered to think what they'd do over a few million.

They pushed past the drugs and found where the cave led outside. The entrance had been blocked with plywood. Duff pulled back the plywood to reveal another hidden cave mouth, complete with dangling weeds and brush. "They were artists at making sure these entrances couldn't be found."

"The Laskeys were helping someone make a ton of meth. Their son cooked it in the cave, and he packaged it in the cave. Obviously, this was done to keep the cops from finding it. But what if it was more than that? What if they were doing it to keep the organized crime guys from finding it?"

"Makes sense," said Abe.

"Might be the reason why the Laskeys were killed, and someone tried to go through their maps to figure out their secret. If they were holding back three million in product in an attempt to barter for their freedom, the dealers would be none too pleased." Duff crawled out of the cave and into the chilly night air. He huffed a misty breath into the air like a dragon.

Abe was grateful to be out of the cave. He could feel his pulse decreasing the second he cleared the hateful space. The cold air felt good on his face and head. He inhaled heavily and blew out a long breath through pursed lips. It helped calm him even more. "Where are we now?"

"Other side of that hill we were on, I suppose." Duff pointed in the darkness. "I see a little light that way."

They plowed through the dark toward a blue-white halogen light in the distance. As they got closer, they saw a building. It looked a little like a house, but slightly bigger, with a long, low room off one side that looked added-on. Dark, floor-to-ceiling windows were all around the added-on section and a little wall of shabby and overgrown evergreen hedges defended the glass. The house was in serious disrepair. It needed new paint badly. A little garage behind the building was in even worse shape. It looked like a good wind would knock it down. An area at the back of the house looked industrial, with a strange extension of a steel room and vent fans jutting off it. There was a large parking lot around the three sides of the building, too. "Looks like a restaurant," said Abe.

"Supper club," Duff corrected him. "It's a Midwest thing. Little backwoods restaurants that function as classy, but affordable dining."

"I know what a supper club is." Abe was offended. He had grown up in Chicago; he wasn't oblivious to the world of supper clubs. The idea of the supper club was started by a Milwaukee native who opened the first one in Beverly Hills, California in the 1920s, but in recent years, the institutions had all but died out everywhere except Wisconsin and Michigan's upper peninsula, which as far as Abe was concerned, was more like Wisconsin than Michigan, anyhow.

"Looks abandoned." Duff pushed through the brush and trees toward the supper club. As they got nearer, a realtor's *For Sale* sign was posted near the road. The sign begged people who were interested in viewing the property to call a number and ask for Maggie Gustafson at Viking Realty. Duff gave a grunt of surprise. "I would have bet money that Chris Collier would have been the Realtor involved with this place. That would have made sense, right?"

Abe had to admit it would have. It would have tied Collier to the drugs and put him on the suspect list for the murders. There was something fishy about Chris Collier, but was it just a general vibe he gave off by being some sort of frustrated alpha male type, or was it more insidious? Abe didn't know, and he couldn't make that call. Growing up as someone who often bullied in school, Abe had to learn to separate his deeply inherent suspicions about people based on his history with guys like Collier from the truth facts presented. As it was now, he didn't even know for certain if Collier slashed the tires on the van. For all they knew, it could have been done by a random idiot just looking to cause trouble like Buddy said. It certainly felt like Collier could have slashed the tires, but there was no evidence pointing to it. That was where Abe was having issues. Collier was a little suspect, no doubt. He gave off that vibe. But giving off a vibe doesn't automatically make someone capable of murder.

The halogen lamp they had been following was a single light mounted high on a telephone pole next to the supper club. It lit the parking lot area with a sickly blue light. It was enough to make people feel safer getting to their cars, but not by much. It gave off just a tiny bit more light than what a full moon cast on a clear night.

Duff gestured to the parking lot then to the supper club building. "Lots of vehicle tracks in this lot for a building that hasn't been in use this winter."

"This is probably where whoever was picking up the finished product came to get it. Drop-offs at the Laskey house, pick-ups here."

Duff walked to the nearest window of the supper club. He pressed his face to the glass and shielded his eyes with his hands to peer inside. "It's not empty. I see boxes."

Abe followed Duff's lead. There were stacks of boxes just past the foyer of the place where the hostess's stand would have been if it were still a functioning supper club. "Think those are the pills or the meth?"

"Meth. This must be how it gets distributed. I think the pills all got delivered to the house. When the coast was clear, Art would ATV them to the caves. Marcus would use the supplies in the caves to make the meth. He put it in the big room for distribution. Art would ATV the boxes of finished product to the supper club. Whoever was supplying the pills picked up the boxes, then they ran them back to Chicago for selling with some local LEO providing cover for them. Seems like a good plan, right?"

Abe felt his gun at his waist. He was glad he had it. His mouth was dry. "I think we have to go in there, don't we?"

Duff already had his lockpicks in hand. "Think they have an alarm system?"

Abe scanned the electrics going into the building from the outside. It looked like it had been wired in the late '50s and forgotten. "Doubt it."

"Good." Duff walked to the kitchen door in the rear of the building so he would be hidden from passing cars, not that there were any on that lonely stretch of farm road. He knelt and swept the lock in seconds. The old door had been keyed into so many times it offered no resistance. As predicted, there was no alarm.

The supper club was cold, but not freezing. The place had a musty smell of disuse that mingled with decades of beers, fish frys, and Saturday night prime rib specials. The large, oval-shaped dining room was dotted with small, dusty circular tables each surrounded by four comfortable-looking faux-leather chairs. There were the requisite mounted deer heads hanging on the wall, and someone long ago had decorated the eight-pointer with a few strings of green and gold plastic beads. The bar was stripped of all alcohol, but there were still racks of pint glasses, brandy snifters, highball, lowball, martini, and a dozen other glasses needed for the full menu of cocktails and boozy beverages patrons would have ordered with their walleye, potato pancakes, and coleslaw.

The boxes at the foyer were full of drugs. Abe found that out when he slit the packing tape on the top box. "Figure another, what? Half-million in street value right here?"

Duff shrugged. "Three-quarter million, maybe."

Abe sighed and leaned against the wall. "What do we do?"

"Retire to a non-extradition country after selling all this."

"Seriously, though."

"Gotta call it in, right?"

It was a no-brainer. "We have to call it in."

Duff checked his phone. "Still no service." His head inclined toward a dusty brown land-line phone on the wall. "Think they still have service here?" Duff tried it anyhow. Not even static on the line.

The dining room of the supper club was illuminated with a dull yellow light as someone's car came around the corner on the road. A pickup truck rolled past the place, its tires causing a faint drone. Normally, the sound of merry conversation and maybe some soft music would have drowned out that noise.

Before Abe and Duff could say anything, another pair of headlights lit up the restaurant casting a bright beam into the dining room. A large Lincoln SUV pulled into the parking lot and quickly drove behind the building.

"Holy shit. They're here to pick up, aren't they?" Duff ran to the door they entered from and locked it.

Abe was suddenly glad he had his gun. He felt his heart start to race. "We have to hide." Abe pointed to a pair of wooden saloon doors that led to the kitchen. "Go! Go!"

They sprinted through the doors. Abe had enough foresight to turn and stop them from swinging after they passed them. The only place to hide in the kitchen was a large walk-in cooler on the far side of the room. The idea of jumping into a cooler that could be easily barred from the outside was not the best idea, but there weren't many other options.

Duff ducked behind the stainless-steel prep table. It was a flat metal surface propped up by thin metal legs with two shelves for pans open to the world beneath. There was nothing to keep him hidden from view should someone want to look into the kitchen, but it was better than the cooler. In the dark shadows of the windowless kitchen, it was as good a hiding place as anywhere else. The cooler could be locked. If they were discovered in the kitchen, they had a fighting chance. Abe followed Duff and hunkered down beside his partner. He drew the Smith and Wesson from his holster and gestured for Duff to do the same. With great reluctance, Duff reached up and under his sweatshirt and pulled the sleek little Walther from his hidden holster.

In a hushed whisper Duff said, "If Buddy ever finds out we actually needed these, we'll never live it down."

12

THREE MEN ENTERED the abandoned supper club unaware of the two detectives in the kitchen. They keyed into the room and looked around for a moment. One of them pointed to the boxes. "That's them."

"I guess you better load 'em up, then," said the man who keyed into the room. As if to stress his point, he spun a keyring on his finger like a six-gun. In the dim light, Abe could make out his shape, but that was all. The man looked like average height and weight. His accent wasn't typical Chicago; it was flatter and more generic Midwestern with the barest hint of an ethnic edge to it, Italian or Greek. The man giving the orders paused to light a cigarette. He used a Zippo and when the flame lit his face, Abe got a good look at him. He had a Roman nose and square jaw. His hair was slicked back with product. He looked like a stereotypical Italian mobster.

The two men with him dutifully grabbed a box each and carried them back outside to the Lincoln. The guy with the keys stood near the door and smoked his cigarette, the smell of the tobacco was sharp and carried into the kitchen where Abe and Duff were hiding.

The two box-carriers returned, grabbed more boxes, and left again. They made a third and fourth trip. Then, they came back for the final box. One of them took it out to the Lincoln while the other stood with the smoker. He gestured to the half-burned Marlboro in the smoker's hand. "You got one of them for me?"

"Sure do, Marco." The smoker took out the pack and held it out. The other man grabbed a cigarette from the pack and leaned closed to the Zippo lighter to hit the tip to the flame. Abe inhaled involuntarily and held it. He recognized the man from the pictures in the Laskey house. The second man was Marcus Laskey. The meth chef himself had come for his product.

The third guy returned from the Lincoln. He stood at the door of the restaurant. "All loaded up, Renato."

The smoker turned to look at him and nodded. "Thanks, Donny."

"Is that it, then?" Marcus looked to Renato and Donny. "We're square?"

"We're almost square." Renato pulled a little wire-bound paper notebook from his pocket. "You and your old man still owe me about ten more boxes of product."

Marcus coughed mid-inhale. "Are you outta your mind? Ten boxes?"

Renato held out the notebook to Marcus. "See for yourself."

"This was it—this was the last of it."

Renato shook his head. "Given the amount of the pills we got you, you should have been able to cook at least ten more boxes of drugs for us. Where is it?"

Abe heard Marcus's voice pitch a tad higher. He was panicking. "I told you, this was it. Those pills weren't as good as pseudoephedrine. If you could have gotten me that shit, I would have easily made you another ten boxes."

"Are you telling me I'm bad at math?"

"No, I'm saying you're not a cook."

Renato snatched his notebook back from Marcus and slipped back into his jacket pocket. "Ten more boxes. Then you can be done."

"I'm gonna need more supplies—"

Renato cut him off. "Ten. More. Boxes."

Marcus was quiet for a long moment. "I'll need to talk to my old man, first."

"He ain't got nothing to do with it no more. Ten more boxes."

"No—he's got the line on the other supplies I need, the chemicals."

Renato jabbed a finger into Marcus's chest and repeated, "He ain't got nothing to do with it no more. Just get us ten more boxes."

"Without the chemicals, I can't cook anymore—" Marcus stopped short. There was a long pause. Renato looked down at his shoes, unable to make eye contact with Marcus. The third man, Donny, didn't make a sound.

In the brief silence, Abe suddenly realized two things: Marcus had not known his parents were dead, and he had just figured out they were.

"You son of a—" Marcus lunged toward Renato.

"Hey now, don't do something stupid."

Marcus grabbed the lapels of Renato's jacket and was walking him into the dining room. "You filthy fuckin'—"

"Don't say something you're gonna regret, Marco. You came to me, remember? You and your dad and your little buddy. You came to me. I took you on, and that was my risk."

"What risk? What fucking risk? We had the knowledge. We had the location. I even figured out how to neutralize the risk!"

Renato pushed Marcus off of him. "Ease up, Marco. You knew the rules."

"Why'd you do it? What did they ever do to you? They were my parents!" Marcus suddenly turned and swung at Renato. He clipped the much smaller man in the jaw and knocked him to the floor.

Donny pulled a handgun from the waistband of his jeans. Marcus went for his own gun, but it was tucked at the small of his back. Donny won that race. Donny pulled the trigger twice. The gun was small, but accurate. The shots shattered the quiet of the restaurant with ear-splitting volume. In the kitchen, where Abe and Duff were hiding, it seemed to echo off of every metal surface making it all the louder. Abe tensed, turning to fire. Duff grabbed his arm. In the darkness, Abe made out a slight shake of Duff's head. The Brewers cap brim turned side to side quickly, and then stilled. Duff raised a finger to his lips.

Marcus stood stunned by the impact of the bullets for a moment. His hands clutched at his body. He staggered backward, bumped into a table in the dining area, and collapsed on the floor. His body was still.

There was a long, terrible moment of quiet. The acrid smell of discharged gunpowder wafted through the air. Renato picked himself up off the floor. "I guess that's that, then. Shouldn't have fucked around, Marco."

Donny spoke, his voice was high-pitched and carried a hint of a whine. "He still owes us product."

"Yeah, well he ain't gonna make it now, is he?" Renato adjusted his suit coat. "Nothing we can do about it now. Get in the truck."

The two men left the restaurant locking the door behind them. After a moment, the sound of the Lincoln's wheels on the gravel lot could be heard. Then, the big V-8 engine roared off down the quiet country road and faded into silence.

ABE LET OUT an extended breath. He felt weak and jittery from the stress and adrenaline. Next to him, Duff slumped to the floor and breathed several deep breaths. "That was close."

"I feel like we should have done something, we should have tried to take them by surprise or something."

Duff shook his head. "That sort of cowboy shit never goes as planned. I have zero designs on getting shot. We know names now. We know what's going on now. That's better than a bullet hole any day. We're about to wrap this whole case up and be home in time for the second half of the Red Wings game on ESPN tonight."

"You think Meyer Himmelman will be able to tell us who is running meth if we give him the names Renato and Donny?" Abe knew their landlord, Himmelman, was a high-ranking player in the Jewish mob of Chicago. Abe and Duff didn't know how exactly high he ranked, and they had no actual proof that he was involved in the mob in the least. It went as an unspoken truth between them. Himmelman knew they knew, and they knew Himmelman knew they knew, but none of them would ever speak about it. When they called him for information, he never answered them directly. He always said he'd ask, and the answer always came through an unknown associate to give Himmelman the illusion of blamelessness.

"I think we stand a better than average chance. If Meyer doesn't know, he will know someone who will."

"We need to call this in." Abe checked his cell signal. Still no bars. "We need to get to higher ground. This valley we're in is a dead zone."

"Long, cold walk to higher ground from here." Duff inspected his own phone in the vain hope that he might see enough signal to call for an Uber. "I don't suppose this restaurant has Wi-Fi, does it?"

"Sure. It's only been shuttered for a couple of years, but I'm sure they kept paying their cable bill." Abe holstered his gun. "I still feel like we should have done more."

Duff holstered his Walther, too. He slipped it under his arm and pulled his sweatshirt down over it, patting it in place. "I feel alive. That's probably better than we'd be feeling if we had tried to do more."

Abe had to agree with Duff. Even at close range, and even with the jump on them, those guys looked like men who had killed before, and they'd certainly have no problem pulling the trigger on two guys who could be witnesses in a murder trial. Staying hidden was the safe way to play the moment, but it didn't feel very Jim Rockford to Abe.

Abe moved toward the door. He pushed the bar in the center. A cold blast of air from outside curled into the room. Abe really wished he'd worn his hat. Before he could take another step, there was a low groan from Marcus Laskey. He wasn't dead.

Abe and Duff wheeled to Marcus's side. Abe felt for a pulse. It was weak, but it was there. "Go see if there are any towels left here."

Duff turned and ran into the kitchen. He started opening and closing drawers.

Abe used the light on his phone to assess Marcus Laskey's injuries. One bullet had hit him high in the right shoulder. The other was lower on his right side. Neither one was necessarily a fatal wound if they could get help in time, but both of them together made for a bleak prognostication.

Duff returned with an armload of kitchen towels he'd found in a drawer. They had been laundered and folded, but over the last couple of years, they'd laid in a drawer gathering dust where who-knows-what kind of vermin and insect life had crawled on them. Still, it was better than letting the man bleed out. Duff folded a couple of the towels and put them on the wounds, he applied pressure. "You're a better long-distance runner than I am, Dr. Bannister."

That went without saying. Abe ran three miles on a treadmill every morning. However, three treadmill miles was a lot different than running uphill on a hard road in thirty-something degree wind and cold. Still, he knew he would fare a lot better than his portly compatriot. "I'll do my best."

"If someone stops and offers you a ride, take it."

Marcus Laskey groaned and licked his lips. He spoke in barely more than a whisper. "Four-wheeler…in the…garage. Use that." His eyes fluttered for a moment and then his head lolled to one side.

Duff slapped the man's face. "Hey, now. Stay here. Stay with us." Duff jabbed two fingers to the man's neck and felt his pulse. "I think he's going into shock. Get moving."

Abe didn't have to be told twice. He nodded and bolted for the door. When he got to the door, he paused. "Will you be alright?"

"Oh, I'll be fine. It's Marcus that's going to have issues. Now run, fool!"

Abe ran to the decrepit garage behind the restaurant. The door was one of the old styles of garage doors, a large, heavy single panel that pivoted on a fixed point. When Abe lifted it, he found the little Rancher ATV missing from the Laskeys' garage. It was mud-splashed and scraped as if it had been making frequent runs through brushy woods and crossing some creeks in the valleys. On any other day, Abe would have been thrilled to try driving an ATV. Now, too much depended on him. He also noticed there wasn't a helmet in sight. He did not relish the idea of taking his virginal ride on a type of vehicle with a well-documented and highly questionable safety record, but beggars could not be choosers.

Abe had climbed onto the machine, turned the key to the run position, and thumbed the electric starter. It jumped to life beneath him, loud and aggressive. Abe knew the basics of driving an ATV, but it suddenly seemed too complicated and dangerous. He said a silent prayer to any passing deity that might be listening and jetted out of the garage.

The ATV responded to the throttle like a rocket. It sprayed loose gravel as the tires tried to bite into the frozen ground for traction. Abe hunched over the handlebars and tried to control it as best he could. It was nothing like driving a car. It felt nimble and tippy beneath him, like he could roll it with one errant move. Within three seconds of driving the four-wheeler, Abe decided he never wanted to drive one again. He was a minivan or station wagon guy. He was a ten-speed bike on city-approved, paved, off-street biking trails guy. He would never be an action vehicle guy.

Abe hunched low over the handlebars and tried to ignore how cold his head was getting as he flew down the road. The road he was on was unfamiliar to him. He did not know which way the roads turned, and the headlight on the four-wheeler was barely enough to light the road in front of him. The headlight cast strange shadows in the trees alongside the road, and in his peripheral vision it looked like something was following him in the woods. It made the hairs on Abe's neck stand on end and gave him the sensation that he was prey, that he was being hunted.

Abe climbed out of the valley as fast as he dared. Someone more confident on the ATV probably could have done it far faster, but Abe needed to make sure he was still alive when he reached an area with cell signal. Flipping over the handlebars of the ATV and cracking his head like an egg was the last thing he needed to do.

Near the apex of a steep ascent, Abe started climbing out of the trees that filled the valleys and started to see the expanse of open farm fields along the ridges that meant nothing would be blocking signals soon. He started feeling a buzzing on the top of his right thigh. His phone had grabbed enough stray 4G signal and a bevy of unreceived text messages and phone alerts were suddenly swarming to come through on the data stream. Abe waited until he got to a crossroads so he could read the street sign at the corner; he was at the junction of Pastor Road and Bloomer Road. Abe released the throttle and eased onto the brake. He pulled the ATV into the tall grass on the side of the road and killed the engine. The area was plunged back into darkness with only the sky above lighting the road.

Abe pulled his phone and made a hurried call to Buddy, first. He told the old sheriff about the shooting of Marcus Laskey, the location of the supper club, and to get there in a hurry. Buddy said he and the deputy would be on their way in two shakes. They had just dug a bullet out of the Laskeys' wall that would prove Art Laskey was killed by a different gun than Michelle.

Abe called 911 after that. A sleepy-sounding operator asked for the nature of emergency. Abe gave his name, his PI license number, and explained he and his partner had just witnessed a shooting. He gave the name of the road the restaurant was on, and explained the location was an old supper club down that road. The operator asked him to remain on the line, but Abe tried to explain to her that he needed to get back to help his partner, that there was no cellular signal in the valley. She asked him if he could wait at the crossroads for the sheriff's department to get there, and then he could ride with the deputy to the scene.

At that moment, a pair of headlights came over a small rise in the road. Abe felt like a deer caught on the road. He froze. The high-beam headlights were blinding him. Abe had to throw an arm in front of his face to block the light. An

SUV roared past Abe and turned right down the road toward the supper club. Abe saw the Illinois license plate as it passed him. The big black Lincoln was returning to the supper club. Abe's heart froze in his chest.

Abe told the 911 operator to get deputies to the restaurant on the double. Then he hung up and dialed Buddy. "The gangsters are heading back to the restaurant."

"Well, that ain't good."

"Duff is there alone trying to keep a man alive."

"How good a shot is he?"

"He's not. Not at all."

Buddy's voice was grim. "Well, let's hope the prospect of life or death grants him better aim."

DUFF SLAPPED MARCUS Laskey's face again. "Stay with me, boss. You gotta stay with me."

Marcus Laskey's eyes fluttered. He licked his lips with a dry tongue. "Tired."

"Not tired; dying." Duff slapped him again. "You gotta stay awake. If you pass out, you're done. Stay awake. Talk to me."

Laskey came back to life again with a small shake of his head. "Stop hitting."

"Stop passing out, then. You gotta fight it, man."

Laskey inhaled sharply and groaned. "Hurts. Feels like weight on my chest."

"That's because I'm trying to keep your blood in your body." Duff kept the pressure on the dish towels. He pressed hard into the wound nearest Laskey's head hoping the sudden stimulation of the wound would flair some life back into the man. Pain was a great motivator. If it hurt enough, it might help him outrun death. The gambit paid off. Laskey gave a yelp and tried to slip his shoulder away from the pressure. Duff eased up slightly.

Duff knew that Laskey might not make it to the ambulance's arrival. He had organ damage. He had blood in his lung. It wasn't going to take much for him to circle the drain and go. Duff also knew this might be the only time to get the full truth out of the man even if he lived. "Don't talk, Marcus. Just lie there. Don't struggle. I need you to listen to me. My name is Duff. You might know my friend, Buddy Olson. He's a friend of your parents."

Laskey gave a short nod to show he was understanding.

"Good. Buddy Olson hired me and my partner to figure out who killed your parents. I'm guessing it was that Renato guy."

Another nod.

"Renato is a gangster, isn't he? What's his last name? Which family is he with? DiCaro? Orlando? Colosimo? Someone new?"

Marcus gave a slight shake of his head. His voice was a whisper. "Mexican."

"An Italian hitter working for the Mexicans? Seriously?"

Marcus coughed lightly. There was a slight, wet burble in the back of his throat. That wasn't a good sign. "Unaffiliated. Wants to be...a big shot."

"So, he signed on with anyone who would have him. Where'd he get the doggy drugs?"

"Stole...from the Mexicans."

"So, he's double-crossing his own gang in order raise the cash to bankroll his own syndicate. Dude is playing with fire, isn't he?" Duff was impressed by the guy's chutzpah. "How'd you and your parents get involved?"

A tear sprang to the corner of Marcus's eye. "I fucked up. Dad fucked up." He coughed again. The wetness in his throat sounded worse. "Desperate. We needed money."

"How'd you and your dad fuck up?"

"I gambled. For Dad, it was hospital bills and a stock market scam." Marcus's whisper was getting thinner and more distant. "We were broke."

Duff dug his index finger into the wound on Marcus's shoulder to flair him back to life. "Stay with me, hoss. Keep it in the present. You gotta stick around to watch that niece and nephew of yours grow up."

"Trying."

"The hospital bills—was that from your mom's dementia?"

Marcus looked confused. "No dementia. Dad's back surgery."

The dementia had been a ruse. Someone had planted the drugs to make it look like the mom was having a break from reality to fool the coroner. Duff said, "So, tell me if I'm wrong. You knew how to cook meth, probably learned somewhere, right? Your dad had the land with the tunnels on it, found them when he moved in and was doing research on the land plats, I imagine. You get in over your head on some gambling debts. Your dad can't keep up with hospital bills and then tries to make money through a stock market deal and gets scammed. How'd you meet Renato, then?"

"Through a friend."

"Renato gets you the drugs. Dad gets you the chemicals and knows of the caves. You and Dad haul stuff to the woods to cook underground, well hidden from the prying eyes of the law, and then you move the stuff to this abandoned restaurant for pickup and get it back to Chicago where Renato's guys can make bank on the meth."

Marcus nodded.

"Let me see if I can guess where it goes from there. Your dad is laundering money for Renato because he can't deposit that much into his accounts. He's rolling big. He gets the truck, the boat, the car, the furniture—maybe he renovates the house with cash under the table to contractors who don't ask a lot of questions. When he and your mom clear the debt and roll up a tidy sum in some hidden account, they want out. They call Renato to the house, tell him they want out, and then he caps them. You're unaware of this because why?"

"Down in Chicago."

"Helping move product?"

Marcus nodded. Another tear slipped out of the side of his eye leaving a glassy trail down the side of his face. "Didn't have much else going for me." There was a long pause as Marcus summoned the strength to finish his sentence. "Thought maybe I'd make enough money to do something with my life. Maybe make enough to get out of stupid things, make Dad proud finally."

"Why didn't you become a cop like your old man?"

"Got busted in the Army for dealing weed."

"Dishonorable discharge?"

Marcus nodded. He coughed again. The wetness was thick and filmy. A glob of spittle exited his mouth and landed on his cheek. Even in the dim, phosphorescent glow from the halogen light outside, Duff could see it was dark in color, more blood than saliva.

Duff pressed the wounds on the man's body again. "Stay with me, Breaking Bad."

Marcus's head lolled to the side. His eyes fluttered. He did not respond to the pressure. Duff wrenched the wounds with more force. Nothing. Marcus Laskey had passed out. His breathing was shallow. He didn't have long. Duff wondered how long it would take the ambulance to get there. Probably too long. They'd show up with Laskey dead on arrival.

The restaurant was momentarily lit up with headlights. Duff didn't see what vehicle made them but inferred the lack of red-and-blue emergency lights meant it was a private vehicle. He hoped it was Buddy and Shelby Ree. He should have known that his luck would not have allowed that.

"Who da fuck are you?" Renato's voice boomed out through the supper club the second he opened the door. Donny was right behind him, the gun in his hand pointed at Duff.

"I'm the magic supper club fairy. I bring fried cheese curds to little boys and girls who finish all their asparagus." Duff squinted at them. The light from the SUV was shining through the window of the door and backlighting the two men. Duff could only see them in silhouette.

"Wrong answer, fucknuts." Donny strode over and pressed the barrel of the gun to the back of Duff's head. He pushed into Duff's flesh. "Want me to spray his brains all over the floor?"

"Let him tell me who he is and what he's doing here, first."

Donny thumped the barrel of the gun off the back of Duff's head. "Talk, dead man."

Duff looked back down at Marcus Laskey. He was dying now. He was about to give up the ghost. "I'm a private detective. I was hired to find out who killed Art and Michelle Laskey."

"Oh, a de-tect-tive!" Renato let each syllable fall out of his mouth with a mocking tone that sounded like he lifted it straight out of a Joe Pesci movie. "You figure out who killed Art and Michelle?"

"I did. It was you."

Renato snorted. "Of course you think that. I'm the guy with a gun to your head."

"Well, technically, Donny had the gun to my head."

Renato pulled out a big black .45 semi-auto from a shoulder holster beneath his coat. He shoved Donny aside and pressed the steel barrel behind Duff's left ear. "Now I'm the one with the gun to your head."

"Hey, I guess I stand corrected." Duff looked down at his legs. "Well, I kneel corrected. Regardless, I'm corrected. But Donny didn't do it if that's what you're going to say."

"How do you know that?"

"Because Donny's your bitch. He's second tier. He does what you tell him to do. Art Laskey was a former cop. He and Michelle aren't breaking out the good china for little fuckin' Donny. He's eating off the generic plates like everyone else. Maybe, if he's lucky, he gets to drink from the special Phantom Menace promo glass from Burger King—Qui-Gon, not Jar Jar—but he isn't a big deal. Donny didn't put the Laskeys on the payroll. My only question was exactly why you knocked them off. I figure it was because Art was done moving money and cooking meth for you, so he became a liability, and liabilities have to be censured."

Renato laughed aloud. His laugh was much higher-pitched than the tough-guy voice he tried to use. "Is that what you think, then? Tell me, Mr. Sherlock Holmes—how'd I do it, then?"

"Well, I figure they had you over, brought out the good china, you had a nice sit-down and a discussion on numbers. I figure Art must've given you all the paperwork he had about the money drops. He explained politely that he and Michelle were out of the drugs game, and you shook hands. Then, when he got up to help you out, you probably blew out his brains when he wasn't looking with that cannon you're holding, then smashed Michelle with the butt when she started screaming. You staged the bodies to look like a murder-suicide and used Michelle's gun to finish her off before putting her hand on it."

Renato looked amused. "Oh, this is rich."

"Only thing I haven't pinned down for certain is the dementia drugs. I figure you must have given her a partial injection of them before you knocked her off. Just enough to throw off the coroner, right? Some real hitter taught you that, right?"

Renato gave Duff an appraising look. "Bingo, hot shot. Got it in one. You must be a good detective."

"I'm better than average," said Duff. "I mean, I'm no Encyclopedia Brown, but who is, really?"

"I used to love those books when I was a kid," said Donny.

"Shut up, Donny." Renato kicked Marcus Laskey's foot. The nearly dead man did not react. He was as good as gone.

"Bet you're bummed you didn't learn the secret of the maps, though. Probably killing you that you can't find where he's cooking the product. I bet you and Donny spent a couple of days traipsing all over the hills and valleys around here looking for the spot, but you never found it."

If that jibe rattled Renato, Duff couldn't tell. The gangster ignored him. "We came back to make sure Marco was dead. We got down the road a little bit, and I says to Donny—Marco was dead, right? And Donny says, I dunno; we never checked. So, we come back and find you trying to keep him alive even though we expressly wanted him dead."

"I decided I needed a hobby. Lifesaving seemed interesting. Turns out, I'm not really good at it."

Renato backed away from Duff and jerked his head back toward the kitchen. "Check the rest of the place. Make sure there ain't no one else here." He kept the .45 trained on Duff, center mass.

"I work alone," said Duff.

"Forgive me if I don't take your word about that."

Donny switched on the light on his cell phone and did a quick sweep of the restaurant including the basement storage area. He came back, the bouncing light preceding his arrival. "Nobody else here, boss."

"Well, I guess your work here is done, detective."

Duff saw Renato aim the gun at him, and he did the only thing he instinctively knew how to do: he cowered like a rat. He threw his hands up to protect his head and tried to make his overly large body as small a target as possible. He wondered for a fleeting second, despite his profound atheism, if some version of the Afterlife might be real and if he might see Becky there. He wondered what he'd say to her. He wondered if she would be happy to see him again. He hoped she would.

The gun fired.

Duff didn't even feel it. Everything just went finally, blessedly dark.

13

ABE KNEW BETTER than to fly into the parking lot on the ATV, so he killed the engine and ditched it in the heavy scrub on the side of the road next to the restaurant. His heart was racing. He wound his way around the building, gun up and in the ready position, hoping to take the men by surprise. Then, he heard a sound he never wanted to hear: the loud, single report of a large-bore handgun. The gunshot was unmistakable. There was only one shot, though. There were two bad guys and only one Duff. If Duff had started shooting, there would had to have been more than one shot unless he somehow had used the shot to convince the men to surrender their weapons, and knowing what Abe knew about Duff, that seemed impossible. Besides, the gunshot had been loud; it was a big gun. Duff's little Walther made a noise like an angry smack. This had been a cannon. There was force behind it. Abe's heart leapt into his throat. Tears started to prick at the corners of his eyes. In the back of his mind, he started trying to figure out how he was going to tell Katherine and Matilda that Duff was dead.

Abe kept his Jim Rockford special at the ready and ran behind the building to the back door. He slipped to the side of the door and pressed his back against the cold wooden siding. Where was Buddy Olson? Where were the police? Panic was rising in Abe's gorge. He knew he needed to play hero, but he also knew he didn't have much hero in him. He wasn't wearing a flak jacket. If he caught a bullet, he could die, too. He wondered how Matilda would go on without him. How much would she cry at his funeral?

For some unknown reason, Abe remembered his undergrad Shakespeare class at that moment. Like a bell ringing in the dark, he heard Professor

Neuhaus's voice bellowing in the crowded lecture hall, *Hamlet's fatal flaw was indecision! Act! Act fast! That's what Shakespeare was telling us. You know the correct moral course of action in your heart, so act upon it without haste!*

Abe smashed the butt of his gun into the glass of the back door. If it had been a movie, he would have shattered the glass. This wasn't a movie. The window splintered and spider-webbed, instead. That was not what he wanted. Abe turned and ran away from the door. He knew the gangsters would be out in a flash. Abe hid behind the SUV. Donny was out the door first, gun raised. Abe tried to lower his voice to sound tougher, more masculine. "Drop the gun!"

Donny fired two shots toward the direction of the sound and ducked back inside the restaurant. A second later, Donny fired a third shot through the glass, and it broke away from the frame and fell to the ground in shards. "Go fuck yourself!"

"You're surrounded. Drop the guns and come out with your hands up!" Abe hoped he sounded as intimidating as he was trying to sound.

"I don't see nobody." Renato's voice carried strongly through the cold air. "You're alone, aren't you?"

The panic was surging through Abe now. "Comply now! Drop the guns and come out with your hands on your heads."

Renato laughed. "You get on the ground and throw your gun out, and maybe we kill you fast instead of slow."

"I don't even think he has a gun," said Donny.

"Yeah, prove you got a gun."

Abe briefly considered winging a round through the door, but if he did that, they'd know where he was, and he'd be down to five bullets instead of six. "Last chance! Drop the guns, or we're coming in!"

"Bring it!" Renato kicked the back door open and strode through, his gun leveled and swiveling from side to side as he looked for signs of movement. "I'm out in the open! Shoot me!"

Donny was right behind him, He moved to the other side of the SUV. They both opened the doors and climbed into the truck. They never saw Abe crouched behind it.

Abe saw the taillights flare as Renato stepped on the brake and shifted to reverse. The backing lights flipped on, and Abe realized he was lit up like a deer on the highway in the camera on the rear hatch, and his image was being projected into the cabin on the LCD panel on the center console. The SUV jerked to a stop as Renato slammed it back into park.

Abe had no choice. He fired blindly at the SUV and ran at the same time, sprinting for the woods at the edge of the lot. He emptied his entire cylinder into the Lincoln and dove behind a downed tree. A second later, the sound of gunshots filled the air and bullets plunked into the woods all around him. Abe fought to reload the six-shooter, slipping new bullets into the cylinder as fast as his frozen fingers could do it.

"He hit the fuckin' tire!" Donny gave a plaintive wail.

"Let's kill him, and then get down the road. I saw a dark field road a little ways from here. We can change the tire there. It'll ride for a bit, yet." Renato popped the clip from his gun and exchanged it for a fresh one. Another eight bullets looking for a target.

Abe's fingers trembled, and his heart pounded in his ears as he slipped the last bullet into the cylinder and snapped it closed. He could hear footsteps on gravel. The two men were approaching cautiously. Abe knew they had guns raised. They were looking for any sign of movement in the darkness. Any movement at all would unleash a barrage of gunfire in the direction of said movement.

Abe felt around by his head and scooped up a hunk of mud and debris, damp and cold. He hucked it sidearm through the scrub. The sudden movement and noise caused Renato and Donny to stop walking and fire into the darkness. Both men popped off two rounds. That meant that Renato was down to six bullets, and Donny was down to eleven, maybe twelve depending on how he loaded his gun and what clip he favored. Either way, they both could miss a whole lot more and still have more than enough to put a few rounds in Abe's chest. Abe didn't like those odds.

Abe inhaled through his nose and out through his mouth as silently as he could. He was trying to get the trembling out of his fingers. If he was going to have any shot at this, he needed one clean round to land and either incapacitate or kill one of the two men. Then, he'd have five shots left to deal with the fallout. He just hoped he could get the shot off without them seeing movement.

Cautiously, Abe raised his gun above the edge of the fallen log. He tried to ease himself up to see over it, but that was too much movement. He heard Donny call out a warning, and then several shots plunked into the rotting tree next to him. Abe fell back flat on the ground. He was running out of time. They were almost on him.

Abe always knew his job might get him killed, but he'd prided himself on being one of those detectives that tried to avoid any sort of gun fight. He and Duff had been shot at before once or twice, but it was never like this. It was always by people who weren't cold-blooded killers.

"It's over, man." Donny's voice called out. There was no fear in it. "Give up now and we'll make sure to kill you fast."

Abe took one last deep breath. He hoped he could kill one of them before they killed him, at least.

Abe brought a knee up so he could quickly raise himself off the ground and shoot from a kneeling position behind the log. Having the protection of the log might keep him alive long enough to squeeze off two rounds, three if he was lucky. He wished he had something clever to say. He hoped his life would flash in front of his eyes before he died. He wanted to see his mom again. He wanted to see Katherine and Matilda back when they were still a happy, unified family.

Abe popped to a kneeling position and fired.

14

A T THE SAME instant Abe popped up to shoot, there came a sudden roar of engine noise from around the bend in the road. It was enough to distract Renato and Donny. Abe's first shot flew wide of Donny. Abe squeezed a second round, and that bullet found purchase in Donny's left calf muscle. Donny gave a shriek of pain and collapsed. He flopped onto his side and fired into the woods. Abe threw himself down behind the log again.

Like an avenging angel, a white pickup truck bounded over the drainage ditch next to the parking lot, launching hard into the air as a grizzled former county sheriff hit the rut at nearly sixty, popping the front end of his Ford into the air as he did.

Renato turned and fired at the truck, but Buddy did not know the meaning of the word brakes. Renato had to stop firing to fling himself to the side to avoid getting a mouthful of truck bumper. In the distance, the tinny whine of ambulance and police sirens could be heard. The cavalry was coming.

Renato knew when he was outgunned and outnumbered. He scrambled for the Lincoln and threw it into drive. Even with the flat tire, he managed to spray gravel as he fled. He turned left toward the lower part of the valley and disappeared around the corner.

Buddy was out of the truck an instant later, firing two rounds after the truck, but hitting the body, causing two dull metallic thuds to ring out.

Shelby Ree had her gun leveled at Donny, the body of the Ford as her protection. "Drop the gun, or I drop you!"

Donny moaned and gave up. He tossed the gun to the side and lay back on the cold gravel. "My fuckin' leg is broken!"

"Ambulance is coming." Shelby approached with her gun leveled at the gangster. She kicked away his Glock and rolled him onto his stomach with her foot. Donny cried out in pain. She quickly handcuffed him and left him trussed facedown.

"Abe? Duff?" Buddy called out to the darkness.

"I'm alive," Abe called back. "I'm coming out. Don't shoot me."

Abe crawled over the fallen log and walked out of the darkness. "Good timing."

"I'm nothing if not punctual." Buddy looked around. "Where's your partner?"

Abe tried to speak, but no sound came out. A lump rose up suddenly and stuck in his throat. His mouth was suddenly dry as dust. He just looked down and shook his head. He gestured toward the restaurant.

Buddy holstered his cannon. His voice was hoarse. "Well, fuck. I figured that little bastard would outlive me just to spite me."

Abe started stumbling toward the restaurant door. He coughed out the lump in his throat. His voice was hoarse. "Marcus might still be alive. I only heard one gunshot."

Ree pointed at the road. "We gotta go after that guy."

Abe gestured toward Donny. "What about him?"

Ree shrugged. "Where the hell is he going to go? He's cuffed and on one leg. If he runs, he won't hop very far before someone drags him down."

Buddy gave Abe a sympathetic look. "She's right. Abe, stay here. Wait for the ambulance. Should be here in another minute. When the deputies or the local police get here, tell them where we went, and tell them to send backup."

Abe could barely understand what Buddy told him. The old sheriff and the deputy jumped into Buddy's pickup, and they bolted after the damaged Lincoln.

Abe looked down at the guy who was bleeding from the lower leg. The wound was superficial. It had grazed the kid's calf, taking a hunk of meat with it, but not lodging into it. It was painful, no doubt, but far from life-threatening. The kid would probably walk with a slight limp for the rest of his life. "Sorry about your leg."

Donny shrugged as if he held no grudge. "I would have done worse to you, man."

"I suppose so." Abe paused for a second. He couldn't bring himself to say the next words. He stumbled over his tongue as he tried. "The guy...in there...did...?" Abe couldn't manage to finish the thought.

Donny knew what Abe was asking. He shook his head. "I didn't kill him. That was Renato's work."

Abe nodded. The ambulance siren was getting louder. Abe could see the red-and-blue lights flashing in the trees down the road. It would be here in less than fifteen seconds. Abe needed a moment with Duff alone.

Abe forced himself to go into the restaurant. With the window shot out, the cold air was seeping in like a blanket. In the half-light of the dining room, Abe could see Duff's body slumped over Marcus Laskey's body. They were dark shapes without detail, but the silhouettes were evident. Duff was curled fetal. Laskey was still prone, flat on his back. A tear was threatening to overflow from Abe's eye, and he wiped it away with the back of his wrist. He didn't know what to say. A moment like that needed some sort of speech, some sort of fitting finale, but what could he say to the man who had been by his side almost every day for more than two decades?

Abe stood in the darkness silently until the ambulance pulled into the restaurant parking lot, a Mount Horeb police cruiser on its tail. The first responders tended to Donny in the cold. Abe knew the cop would be inside in a moment. Abe had to say something poignant fast or lose the moment forever. He thought about all the times Duff had solved a case for them. He thought about Duff antagonizing some guy until he swung at him, just to make sure Abe didn't get hit. Duff was the guy who showed up in the hospital first when Matilda was born, even before Katherine's parents got there. He'd bought a Milwaukee Brewers onesie for her. Other than Abe and Katherine, Duff had been the first person to hold Matilda. He'd been there for Abe at every milestone. He was gruff, sure. And he was odd. And he was set in his ways. But he was still Abe's best friend.

Only friend.

Abe tried to summarize more than twenty years of friendship, and the words weren't there. He couldn't encapsulate their time together with a sentence or two. It was impossible. Abe licked his lips and summoned the only words he could think to say. "I'm sorry, Duff."

"For what?"

Abe leapt backward. His heart was in his throat. "What?"

Duff groaned and spoke again. "Why are you sorry?"

"You're alive?"

"For now. Might die later if I'm lucky."

"But how?"

Duff still hadn't moved. He remained curled fetal. "Magic? Miracle? Or maybe the sumbitch shot me in the ribs where my gun is, and the gun stopped the bullet, but the impact broke every rib in my chest? The pain was so bad it knocked me unconscious for a couple of minutes."

Abe dropped to a knee beside his friend. He gingerly lifted Duff's sweatshirt. Even with Abe trying to be careful, Duff howled like his leg was getting hacked off. He seethed through gritted teeth. Abe saw the damage. A bullet had lodged in the side of the Walther rendering it unusable for future action. If the gun had not been there, the bullet would have easily punctured Duff's heart. As it was, Duff probably had five or six ribs that were cracked. Abe said, "I guess Buddy was right. You never know when you're going to need a gun."

"If you tell that old bastard the gun saved my life, I'll never speak to you again."

The Mount Horeb cop entered the restaurant with his gun drawn. Abe raised his hands to show he was unarmed. "I'm the guy who called nine-one-one. I'm a private detective from Illinois. We need help in here."

"You armed?"

"I am. Right hip." Abe kept his arms raised and turned so the police officer could see the weapon.

"Don't move." The cop approached Abe with his gun at the ready.

"I won't."

The cop disarmed Abe and checked the gun. "This has been fired."

"I winged the kid in the parking lot with it. You need to send units south of here. You need to find a Lincoln Navigator riding on three wheels being chased by a white Ford F-150 pickup. Likely the F-150 will be excessively exceeding the speed limit. After you get other units on the road after the bad guy, I'll explain everything."

"You winged someone?" Duff sounded impressed. He still had not moved out of the fetal position.

Abe nodded sheepishly. "First time for everything, I guess."

SHELBY REE WAS hanging on for dear life. She had buckled her seatbelt, of course, and she held firmly to the Oh Shit handle above the passenger door. Her left arm was straight out and braced against the passenger dash for a third point of contact in an attempt to stabilize herself, but it did not help much. Shelby had been involved in high-speed chases before, but screaming through the darkness on a twisty, turning, up-and-down county road with Buddy Olson at the wheel of a pick-up truck was as close as she had ever come to feeling like she was going to die.

Buddy's reckless disregard for safety combined with his generous belief in the cornering abilities of a pickup truck had caught them up to the hobbled Lincoln in no time. The gangster in the SUV had the vehicle floored, but the flat rear tire was preventing the SUV from gaining torque and handling properly. The Navigator was limping along like a lame horse.

Buddy gripped the steering wheel hard. "Brace yourself. I'm going to PIT him."

"You think that's wise out here?"

"You think I should wait until he hits a bigger road?"

The Lincoln's dashboard was casting enough light in the cab that Shelby could make out a silhouette at the wheel despite the heavily tinted glass. She saw a very particular movement, one for which any cop is always on guard. "He's going to shoot!"

Shelby threw herself down behind the dashboard as a pair of gunshots rocketed through F-150. The blast punched two ugly holes in the front windshield and splintered the rear window. Cold air flooded the cab.

The bullets narrowly missed Buddy. "Shoot him back!"

Shelby opened the window and leaned her arm outside. She squeezed off four rounds at the SUV.

The driver of the SUV returned fire. This time, one of the big slugs from the gun hit the radiator of Buddy's truck and probably lodged into the engine block. Several lights began to blink on the dash. The old sheriff cursed loudly and accelerated. "Aw, hell. It's now or never, I guess."

Buddy stomped the gas pedal. Whatever damage the shot had done to the truck was impressive. The F-150 no longer had great acceleration. It lurched forward gamely, but it was clear that it was no longer the vehicle it used to be. "I'm going to run up his ass. Should do the trick."

The F-150 contacted the Lincoln. The bumper of the Ford smashed into the trailer hitch for the Lincoln. The Lincoln crow-hopped to the right and the driver lost control. The Lincoln pitched over an embankment on the starboard ride of the road and disappeared from view. Buddy's truck crow-hopped left and the engine gave out. Buddy was able to guide it into a ditch before the steering gave out entirely and the column locked. The brakes worked just enough to stop the truck before it smashed into the hillside beyond the road. Dark smoke started to pour out from under the hood.

Shelby and Buddy sprang into action. With guns drawn, they made their way across the road and sought cover behind trees. Buddy called out, "You're done! Throw your gun down and come out with your hands up."

No response.

Shelby could see the Lincoln on its side. The headlights were out, but one of the taillights still glowed an eerie red, splaying the bloody color over the dead, dry winter grass. "Cover me."

Buddy shook his head. He was already moving out from behind his tree. "No, you cover me. I'm old. If he's going to kill one of us, it should be me."

Shelby wanted to argue. She was the one who was still an active-duty deputy. He was retired. Buddy moved too quickly for her, though. He was down the embankment in a few steps and moving to the SUV.

Buddy's baritone cop voice thundered in the night. "If I see a gun, I swear to God and Holy Jesus I'm going to empty this .44 in your mouth." He moved around the top of the SUV using the opaque body for a shield. When he got to the front window, he moved around, gun raised and ready to shoot. He froze. He called back to Shelby, "Nobody in the truck."

"What?"

"You heard me. He's bailed. Kicked out the front window. He's on the run."

Shelby wished she had her police unit with the spotlights. She wished she could radio for a K-9 unit. She squinted into the darkness. The guy could be anywhere. He could be right in front of them. She wouldn't be able to see him until it was too late. "We're targets out here."

"Big ol' targets." Buddy hustled up the embankment.

They waited for a few moments using the trees as cover. They waited for gunfire or the sound of someone running, but there was only silence and the sound of the two vehicles crepitating as the cold worked to chill the hot engines.

"He's gone, isn't he?"

"Not entirely gone." Buddy gestured to the distance with his chin. "Got to be a road over there somewhere. Got to be some houses. We're going to need to get over that way. People need to know a dangerous man is on the run. I worry about what he might do if he gets into someone's house."

"This is Wisconsin. People own guns. He kicks at the wrong door, he's liable to get a face full of bird shot or worse."

"Still. Backup better get here quick."

As if speaking it into existence, the flashing lights of a county deputy's SUV came around the corner. Ree recognized the driver right away. Bill Paczech was a good guy and almost a thirty-year veteran of the department. He had the paunchy belly of a guy who ate too much fast food on duty, and the lackadaisical air of someone too close to retirement to risk getting shot.

Ree pulled her badge from her pocket and held it up so it caught in the spotlight on Billy's cruiser. Billy pulled up and rolled down his window. "Shelby?"

"Evening, Billy. The bad guy went thataway." Shelby jabbed a thumb over her shoulder. "Going to need a lot of backup for this one." She explained the situation.

Billy gave a nod and reached for the radio mic. "I guess we're going to need a whole lot of backup."

DUFF WAS A bad patient. He hated being sick or injured, and he made sure the EMTs knew he was hurt. Every little motion caused him to unleash a string of creative invectives that denigrated everything from the EMTs' intelligence, to their hairstyle, to their choice of footwear. And sometimes it was all three. They managed to get him loaded onto the gurney and get him into the back of the ambulance with a minimum of fuss, but Duff still seethed and groaned like a dying man. Abe had no doubt Duff was in tremendous pain. Abe had cracked a rib before; he knew what sort of pain that brought. Duff was in exponentially more pain. It was the sort of injury where thinking about breathing could cause the body to tense in anticipation of the pain a breath would cause, and the anticipatory tension would cause debilitating pain. And heaven help him if he had to sneeze or cough.

Once the EMTs got him on the ambulance, they gave Duff a shot of Demerol. It hit him quickly. He sighed lightly as the drug ran through his system at warp speed. "Took you idiots long enough."

Abe reprimanded his friend. "Duff, we try to be nice to the people who give out the happy juice."

Duff leaned back and closed his eyes. "Tell them to hit me again and put it on my tab."

"I'd like to hit him again," one of the EMTs said. She was a tough-looking middle-aged woman with a short, mannish haircut and eyes that looked like they'd seen too much drama over the years. She made a fist and mimed punching Duff in the jaw.

Duff caught the motion and smiled. "I like you. Let's start a home-based crafting business together."

At that moment, the call for backup from Bill Paczech's radio came out. Suspect was armed, on foot, and to be considered very dangerous. More units were being dispatched.

Duff's smile did not leave his face. He snapped his fingers at Abe. "Ask one of those cops if that friend of Shelby's is working, Lonnie."

"Why?"

"Don't ask questions! Just do! Just do!" Duff's voice had a strange, dreamy, sing-song quality to it. It was unsettling.

Abe turned and found the nearest brown-shirted deputy. "Is Lonnie Rostenbach working tonight?"

The deputy thought about it for a moment before shaking his head. "Nah, he worked the weekend shift. He's off. Why do you ask?"

"No idea. My partner wanted to know." Abe walked back to Duff but found the big man fast asleep thanks to the drugs. Abe looked to the EMT. "Can I wake him up?"

"You do, and I'll kill you."

"Noted." Abe backed up from the ambulance. Why had Duff asked about Lonnie? What did he know?

Abe hated it when Duff did things like this. Duff's observational skills were inhuman, and Abe tried his best to replicate them, but he was rarely as successful. Abe knew that Duff didn't have any sort of superpower; he just saw the world through a different sort of lens. When it came to mysteries, Duff somehow knew what things were important and what things weren't, and combined with his far-better-than-average memory, it turned his ability to pick out clues into a wild parlor trick.

So why did he ask about Lonnie?

Abe looked around the parking lot of the restaurant carefully. He tried to see it how Duff saw it. There was the activity, of course. Two police cruisers, an ambulance, and an unmarked squad were there. The first ambulance with Donny in it had left for the hospital, a Mount Horeb police officer riding with them to the hospital so the suspected murderer of Marcus Laskey could not try anything stupid. Police were waiting for the county coroner to show up to take Marcus's corpse. They were waiting for detectives to come and clear the scene. No one was really paying attention to Abe.

That was Abe's superpower: the ability to disappear in plain sight. Even in dirty khakis and a bulky winter coat, Abe stood in the midst of the activity unnoticed. The police weren't speaking to him. They hadn't given him back his gun, confiscating it as evidence in the shooting. No gun meant he wasn't a threat in the least, and thus his invisibility was complete. Abe casually and calmly moved toward the door of the restaurant. Not a single cop asked him what he was doing. Abe simply walked back into the cold dining room and let the broken door close behind him. No one said a word.

Abe looked around the dining room. What had Duff seen that he hadn't? Abe walked into the kitchen and used the light on his phone to scan the room. Nothing unusual. Nothing out of place. Abe remembered that most of the time they had hidden in the kitchen, the room had been dark. It wouldn't have been here.

Abe walked out and looked at Marcus Laskey's body. Duff had spent several long minutes draped over the corpse, struggling to breathe. Duff had lain in a fixed position, unable to move. The only part of him that didn't hurt to move was his eyes. Whatever Duff saw, it was from the fetal position atop of Marcus Laskey. Abe lowered himself to the same level and tried as best he could to approximate Duff's position on Marcus. He turned his head and looked at what Duff could see.

It wasn't much.

The dining room walls were mostly glass with a narrow strip of wall above the lintel. The strip of wall was where kitschy knick-knacks were mounted, aged from light and cigarette smoke, and covered in dust. There were wooden plaques displaying stuffed and mounted fish—mostly bass. There were pictures of Wisconsin things like Packer and Badger football players, a few pictures of Robin Yount and Paul Molitor in their powder blue Brewers uniforms, and plenty of beer signs.

When Abe's eyes found what Duff had really been staring at, just like odd piece of plaster that hid the witchball in the Laskey's basement, it suddenly jumped into such focus that it was amazing he hadn't seen it the whole time. Nestled between a photo of Ray Nitschke and an impressive largemouth bass was a woodcut sign painted John Deere green with white lettering. The sign was small and narrow. In the darkened half-light of the restaurant's glass-enclosed dining area, it was almost invisible. The sign said simply: *Rostenbachs' since 1941.* Abe stared at that simple little woodcut, and a few more pieces of the puzzle fell into place.

Renato and Donny had a key for the building. They didn't break in. They had a key. That meant they were either tied to the agent listing the property or the former owner. Shelby Ree had said that her friend in the Dane County Sheriff's Office was named Lonnie Rostenbach. It didn't take a genius to connect his last name to the supper club based on that sign. Duff had also already figured out that moving the amount of drugs Renato and Donny were moving through Dane County would have required law enforcement support. They had secured ex-law enforcement's help to manufacture the drugs, but shipping was something else. They needed someone who could get them through the county fast with minimal fuss. It probably helped that the same law enforcement official had keys to an unoccupied space that backed to the Laskeys' property. Abe would have been willing to bet Lonnie had something to do with Bob Benedict's missing files, too. As Abe knelt over Marcus Laskey's corpse, the only question that remained was whether or not Lonnie Rostenbach was working alone.

15

BUDDY AND SHELBY Ree returned to the Rostenbachs' shuttered supper club in Billy Paczech's county cruiser. Already, other deputies were setting up the crashed SUV as a crime scene. Buddy was relieved to learn that Duff had refrained from joining the Choir Invisible and was instead in the back of an ambulance zonked out on painkillers. He looked over Duff's sleeping form in the back of the ambulance and patted him on the foot. "I told him he needed to carry a gun."

Abe briefed them on what he and Duff went through with Renato and Donny, what he learned about the supper club, and about his ventured guess that Lonnie Rostenbach was involved in this mess. Shelby confirmed Abe's working theory by telling him about the photograph Buddy found at Lonnie's apartment, and then she told him about Renato being on the run.

Abe considered the predicament Renato was in at the moment. "You're a wannabe Chicago mobster on the run in the middle of the countryside in Wisconsin. You're on the hook for multiple counts of murder, at least one count of attempted murder, and possession with intent to distribute. That'll be a life sentence without parole. It's cold. You're improperly dressed. Your partner is in police custody on the way to the hospital. You've just lost a couple hundred thousand dollars' worth of drugs. What do you do?"

Buddy didn't need to think about it. "I call for help."

"Who do you call?"

"A guy who can get me out of this mess, or at least get me to a safe spot where I can think about the next step."

Ree said, "That's got to be Lonnie. We don't know that Renato knows anyone else in the county."

"So, logically Renato would need to get to higher ground—somewhere his cell phone would work—and he would call Lonnie for help. Then, he'd lie low. He'd have to be sure he doesn't get spotted by any of the cops cruising around."

"Where does he lie, though?" Buddy put his hands on his hips and tilted his head south, toward the direction of the crime scene involving his truck and Renato's Lincoln. "Kid drives a Navigator. That doesn't strike me as the type of person who will be content to chill out in a ditch or hide in a culvert."

"We got K-9 units en route to track him. He can't stay outside unless he can run faster than a Malinois. How was he dressed?"

"Fancy," said Abe. "Good shoes."

"Then he'd break into a house," said Ree. "If someone is in the house he chooses to break into, they're now up the proverbial creek without a paddle."

Abe tried opening the map app on his phone. It wouldn't refresh, but thankfully the last map it downloaded was available, and that was enough of the local area to give him a solid look at the likeliest path of escape. Abe tried to envision the route the way Duff would. Duff would somehow look at the map, judge the terrain and figure out where Renato was making a beeline, even if it wasn't the straightest or most logical route. To Abe, it should be a direct line.

Abe scoured the road in front of the supper club on the map. It led into a valley. Ree pointed out where the SUV wrecked. Abe zoomed into that area on his phone with his fingers. He readjusted his glasses and tried to focus. The valley wouldn't get Renato better signal. Higher ground was to the east of the crash site, but the south was the logical escape route. It was easier to run downhill than uphill. Abe wondered if that would factor into Renato's plans. He needed to escape. Downhill would give him more speed. Abe looked at the map and the terrain. Straight south would run him to a creek. "We need a car," said Abe. "I can figure this out."

"Someone can give us a ride back to my Jeep." Ree stuck two fingers in her mouth and gave a whistle. "Billy, we need a lift, quick."

Billy Paczech glanced around at the activity in the parking lot. "You haven't given a statement, yet."

"Billy, there will be time for that later. Right now, we have to catch a murderer."

WITH REE AT the wheel, Buddy in the backseat, and Abe riding shotgun as navigator, Ree drove her Jeep out from behind the shed where Abe left it and flew up the Laskeys' driveway. "Where to?"

Abe was trying to get bearings on the map. His phone, flush with newly acquired 4G signal, suddenly refreshed itself. He bit back a curse and waited. "To the left."

Abe was trying to use the zoomed-in feature on Google Maps to determine the locations of houses. On a computer with a normal monitor, this was not much of a task. On a five-inch cellphone screen while riding in a bouncy Jeep, this was a difficult chore where the slightest finger touch in the wrong spot would send the map spinning to a location a dozen miles away.

Abe took a guess. He didn't like guessing, but in this case, it was all they could do. "If I were Renato, I'd get out of the valley to high ground on this path. It looks like he had about a half-mile or more to cover to the nearest house. I don't see him as a sprinter, so he might not actually be at the nearest house, yet."

"Where's the nearest house to his likely path, then?" Ree had yet to make the turn out of the Laskey's driveway. She wanted a destination point, first.

"If he runs a straight line, he'll end up here." Abe zoomed into the map and found a house not far from the Laskeys' house. It was on a road that ran parallel to the road they were on now, but east a quarter mile from the county road by the Huseth house.

"It's as good a place as any." Buddy checked his gun. He emptied the shells from the spent chambers and put in fresh bullets. "Hit it, Deputy."

"Might not be a deputy much longer after this." Ree stepped the gas and the Jeep launched out of the gravel road. Billy Paczech followed in his squad, no lights.

They roared down the road and rounded the corner hard. The house Abe had located on the map was an older farmhouse that had fallen into some disrepair. A rusty tractor had been abandoned near a windbreak of trees on the north side of the house. On the south edge, an old Chevy Lumina sat next to a Chevy Silverado that was long past being serviceable. A barn that hadn't been used in years was off to the south edge of the property. Weeds were overgrown all around the place with only a small, serviceable lawn around the house itself still trimmed short enough to not be considered wild lands.

Billy Paczech parked his car just off the road opposite the house. Ree pulled into the driveway but parked at the end of it.

Buddy lurched out of the back of the Jeep, too big to be comfortable in the backseat. "Pistols out, Mouseketeers."

Abe pulled his .38 and inspected the cylinder. "I don't remember Annette or Cubby having to shoot anyone."

"You're too young to remember the Mickey Mouse Club at all."

"What's Mickey Mouse Club?" Ree pulled her service weapon.

Buddy huffed into his mustache. "Ignore her. She probably doesn't even know Annette Funicello sold peanut butter."

"Who?" asked Ree.

"Exactly." Buddy took command of the scene. "Here's the plan: I go left, Ree goes right, and Abe goes straight up the middle to the house."

Billy Paczech waddled after them, his weapon drawn, as well. "What about me?"

"You got the flashlight; you go around to the barn. He might be hiding in there. If he's not in the barn, start sweeping the fields around this place."

"What if we don't find him?"

Buddy shrugged. "Given that only one of us has a flak jacket, maybe it's best we don't."

"If you see him, call it out." Ree hustled to the right of the house. Billy took off to the far right. Buddy went left using the trees in the windbreak for cover.

Abe ran up to the house and knocked on the door. He knocked like he thought Buddy would knock, loud and decisive. After a moment of waiting, a short, round elderly woman in a sweatshirt and jeans opened the door and peered out at him through the screen door. "Hello, there. What can I do for you?"

Abe pulled his PI folio. He quickly explained what he, two current deputies, and one retired sheriff were doing on her property.

The old woman nodded as if a crazed murderer roaming the countryside was a common occurrence. Then, she reached off to the side of the door and pulled back a pump-action shotgun. "I'm ready if that sumbitch shows up here."

Abe took a step back. "I guess you are."

The woman racked the shotgun once to show she knew what she was doing. "My husband died six years ago. I'm seventy-six. If you're going to be my age and live alone in the country, you keep things like this handy. Them goddamned Jehovah's Witnesses don't come 'round here anymore, I'll tell you that."

"I would imagine they don't." Abe stepped back from the woman. He didn't fear she would shoot him, but he also did not necessarily want to appear as a threat. "Do you mind if we search your property?"

"Cops will do what they do. They don't give much of a care what I think. I hope you get the little pissant." She closed the door, and Abe heard a heavy lock click shut.

Abe jogged around to the left side of the house following in Buddy's wake. He could see the old man moving fast, but not jogging, along a sparse line of trees. Abe got behind the house and saw Ree moving out into the overgrown fields beyond the lawn. She was crouched low and moving fast. She looked like a big cat on the hunt, her body taut and ready for the worst. Abe was squinting against the darkness of the valley splaying out before him. He crouched like Ree and watched for movement against the tops of the grass. And then, like a clarion call from on high, a voice screamed at him in the back of his mind. *What in the hell are you doing?*

Abe dropped to his knees in the weeds and fell forward clutching at the ground. He wasn't a cop. He wasn't a hero. It was ludicrous that Aberforth Allard, chosen last in every gym class he'd ever had, was cruising through a field with a handgun to attempt to apprehend a bona fide murderer while actual law enforcement officials with training were leading the charge. Abe did not know their tactics. Abe did not know their mindsets. He would be more likely to get in the way and hamper the operation than assist it. Abe lay flat on the ground and hoped it would all be over soon.

A single gunshot rang out in the night somewhere in the distance. It was too far away to be Buddy, Ree, or Billy Paczech. Buddy's voice called out, "That house! Over there!"

Abe chanced pushing himself up to see where Buddy was headed. The shot apparently came from the Huseth house where Buddy, Abe, and Duff had interviewed Birgit Huseth. Abe's calculations had been incorrect, or else Renato had just veered to a longer, more difficult course than Abe had anticipated. Either way, the action was a quarter mile to the southwest from his position.

Shelby Ree, far and away the most athletic of the quartet, was already hustling through the weeds, moving like a deer. Buddy was stumbling after her, more drunken rhino than deer. Billy Paczech called out to them, "I'm getting my truck!" He turned and ran toward his unit, which given the circumstances made sense. There were supplies in the truck, a light, a first aid kid. They would need it. Paczech was also calling in the shots fired alert on his collar mic. Abe watched Shelby Ree charging through the night and realized if anything happened to her, he would never get over hiding in the grass like a coward. Even if cowardice was what was in his heart.

Abe drove himself from the prone position like a sprinter and started to run toward the sound of gunfire, something he had always hoped he would never have to do.

16

SHELBY REE HAD always been fast. Even as a kid, whether it was on the rez or in the suburbs near Madison, she had been one of the fastest kids on the playground. In a shorter distance race, she could beat most of the boys, even the older ones, by the time she was twelve. In high school, she won more races than she lost, and even went to the Wisconsin State Track and Field Championships her junior and senior year. She didn't medal in either of those years, but she didn't embarrass herself, either. When her adrenaline started flowing, she was even faster than normal. The sound of gunfire was invigorating. Equal parts fear and excitement were like rocket fuel. With hardly a thought to how cold it was or how tired she was, Shelby Ree was flying over the uneven turf and bounding over the ruts and matted weeds. Every sense nerve in her body was fully alight. A 400-meter sprint in college took her around seventy seconds on a normal track. With the fear of a gunfight propelling her, she felt like she was going even faster.

Shelby kept her eyes darting. She was looking for any sign of movement. She had no idea what was going on at the house. She did not know what she would find when she got there. Moving as a fast as she was, even in the dark, made her a target. She wished she'd had the foresight to put on a vest. She felt exposed.

Shelby covered the distance between the houses in record time. As she approached the Huseths' from the rear, she saw light streaming out of the patio doors that opened to the rear of the house. A curtain was blowing in the breeze. As she got nearer, she saw that someone had used a cement block to smash in the glass on the patio door.

A man was standing on the patio with a shotgun. Jerry Huseth, Birgit's husband, was burly and older, a bald pate glistening in the night and a bushy beard hanging from his chin. He turned and pointed the gun at Shelby when he caught movement in the field.

Shelby froze and raised her hands. "I'm a cop! Dane County sheriff's deputy!"

Huseth relaxed. "You got a badge?"

Shelby pulled the badge from her back pocket and held it up. "Where is he?"

Huseth shrugged. "Son of a bitch broke my patio door and walked into my kitchen. I was in the basement, thankfully. I grabbed my shotgun and ran up the stairs. He caught sight of what I was carrying and ran out through the door. Figured he was a tweaker or something."

"Something like that," said Shelby.

"I run out on the deck here and shot after him, but I don't know if I hit him or not. Probably didn't. It was dark."

"What are you loading in that?"

"Bird shot. If I hit him, he ain't likely dead, but he ain't likely happy, neither."

"Which direction did he go?"

Huseth waved his arm straight in the direction the steps on the back deck led. "Somewhere out there."

Shelby nodded her thanks. "Get back into the house and guard the door."

"Don't got to tell me twice. Me and the wife are both carrying."

"I'll be back as soon as I can." Shelby jetted in the direction the man indicated.

Shelby ate up ground, a sweat breaking out on her forehead. She felt like she was close now, like the hunt was almost over. She remembered an old hunting trick one of the old men on the rez taught her one year. She knelt down and lowered her head to the level of the grass. In what little ambient light there was, a faint trail through the matted weeds appeared. It was clear something had disturbed the grass recently. Shelby judged the direction and took off in pursuit. The man was heading toward the road.

Shelby chanced a glance behind her. In the darkness, she could see two faint shapes, both cutting a fair shadow in the night. Because of their proportions, it was easy enough to tell Abe from Buddy. Buddy was walking, his stocky outline's movements reminding her of Jason in the *Friday the 13th* movies, a relentless pace, but never a run. Abe was jogging, moving fairly well over the terrain for a city boy. Already he had passed Buddy. Shelby chanced a glance toward the road and could see the distant headlights of Billy Paczech's squad maneuvering toward the county highway. He had not fired the light bar, and at this point, it would have been pointless anyhow. Renato knew they were coming. He could be anywhere, and he knew they were coming.

ABE IGNORED THE angry pounding of his heart in his chest. He passed Buddy, and the old sheriff waved him by. "Don't do something stupid like get shot."

Abe assured Buddy that he would do his best. He kept running. He was sweating profusely now, a combination of exertion over uneven ground and fear. He had a sick, squishy feeling low in his stomach, almost like a precursor to food poisoning, but not quite. It was sharper, and less sickly. It twisted in him and told him to turn back and run the other direction. He had to ignore that feeling. Abe missed Duff. Somehow, in the past, every time someone had shot at them, Duff had always managed to move in front of Abe. He'd never been hit, but he was always there, ready to take a bullet. Abe noticed it the first time it happened, which happened to be shortly after Matilda was born. It was as if Duff had just assumed his greatest value in life would be to be a shield for Abe if that meant Abe got to go home to his little girl. Their brand of detective work was slower and less dangerous than most TV shows would have you believe, but people had taken shots at them over the years, usually more out of frustration and warning than a desire to kill. Abe took comfort in that. Most people did not want to use lethal force on others if it wasn't necessary. Those that will, though—they are the ones who made Abe worry. This was a little different, though. Somewhere in the darkness was someone who had already killed and would kill again to stay out of jail, and Duff was nowhere to be found.

Abe ran past the house and saw Jerry Huseth standing guard with his shotgun. Behind him, Birgit was holding a sleek, black handgun. Judging from how she held it at her side, easy but firm, she was not a novice with it.

Abe continued to plow into the darkness after Shelby Ree. He veered to the right slightly in order to cover more ground. Shelby looked like she knew where she was going. Abe wondered if she could see Renato. She was younger than he was, and she didn't wear glasses. She probably had better night vision than he did. Abe heard a shout from behind him. He didn't look back. It was Buddy greeting the Huseths, or maybe the Huseths greeting Buddy. He didn't know.

SHELBY REE COULD see the road. She could not see Renato. That made her worry. When she looked at the trail he'd made, as far as she could tell, he was headed straight for the road. He had to have veered off somewhere, but where? It was an almost wide-open farm field. The nearest trees were over a hundred yards to the north, and if he was wounded from the bird shot, she doubted he would have made the trees.

Shelby dropped to a crouch and squinted hard into the darkness. He was watching her; she could feel it. He could see her, but she had not yet located him. If he could see her, then that meant he could shoot her. If he hadn't shot her yet, it meant that he either thought he could hide it out and avoid being caught, or she was too far away. Shelby considered what she knew about the man and had to assume it was the latter.

If he was too far away to shoot her, that meant he veered south, toward the freeway, which would have thrown him well into the blue-white halogen light that flooded the Huseths' driveway. That meant he had to have veered north, toward the trees, which painted him in darkness and shadow.

Ree turned to her right and saw the dark shape of Abe covering ground. Abe was much closer to the trees than she was. Abe was illuminated against the dark by the light streaming out from the Huseth's broken patio door.

Ree felt panic mode set in hard. She screamed out toward Abe to get down. Abe stopped moving when she shouted, but he didn't drop. Now he was a stock-still target for an angry man.

ABE FROZE; A strange sensation crawled up his spine, scurrying like a centipede. What had Ree said? Abe had heard her shriek his name, but the rest had not translated into his brain because his heart was pounding in his ears. It only took a split-second for him to interpret what was happening, what Ree meant, but it was a second too long.

Abe turned to see a silhouette in the dark. A man was squaring up. Abe could only see the oily black darkness that stood out from the rest of the darkness around it, a nightmare wraith bringing doom. Abe's heart seized in his chest.

At that moment, a brown-and-white missile shot past Abe at incredible velocity. An angry dog honed in on the shooter and sprang at him. The Huseths' dog, Ripley, had joined the battle. Despite the dog not being a fan of guns or loud noises, he somehow sensed that a bad man had tried to break into his family's home. He was seeking retribution. Ripley flew through the air and contacted Renato an instant before he pulled the trigger.

A gunshot rang out in the night. Abe saw the muzzle flash. At that moment, time seemed to stop. Abe threw himself backwards out of instinct and terror. In the slowed-down, stop-motion moment of him falling through the air, he could swear he felt the bullet's wake blow past his face. He could swear he felt the heat from the shot. And then he landed hard on the ground, still in one piece, still unpunctured by a bullet. Renato had missed him. Renato had him dead to rights but missed him. It had to have been because of Ripley's last-second interference. Abe lay flat on his back. He clutched his .38 and tried to look down the length of his body without raising his head off the ground. He was below the level of the grass. He reminded himself he wasn't a target there.

"I see him!" Buddy called out. The old sheriff leveled the hand cannon he carried and fired. The blast was immense.

Shelby Ree twisted into a shooter's stance with a graceful, practiced ease and squeezed off four rounds in Renato's direction.

In the distance, red-and-blue lights began to appear on the road. Dane County SUVs were bouncing over the uneven ground of the fields, having veered off the road toward the sound of gunfire. The headlights illuminated the area with bobbling, wild strobes of yellow. Abe continued to scan the field for a sign of the man who'd shot at him, but he saw nothing. After a moment, Buddy's voice rang out above the din of engine noise. "He's down."

Abe sat up and saw the sheriff pointing his gun at a spot on the ground. He kicked away Renato's gun. Abe stood and jogged over to the spot where the sheriff had Renato in his sights. The wanna-be gangster was lying on his back. Two shots had hit him in the upper thighs, one low in the belly, and one had lodged in his right forearm crippling his shooting hand, hence why he had not been able to return fire when Buddy approached. All of the bullet holes were small, neat shots from Ree's nine-millimeter. Buddy's blast had missed entirely, or the body would have been in very different condition. Renato groaned. His wounds were survivable. Seconds later, uniformed deputies swarmed the scene. An ambulance was brought out to tend to the wounded man.

Buddy holstered his gun and held out a hand for Shelby Ree to shake. "Nice shootin', Tex."

"Blind, dumb, and lucky." Ree refuted the compliment. "I couldn't see shit out there."

Buddy held out a hand for Abe. "Way to not get shot out there."

"I did my best."

"That's all I can ask."

Ripley trotted over to Abe and flopped over onto his side, twisting awkwardly to roll on his back and expose his spotted belly. Abe knelt and ran a hand over the dog's stomach. "Good dog." The dog had probably saved his life. Abe couldn't help but wonder if Duff's rapport with the dog had influenced him to put his life on the line for Abe. It seemed plausible, at the very least. Even when Duff couldn't be there, somehow he was still looking out for Abe.

"We're not done here, you know." Ree turned to face the road. "I'm pretty sure Lonnie Rostenbach isn't going to roll up here with all lights flashing and the like, but I know we have to go see him."

"Kid's not going to like seeing us," said Buddy.

"Then we bring the big man."

"He's in the hospital," said Abe.

"There's more than one big man, Abe." Ree pulled out her cellphone and started dialing.

17

LONNIE ROSTENBACH'S FACE was pinched and tight when he opened his apartment door. Outside, Shelby Ree, Buddy Olson, and Abe Allard were all standing behind a large, beefy man in a dark brown blazer. A sheriff's badge was clipped to the breast pocket of the man's jacket. Lonnie tried to give the man his best smile. "Hey, Sheriff! What brings you by tonight?"

Sheriff Jared Donohue stepped into Lonnie's apartment. He gestured toward the sparsely decorated living room. "Hey, Lonnie. Why don't we sit down?"

A thin African American woman in jeans and a blue blazer stepped in behind Donohue. The sheriff said, "Lonnie, you know Ms. Paris, the department legal counsel, right?"

Alice Paris gave Lonnie a tight-lipped smile. "Hi, Lonnie."

Lonnie's face contorted into a mask of confusion. "What's going on?"

"Don't play dumb, Lonnie. We're here to help you. Tell me the truth and maybe all that happens is you resign from the force." Donohue's voice was like gravel tires on a driveway. He was intimidating at the best of times. With his impressive size blocking the doorway, Lonnie had nowhere to run and no cards to play.

The young man's face fell like a rockslide. He was defeated. There was no getting out of it. He sighed heavily and walked over to the couch in the living room. "C'mon in, Sheriff. I'll tell you what I know."

"Start at the beginning." Donohue walked into the apartment and sat at the other end of the couch from Lonnie. Abe and Ree filed into the tiny kitchen. Alice Paris stood near the door to Lonnie's bedroom. Buddy stayed by the door with his arms crossed like a knight guarding a treasure vault.

"It wasn't really what I wanted to happen, you know." Lonnie rubbed his face with both hands and groaned.

"I know, Lonnie." Donohue reached out and patted Lonnie's shoulder reassuringly.

Paris pulled a small notebook from her interior pocket and clicked a ballpoint pen into action. "When did you get approached by Renato Amato to help him run drugs through Dane County?"

Lonnie looked down at the floor. "I didn't. Marcus Laskey asked me to help him with that. Said we could make a ton of money really fast and then it'd be over. Easy-peasy."

"You knew Marcus?"

"Yeah. I grew up near him. We rode the bus together when we were in high school. He was a couple of years older than I was. After I graduated from college a few years ago, we kind of got back in touch. He was working at my grandparents' restaurant just before it closed. We kind of had the idea that we'd run the restaurant together when they retired, but then their debts caught up to them, and my grandpa died, and that was it. I didn't have the money to buy the restaurant. They couldn't sell it to me because of the liens. So, it got shuttered."

"So, you joined the sheriff's department?" said Paris.

"Not at first. At first, I sort of bummed around. Construction. Painting. I had a degree in Criminal Justice because my parents wanted me to get a degree, but I had always imagined I was meant to be running a supper club, so I was sort of lost. When I saw an ad online about being an LEO, I guess it was meant to be. I joined up. I thought maybe I could work a lot of overtime and make enough to buy back the restaurant before someone else did."

Ree leaned over and whispered into Abe's ear. "Overtime is offered by seniority. Us pups hardly get any to start."

"And when that didn't happen?"

Lonnie gestured around the apartment. He threw up his hands in frustration. "Look around you! I'm not living large, Sheriff. I'm staying within my means as best I can, right? I'm not going on expensive trips. I'm not drinking away my paychecks. I don't even have cable TV. But everything is so fucking expensive now. Everywhere I turn, something costs more money. Houses are getting more expensive by the second. It's ridiculous. How am I supposed to get ahead? Huh? Tell me! How the fuck am I supposed to get the down payment for my grandparents' restaurant, a house, and still have enough money to maybe get married and start a family someday in the future? You can't even find a shitty house for under three-hundred-thousand in Dane County now, and I'm still paying off student loans, for chrissakes! I'm almost thirty; I got nothing! It's going to take years to get ahead, if that's ever even going to be possible. Meanwhile, everyone tells me that I'm supposed to pull myself up by my bootstraps without realizing I can't even afford to buy boots with straps."

The pieces fell into place pretty quickly after that. Marcus Laskey knew his parents were in dire straits. He knew Lonnie was struggling. He, himself, was in bad financial shape due to his drug arrest from college. And then, somehow—Lonnie didn't know how—Renato Amato showed up in Marcus's life. Marcus could make meth. Art and Michelle had the property and the protection to make meth. Renato could get the supplies to make meth. All they needed was someone who could keep those meth trucks moving. They moved products and supplies only on the days and nights Lonnie was working. They made money hand over fist selling bulk to the gangs in Chicago, who in turn sold to the users at markup.

"All you did was run interference?" asked Donohue.

"That's it. I never even saw the product." Lonnie looked over to Alice Paris. "I tried to stay out of it as much as possible."

"You still used county resources to aid in the commission of a crime."

"I won't say I didn't."

"And the files on Benedict's computer? Did you delete those?" asked Shelby.

Lonnie gave a sheepish nod. "I did. Figured no one would notice if it was an open-and-shut case."

Donohue stood and rolled his head toward the door. "I think you'll need to come downtown with me, Lonnie. We'll accept your resignation, and I'll take your gun and badge now."

"You think I'll avoid jail?

Donohue blew out a long breath through pursed lips. He looked to Paris. She gave a barely perceptible shake of her head. Donohue sighed. "Probably not, Lonnie. Probably going to have to serve some sort of time. We'll work with the DA, though. Maybe get you probation, maybe get you less than a year."

"Less than a year? Where I'll have to serve in the county lockup where I'll get to mingle with a lot of guys I helped put in there."

"We'll send you to a different county."

Lonnie fell back against the couch limply. "My life is over."

Ree piped up, "It's not over, Lonnie. This is just a hiccup. You'll come back stronger. You'll put your head down and keep working, keep moving forward."

"Easy for you to say."

At that moment, Ree saw a look cross Lonnie's face. She'd seen it before: it was the face of someone giving up everything. Lonnie slumped to his left, his arm falling on the other side of the low couch. Shelby suddenly knew was he was doing. She knew what was under the couch.

"Gun!" Shelby shifted into motion. It took her three steps to launch out of the kitchen and at the couch. She dove over the cheap coffee table and hit

Lonnie just as he brought the gun out from under the couch. It was a slim, black Springfield XD. It was a personal weapon for home protection, not a service piece. Like a lot of cops, Lonnie walked that fine line between safety and paranoia. He kept a gun within arm's reach for emergency situations.

Shelby somehow managed to grab Lonnie's wrist with both hands before he could get it to the side of his head. The gun discharged, the bullet shattering the glass of the patio door to Lonnie's left. Shelby kept both hands on Lonnie's arm like her life depended on it, which it might have. Donohue was second to react, pouncing and landing his considerable weight on Lonnie's chest and head, pinning him to the couch. "Don't do it, son! Don't do it! We'll get you help!"

Lonnie squeezed off a second bullet that embedded itself in the wall. Shelby stripped the gun from Lonnie's hand by wrenching it back until it nearly broke his trigger finger. He was unable to squeeze another round. The gun fell out of his grip and landed heavily on the floor. Shelby dove on it, expertly ejecting the magazine and jacking back the slide to clear the chamber rendering it harmless.

Lonnie went limp beneath the sheriff. He offered no resistance as Donohue rolled him onto his stomach on the floor and cuffed his hands behind his back. With his face pressed into the carpeting, Lonnie made eye contact with Shelby. "I don't know if I'll ever forgive you for that."

Shelby, heart pumping and blood racing with adrenaline, resisted the urge to say anything mean. "At least you'll live long enough so we can both find out."

18

HOSPITALS WERE NEVER Abe's favorite place. When he was a kid, they usually meant something was seriously medically wrong with him, and it meant that his mother was going to stress and fret about money for the next six months as she tried to find the strength of will to work any overtime she could manage in order to pay off the bill. When his mother was dying, Abe spent far too much time in a hospital room watching her wither away while they watched pointlessly dull daytime TV together. Hospitals depressed him.

"Daddy!" A blur of red out of the corner of his eye made him spin around. Matilda slammed into him like a missile. She hugged him ferociously. Abe held her for a moment. He laid his cheek on the top of her head. He didn't get that many hugs anymore. He missed them. Her hair smelled fruity and clean. He didn't get that many Daddy moments, either. As of late, it was Dad. Or Father. Or Patriarch. Or, more frequently, *Bruh*. He liked being Daddy. It reminded him of when she was little and liked to be carried.

"Did you see him already?"

Matilda pulled back from her father. "Oh, yeah. He's in a rare mood."

"I imagine so."

Duff had been held at the University of Wisconsin Hospital near the shore of Lake Mendota since he'd been injured. The damage was less than initially feared, but still painful. He suffered two serious rib injuries and several more minor rib injuries. He also was badly bruised. A dark purple stain the size of a basketball marked the spot of impact. It was a bad injury, but not nearly as bad as it could have been if not for the Walther's convenient placement under his sweatshirt and Duff's refusal to use it.

Abe had called Katherine the morning of Lonnie Rostenbach's arrest. She and Matilda had come up from Chicago that afternoon, both of them taking a couple of days off of school to help keep Duff company until he was cleared to be released from the hospital. Abe had not been able to spend much time in the hospital. He had been busy with the Dane County Sheriff's Department. He and Buddy Olson helped them fill in the gaps in their investigation and helped them build a murder case against Renato Amato. Investigators tested the bullet Buddy and Ree dug the bullet out of the wall at the Laskeys' house and found it a match to Renato's .45. They started tracing some of the money orders.

The detectives in the sheriff's department were adamant that Marybeth and Chris Collier must have been in on the Laskeys' activities, as well, but they had been unable to draw a concrete line of proof to them. If the Colliers had been privileged to the Laskeys' misdeeds, it was well-hidden, probably by design. It kept the Colliers safe and free.

Abe wondered if that was what was behind Marybeth's display for him when they first met. No doubt she was saddened by her parents' deaths, but how much of it was tinged by perhaps knowing why they died? That was the most frustrating part of detective work: sometimes, all the loose ends couldn't be tied up neatly. Maybe the Colliers would be implicated in this mess someday, or maybe they'd skate free. Maybe Marybeth knew where her parents were hiding the unaccounted-for money, and that'd be something from which she and her husband could siphon for years. Maybe they were truly innocent in this. Abe would never know.

Abe and Tilda walked down the long hallway to Duff's room. They could hear the big man's irascible tone before they got there. He was complaining to someone about the quality of the food served for breakfast. "All I'm saying is that would it kill you to have someone in this dump learn to make a halfway decent breakfast burrito? They're not hard. It's not rocket science."

A woman's voice answered him. There was no disguising the tone of exhaustion in her voice. Clearly, she'd already grown tired of dealing with the esteemed CS Duffy. "You know, maybe you could apply for a job here. Seems like you'd bring the level of breakfast up a notch since you're such an expert."

"All I'm saying is that the University of Wisconsin is a hallowed and prestigious university, fabled in story and song, and you can't manage to make an edible breakfast burrito. Somewhere, John H. Lathrop is spinning in his grave."

"Who's that?"

"He was the first chancellor of the university."

"Well, bully to him."

Abe and Matilda rounded the corner of the room to find Duff still abed, Katherine looking tired in the chair by his bedside, and an even more tired-looking nurse milling about the room. The nurse was in her forties with short, sassy hair. She had tortoise-shell glasses and a pair of well-worn Sketchers on her feet that matched her dark blue scrubs.

Abe gave Duff a nod when he walked in. "How're you feeling?"

"Like a bunch of marbles in a sock. How're you?"

"Not so bad." Abe smiled down at Matilda. "Could be worse."

"Yeah, you could be the one in the bed."

Katherine reached over and put a hand on Duff's forearm. "You wouldn't let that happen to my Abe."

"I might. Depends on whether or not he's pissing me off that day."

Abe gave the beleaguered nurse a smile. "Taking good care of him?"

She rolled her eyes. "Oh, I'm about to take care of him."

Duff held up an unopened cup of lime Jell-O. "I think Bill Cosby there has been dosing my little treats with sedatives to make me nap more."

The nurse narrowed her eyes at Duff. "I have not. I've certainly thought about it, though."

"You're going to miss me when I leave today, aren't you?"

"About as much as I miss a hangnail."

"Okay, we can be pen-pals, then."

"Take care of yourself, Mr. Duffy." The nurse gave him a forced smile and left the room.

"You ready to get out of here, then?" Abe clapped his hands. "I'm sure you're ready to get back to your PlayStation and some of Cesar's burritos."

"That I am. I'll miss the regular doses of painkillers, though."

"You hardly drink, and I've never even seen you take aspirin," said Katherine.

Abe knew that Duff was putting up a front. He was not and could never be someone who enjoyed drugs.

Duff nodded toward his jeans and Carhartt draped over the arm of Katherine's chair. "Why don't you toss me my gear, and we'll get going. I'm ready to blow this Popsicle stand." He tossed back the covers of the bed and swung his legs over the side. Every move made him grimace and suck air, but he kept moving. His left arm was mostly useless. He was keeping it pinned to his side to minimize movement. He was able to step into his jeans and pull them up with his right hand. He moved his left forearm to do the button and fly, and then strained a bit to fasten the belt buckle. His Carhartt was a different story. He was able to get it over his head and get his right arm into it, but he couldn't bring himself to put his left arm into the sleeve. Katherine pulled it down on his left side for him. "Good enough for government work."

Duff slipped his bare feet into his Nikes. He couldn't bring himself to bend over to put on socks, a slightly challenging task on his best days. Instead, he stuffed his socks into the pocket of his sweatshirt. "Let's get out of here."

SHELBY REE WAS waiting for them outside the main doors. She stood by her black-and-brown Dane County unit. Buddy Olson was standing with her. His truck had been totaled. It was now resting in a scrapyard outside of Arena, Wisconsin. He had gotten a rental pickup from Enterprise pending his insurance company's decision on the payout on his policy.

When the group emerged from the doors, Duff tilted his head toward Ree's car. "Officer, I'd like to report a county vehicle parked illegally in the fire lane."

"I'll get right on that."

"Heading home, then?" said Buddy.

"I think I've worn out my welcome for Wisconsin."

Buddy shook Abe's hand. "Thanks for finding out the truth. The answer wasn't what I was hoping it would be, I knew it wasn't murder and suicide." He didn't bother to offer to shake Duff's hand; he knew better.

Abe introduced Katherine and Matilda to Buddy and Shelby. Ree shook both of their hands. "I didn't peg you as a fatherly type."

"Not many people do," said Duff. "I think it's because he looks like he's incapable of having human sex."

"What other kind of sex would I be having?"

"Praying Mantis sex."

"Can we stop talking about my father and sex, please?" Matilda covered her ears with her hands.

Abe broached a touchy subject with Ree. "Is the department going to bring the hammer down on you?"

"Probably a little. I was sort of friendly with Lonnie Rostenbach. I'm sure they're going to want to know everything about our relationship and how much I knew."

"How's the case against Renato going?"

"He was arraigned yesterday. Three murder charges and one attempted murder with additional charges for drug trafficking pending. That pretty much means he's getting held without bail until trial. Those three murder charges will stick because his little buddy already made a deal to turn state's evidence and pin Amato permanently to the wall. He'll never walk outside a free man again."

"Couldn't happen to a nicer guy," said Duff.

"What about Lonnie?" asked Abe.

"He's already resigned from the department. He's lawyered up. They're working on a plea deal for him. I hope it won't be too bad for him, but I think he's probably looking at least one to three years."

"I'm sure he'll come around to understanding what you did for him, for keeping him from killing himself. I'm sure he'll thank you someday."

"Maybe he will. Or maybe he'll just kill himself later. The county already confiscated all the weapons from his apartment, but if he's really serious about doing it, he'll probably do it before the trial. Without a trial, in the eyes of the state, he'll forever be innocent of his crimes."

There was a sad lull in the conversation. No one knew quite what to say next. Ree summoned the energy to make the departure. She threw a thumb over her shoulder at the SUV. "I better get back to it. Without Lonnie, there's a few extra shifts that need to be covered for the time being."

Duff raised an eyebrow. "You going to stick with the department, then?"

Ree shrugged. "For now. Maybe something else will come up."

"If you need anything, don't hesitate to reach out," said Abe.

"I will. You do the same." Ree turned on her heel and climbed into her SUV. With a final wave, she shifted the unit into drive and slowly rolled away from the hospital. She turned a corner and vanished, any further view of her was blocked by the parking ramp.

"She's good people." Buddy nodded once. "She'll go far, I'm sure. Tough kid. Head and heart are in the right place."

They walked into the parking ramp. Buddy's rental truck was parked next to Abe's minivan, which in turn was parked next to Katherine's Kia Soul. They paused for a final round of good-byes.

"I owe you boys one. Thanks." Buddy gave them a nod. He turned toward Katherine and Tilda and touched the brim of his cowboy hat. "Ma'am. Miss."

"Nice meeting you, Buddy. Abe has said nothing by nice things about you."

Buddy winked at Katherine. "You're a rotten liar, ma'am. But I appreciate the attempt." He climbed into his truck, backed out of the parking space, and left without another wave.

"Back home, then?" Katherine said to Matilda.

"Back home. I should go to school tomorrow, at least. It's only Thursday. I can make up what I missed the last two days." She gave Abe a hug, and then gingerly hugged Duff.

Katherine hugged Duff. "Thank you for protecting Abe."

"Katy, I don't know what you're talking about."

Katherine pulled back from Duff and turned to Abe. There was an uncomfortable moment, a strange, painful pause. Then, Katherine said under her breath, "Oh, fuck it." She hugged Abe. Abe returned the hug. It felt familiar, yet foreign. There was something different about hugging her now. "I'm glad you're okay."

"Thanks for coming up," said Abe.

Katherine and Matilda climbed into the Kia, backed out of the parking space, and followed the same route Buddy took to exit the ramp. Abe waved as he watched them go. When he turned around, he found Duff was already in the front seat of the van, buckling himself into place with a slow, awkward movement.

Abe climbed into the driver's seat. "You don't look well."

"Good. I'd hate to be in this much pain and not have people notice."

"Home?"

"Culver's first, then home."

Abe checked his watch. It was just after ten in the morning. Culver's would be open. "Sounds like a plan."

Abe shifted in reverse, guided the van out of the space, and started the drive back to the office. Abe cracked his window slightly and took in a deep breath of spring air. Real spring was coming. It smelled pleasant outside. The forecast had the temperature climbing to sixty that day. Sixty in March felt more like seventy does in the summer. The Madison traffic was strangely light for that time of the morning, and the sun was soft and warm. It had all the makings for an extremely pleasant day.

The Bad-Luck Charm took that moment to crunch into an unavoidable pothole, a great crater left as a winter offering to the spring road gods. The suspension didn't staunch an ounce of the blow and Abe and Duff were buffeted about their seats like racquetballs.

Duff sucked in a breath through gritted teeth and belted out a hall of fame string of expletives directed at Abe, the van, the pothole, the Wisconsin DOT, and an elderly woman walking a Shih-Tzu on the sidewalk.

It'd be an alright day.

Acknowledgements

As per usual, this section remains both my most and least favorite thing to write. I always enjoy writing it because it means I got to the end of another book, the editing is over, and I'm not terribly long from unleashing whatever I've done on the world. I always hate writing it because I'm struck with the nervousness and apprehension of wondering if people will like it, if it will sell, how it will be reviewed, and a landslide of other worries that comes with this publishing game.

While I'm no *New York Times* best-selling author, I am lucky enough to have sold more than a few of the Abe & Duff books and been even more lucky to have some of those people who have read them leave nice reviews. So, any thanks to getting to the fourth book in the series is largely due to those people who have taken time out of their own lives to jot down a paragraph or two on Amazon, Goodreads, or any of the thousand other sites where people can leave book reviews. Those reviews help more than you know.

I'm also extremely grateful to the twenty or so people who make regular appearances in the comments section of my Facebook page or on my Twitter feed. It's nice to know I'm not throwing books into the giant vacuum of publishing without someone seeing the work.

And, as usual, I'm grateful to my family and friends who, even though a lot of them have never read my books, still give me a lot of support during the writing, editing, publishing, and promotional process. Thanks to Ann, Emily, Ryan, Dusty, Jamesy, Jack, Josh, Jena, and the rest of you freaks and miscreants for putting up with this nonsense.

Thanks also to the authors whose writing has shaped my own. Obviously, Craig Johnson is a major influence on these books, as is CJ Box, Gareth Powell, Neil Gaiman, and Alex Bledsoe. Thanks as well to the authors around me here in Madison who help out, encourage, and support my work. Thanks to Maddy Hunter, Kathleen Ernst, Jeff Nania, and Alex Bledsoe (the same one as above).

Thanks also to my family for understanding why I'm always somewhere else in my head. (As a side note, my daughter is starting college in the fall of 2023, so any positive thoughts her way will be appreciated.)

I am also grateful that I got to set this book near Mount Horeb, Wisconsin. I grew up Mount Horeb and spent a fair amount of time ranging around the area throughout the course of my life. I highly encourage you to get there at some point in your life and just drive around. The scenery is beautiful, and the hills and corners will get you carsick as hell. You'll love it.

As a special treat, I wanted to drop a preview of my next novel, *Welcome to Meskousing*.

You have my noticed that in this book, for the first time, I actually had a narrative change of view from Abe or Duff to a third character. Deputy Shelby Ree got her own chance to shine for a bit because she's the protagonist of my next novel. I wanted to write a spin-off from the Abe & Duff series to explore a different interest of mine: paranormal horror/mysteries. If that's your cup of tea, I hope you'll stick around for it.

I don't want to give too much of the book away here, but I wanted to include part of the first chapter for your perusal. Initially, I wanted to put out this book simultaneously with Bought the Farm, but life simply would not allow that. If you enjoy this excerpt, please drop a message on social media or email to let me know. The rest of it should be out in early-to-mid 2024, I hope.

Thanks for reading.

Sun Prairie, Wisconsin
August 2023

Welcome to Meskousing

Coming in 2024

1

THERE COMES A POINT IN the fall of the year when night falls like a charging ram, head down, full speed ahead, no concerns about anything around it. There is sunlight. There are a few fleeting moments of dusk. And then darkness slams into the horizon without the slightest concern for those who might still wish to see. Even more disturbing is that moment in the twilight between dusk and dark when the shadows elongate and obscure playing tricks with the vision and making the slightest bit of wind make the trees look like they are suddenly moving, suddenly sentient and alive. It is in this twilight period where car headlights seem to do no good. There is too much ambient light in the sky for the headlights to make a dent in the coming shadows. Instead, for at least a few minutes, drivers have to trust their eyes in the dimming light until their headlights can finally bridge the gap and become effective once again.

Shelby Ree both loved and hated this time of the night. She guided her beat-up rust-bucket of a '94 Jeep Cherokee along the rugged, twisty lane of County Road A. It was equal parts thrilling and terrifying, made even more dangerous along the back roads of Wisconsin because this was the time of night when deer were on the move. They were waking up from their daytime sheltering spots and moving to feeding areas. It was in this time when deer were most likely to appear from the tall trees along the side of the road or bound out of the withering, brown cornfields that had not yet been harvested. Deer are jump-scares waiting to happen. The barest hint of them forces drivers go hyper-alert, eyes darting constantly with their right foot sitting lightly on the gas, ready to make the leap to the brake at the first suggestion of movement.

In the back seat of the Jeep, Shelby's grandfather, Melvin Gokey, spoke. His voice was thin and easy as if he was commenting on the weather. "Deer ahead."

Shelby's foot stabbed the brake pedal bringing the Jeep to an even slower crawl. Her eyes swept both sides of the road, looking for the telltale eye shine of the whitetails that inhabited the area. "Where?"

"To the left." Melvin's face drifted right, toward an imposing copse of trees just off the road. He was well-wrinkled from age, had a closely cropped thatch of white hair, and wore circular wire-rimmed glasses. Like Radar O'Reilly, he used to say. He also wore the dark green uniform shirt and well-worn blue jeans that had been his daily outfit for most of the last fifty years.

"I don't see it." Shelby slowed the Jeep to a crawl. Like her grandfather, she favored a shorter haircut, though some of her Ojibwe relatives gave her some flak for it. She had a pixie cut with a side-sweep that showed off impressive cheekbones. She also wore blue jeans but wore a blue-check flannel shirt with the sleeves rolled to the elbows. She had not started her new job, so the uniform shirt matching her grandfather's would have to come later.

"Wait for it." Melvin's voice never raised above a standard speaking volume, even back in his days as a county sheriff. He never liked it when people yelled; it just begat more yelling. He reasoned that calm always won the battle against rage. He faced forward and smiled up at Shelby in the rearview mirror. "They will be there."

Shelby stopped the Jeep completely. A split-second later, a hundred yards up the road, three whitetail deer emerged from the weathered and browned cornfields to the left. They stepped gingerly out of the withered stalks, crossed the road with light steps, and disappeared into the trees to head for a safer place to bed down for the night. They all glanced at the Jeep as if to bid it a good evening, but none of them were disturbed by the contraption. If Shelby had not stopped, she likely would have spooked them into blasting out of their hiding spot in a panic, and she would have hit one of them in the ensuing chaos when they darted in who-knows-what directions. That would have spelled the end of her beloved old Jeep, and it would not have done the deer any favors, either. Shelby glanced into the rearview. "How do you always do that?"

"Practice." Melvin's smile was serene. It was always serene. Whether he was looking at a newly born baby or arresting a tweaker on a bad trip, the smile was constant and unwavering. Shelby slipped the Jeep back into drive and proceeded down the roller-coaster of a highway.

Meskousing County was deeply entrenched in the notorious Driftless Region of Wisconsin. The Driftless is an area which, for whatever reason, was spared from the massive glaciers that encroached south during the last Ice Age. The glaciers worked like massive snowplows, leveling the land underneath their ceaseless push and smoothing it flat like it did in North Dakota or Minnesota, but the Driftless area remained untouched, and thus it was a wild land of dense forests growing thickly on rolling hillsides and rocky vales. There were tall ridges that overlooked the county, as well as deep valleys where direct sunlight could only touch the depths for a couple of hours a day. Moss grew thickly in those valleys as well as lichens and various molds. Streams and rivers cut paths through the deepest valleys in the county, all fed from the Mississippi or Wisconsin Rivers which flowed in the distance to the west and east, respectively. The farmland cleared by settlers when they tried to tame Meskousing turned out to be rich and fruitful with those streams providing abundant water, but beware their fury in the spring when the winter's snowmelt often caused them to overflow their banks leaving the valley bottoms flooded for weeks at a time.

The lack of glacial coverage meant the hills were never pushed into the valleys like they were across the rest of the state. Thus, all the roads through the Driftless were built where they could be, not necessarily where they needed to be, and they were all wild, winding, up-and-down, twisty paths that caused a lot of wear-and-tear to the brakes in the summers, and constant headaches and dangerous cornering in the winters. Add in the fact that the scenery was unparalleled in the state, and the hills were grand challenges for people who liked to ride bicycles, and the roads were usually dotted with cyclists in the summers despite the fact most of the roads lacked adequate shoulders for them to ride on, so that only added another level of difficulty to driving through the Driftless. Somehow, everyone made it work, though.

Shelby had spent most of the last two years working in the Dane County Sheriff's department as a deputy. Dane was a fairly unremarkable county, topographically speaking, in southeastern Wisconsin that was much closer to the traditional images of gently rolling fields of farmland that people pictured when they heard the word Wisconsin. The Driftless region only touched the northwestern corner of Dane County, and the rest of it was lakes, city, or farmland. Having spent two years on those large, banked corners and wide-open stretches, it was jarring to be driving in Meskousing. The Driftless required an entirely different set of driving skills. Meskousing was about being present in the moment and having a much shorter sense of the road. It required a lot more gas-and-brake coordination to settle into a turn and accelerate out of it in preparation for a sudden steep hill climb. You had to be able to judge speed by feel, and you had to truly understand your car's ability on curves. Meskousing was not the county to be in if you were prone to motion sickness.

As the Eisenhower Interstate Highway System was built in the years post-World War II, Wisconsin had been crossed by Highway 90 to the north of Meskousing County. It was a much simpler task to drive the highway if you needed to get from Madison to LaCrosse, so that took away most of the need for anyone to go into the Driftless Region at all. If you were in Meskousing County, you were there on purpose. If you needed to get through Meskousing, there were easier, faster roads to take with almost as much beauty to see from the road. Visitors to Meskousing could be spotted quickly because they were riding the brake pedal constantly, unable to anticipate the layout of the roads like the locals mastered through years of practice and repetition. The locals could wheel through those back roads blindfolded and delighted in the roller-coaster sensations it brought. For some of them, it was a challenge to do it as fast as their trucks would allow, even up to the point where tires squealing on the corners was a badge of honor.

Shelby guided the Jeep around another blind corner. To the right were thick, dense woods. To the left, a steep drop of maybe twenty feet to a cornfield barely off the shoulder of the road. A ninety-degree corner ahead gave her pause. She lifted her foot off the gas and readied it over the brake. Then she stepped on the brake hard. She paused. Something wasn't right; all of her police senses came alive. She rolled down her window and listened to the night sounds. Prickles of apprehension crawled over her scalp and down her back. She pulled over to the side of the road and hit her hazards.

From the back seat, her grandfather smiled at her in the rearview. "You felt it, yeah?"

"I felt it." She got out of the Jeep and smelled the air. She could smell gasoline and dust mixed in with the normal smell of a late fall country night. Something was definitely not right. She leaned back into the Jeep and pulled her service weapon from the case on the passenger-side seat. She snapped her utility holster around her waist and slipped the weapon into its sheath on her hip. There was something comforting about having a weapon ready to use, even if she did not know if she needed one, yet. She paused and carefully surveyed her surroundings. Then, she saw it: tire tracks on the left side of the road, headed down the small ravine. The tires clearly had to have come from the right lane of the road, flying off the drop-off to the cornfield below. They exited the corner just a few feet from where the heavy corrugated metal guard rail ended. This wasn't someone who missed the turn due to speed because they would have hit the rail if that were the case. This person turned and drove off the road to avoid something.

Shelby ran across the road and glanced down the drop. Sure enough, a Nissan sedan with Illinois plates had done a full belly flop into the cornfield. It had caught plenty of air before slamming squarely into the earth almost two stories below. The tires jutted out at angles, smashed up into the wheel wells when the axles broke. The head-and-tail lights had all been smashed on impact, but the car's interior lights still glowed faintly enough to show the crash had been recent, perhaps only minutes prior.

Shelby cursed under her breath and ran back to her Jeep. She popped the rear gate, pulled out her first aid kit, and shut and locked the Jeep. "Be careful," her grandfather called from his seat in the back.

Shelby ran back across the road and made her way down the steep, grassy slope to the field below. Mattocks of grass had been growing thickly over the drop for decades. It was wild and rough but gave plenty of handholds and places to set her feet so she could mountain goat her way to the ground.

Shelby dialed 911 on her cell phone and hoped she had enough bars to get through. In the deep valleys of Meskousing County, it was not always possible, even despite recent attempts to populate the rolling hills with towers. The phone rang through, and a sleepy-sounding woman answered. "Meskousing Sheriff's Station Emergency Line. What's your location?"

Shelby rattled off the critical info. "This is Shelby Ree. I'm on Highway 25 about six miles south of Mount Bodd. I've got a single-vehicle accident. A car went off the road and plunged about twenty feet. I'm making my way to the driver now. Send an ambulance."

There was a moment of silence. "Is this right by that big-ass corner?"

"I guess so."

"Ah, yeah. I know right where you are. I'll send paramedics, and I'll call Husky Poyden and tell him to bring his wrecker out. Mitch Shangle ain't going to be happy when he finds out another car landed in his field."

"This has happened before?"

The dispatcher was unfazed. "Oh, yeah. Moreso in the winter, but it's happened a few times in the summer, too. Usually when someone's had a few pops of Pappy's special bathtub gin."

Shelby got to the driver's door. The airbags had deployed, a bright red wet smear on the driver's side bag. The windows of the car had all splintered into spiderwebbed messes but were still intact. Shelby used her elbow to punch through the broken glass and pulled the webbed safety glass out into the cornfield so as not to rain it down on the driver.

A single, Caucasian male was leaning back in the driver's seat, his fingers trying to pinch off a bloody nose. The man was groaning slightly. He was clean-shaven with a fresh haircut. He was dressed in a tuxedo, but the bow tie was undone from his neck and hanging loosely.

"Sir, my name's Shelby. I'm here to help. How do you feel?"

The guy opened his eyes and rolled his head to the side. "Feel like I'm about two inches shorter. I think I telescoped my spine."

Shelby looked at the cliff edge fifteen feet over her head. "I don't doubt that for a second."

The guy started trying to open his door. Shelby stopped him. "Sir, I have paramedics on the way. Do not try to move. Just rest easy. Let's let the professionals help you out and see to your injuries. You're safer if you don't move. You might have a spine injury."

The man relaxed. He blew out a big breath of air. "It's just one thing after another, isn't it?"

Shelby leaned into the car. She pressed a bandage to the man's bleeding nose. "Here use this. What's your name?"

He took the bandage, holding it in place beneath his nostrils. "Emerson. Emerson Guthrie."

"Well, Mr. Guthrie. You're moving your arms. That's a good sign. Can you move your legs?"

"Oh yeah. I mean, they're sore. I think I hurt my ankles when I landed, but I can move them. It hurts, but I can move them."

"Both very good signs."

"My lower back is pretty bad, though. Feels like a giant played accordion with my spine." Emerson blew a breath through his nose. Blood spurted like a Las Vegas fountain. "I think that airbag broke my nose."

Shelby could see his beak was at a slightly exaggerated angle. "Oh yeah. No question."

"I never broke anything before."

"Congratulations. You have now."

"It sucks. I don't recommend it."

"Were you on your way to a party?"

"What?" Emerson was confused for a moment. Then he remembered and looked down at himself. The pleated white bib of the tuxedo was stained with drops of blood. "Oh, the suit. I was supposed to get married today."

"Well, can I call the church for you? Or your fiancée?"

Emerson groaned. He tried to open the door of the car again. The impact had crumpled it so that it could not open without tools. "Supposed to is the key terminology here. I got jilted. She got to the venue at nine this morning and turned around and left. I got a text from her saying she wasn't ready to settle down, and that was that. I sat in the church for two hours while people came up and raged and apologized to me, and then everyone left. I didn't know what else to do, so I just started driving."

"From where?"

"Springfield, Illinois."

"Well, you're quite aways from home."

"Didn't know where else to go."

In the distance, Shelby could see red flashing lights being cast to the trees on the far side of the valley. The ambulance was coming down Highway A. They'd be there shortly. "The ambulance is almost here," she told Emerson.

"How's my car?"

"Totaled."

"Got a hotel around here?"

"Sure do. Indoor plumbing and everything, but I think you'll probably be spending tonight at the hospital."

"Good enough." Emerson's head slouched back against the headrest. He tried to blow out through his nose again, but the adrenaline was starting to wear off. He sucked in a sharp breath and groaned.

"Mr. Guthrie—"

"Emerson, please. Call me Emerson. I hate my last name. Not too thrilled about my first name, either. I think I should have been called Butch. Or Spike."

"No offense, but you don't look like a Butch or a Spike."

Emerson looked at Shelby out of the corner of his eye. "Who do I look like, then?"

"You definitely look like an Emerson. Or maybe a Tad."

"Tad is worse than Emerson."

"I have a cousin named Tad."

"No offense."

"His last name is Poleski."

"Tad Poleski? Really?"

"Yeah. My aunt and uncle have a silly sense of humor."

The lights of the ambulance appeared on the cliff top above them. From the other direction, the telltale red-and-blue flashers of a police unit were lighting up the darkening valley. An EMT emerged from the ambulance and shined a powerful spotlight down onto the wreck flooding the cornfield with brilliant white light. "I guess this is the place." The voice was female.

"It is," Shelby called back.

"We'll have to rig up some ropes, maybe get the fire department here with a crane, I think."

"Don't hurry on my account," said Emerson. "I'm all dressed up with no place to go."

"Take your time. The driver seems to be okay, for the most part," said Shelby.

"We'll get someone down to get monitors on him as soon as we can tie off a rope to the truck." The EMT backed away from the cliff edge.

"We'll get you out of there soon. Just relax." Shelby patted the man on his shoulder. "Was it a deer?"

"What deer?"

"A deer that made you swerve off the road."

Emerson turned his head to look at her. "If I told you, you'd make them check me for brain trauma."

"You launched off a cliff, fell about twenty-five feet, and went face-first into an airbag. You've definitely got brain trauma. Besides, running off the road because of a deer is nothing to be ashamed of. It happens all the time in Wisconsin."

"It wasn't a deer," said Emerson.

"A dog? A coyote? A squirrel?"

Emerson pulled the bandage away from his swelling nose. "Promise you won't laugh?"

"I won't."

Emerson sucked in a long breath and exhaled it slowly. "I think it was Bigfoot."

"Bigfoot. Sure."

"I told you you wouldn't believe me."

A rope was thrown down the cliff and the female EMT began to rappel over the edge. She made it down the grassy slope in no time and walked to the car, removing a shoulder bag of first aid gear as she did. She introduced herself. "I'm May August."

"May August?"

May nodded and shrugged. "Don't ask. Got two sisters named April and June and a brother named July. It's a whole thing. None of us have forgiven our parents for it."

"I'm Shelby Ree."

May's face lit up with recognition. "Melvin's granddaughter? The new boss?"

"That's me."

"Pleased to meet you, Sheriff. If you don't mind stepping aside, I'd like to get monitors on this fellow to make sure he's not in shock."

"I'm not in shock," said Emerson.

"Not in shock yet." May shouldered past Shelby in a friendly but firm manner and began tending to her patient.

Shelby used the rope to climb back up the slope to the ambulance. She looked at the back of her Jeep. Her grandfather was no longer in the back seat.

That's the problem with ghosts. They come and go as they please.

Made in the USA
Las Vegas, NV
21 November 2023

81295384R00120